I0654125

ALUMINUM MAGIC

BRUCE DAVIS

Brick Cave Media
brickcavebooks.com

Aluminum Magic

Copyright © 2025 Bruce C. Davis

ISBN: 978-1-938190-94-0

All rights reserved. No part of this publication may be
reproduced, stored in a retrieval system or transmitted in any
form or by any means, electronic, mechanical, photocopying,
recording or otherwise without the prior permission of the
publisher or in accordance with the provisions of the Copyright,
Designs and Patents Act 1988 or under the terms of any license
permitting limited copying issued by the Copyright Licensing
Agency. No part of this book may be used or reproduced in
any manner for the purpose of training artificial intelligence
technologies or systems.

Printed in the United States of America.

The characters and events in this book are fictitious. Any
similarity to real persons, living or dead, is coincidental and not
intended by the authors.

Cover Illustration Artist: Thitipon Decruen
www.xric7.com

Brick Cave Media
brickcavebooks.com
2025

For fans who love Simon and Sylvie as much as I do.

Also by Bruce Davis

Available from Brick Cave Books

MAGIC LAW SERIES
Platinum Magic
Gold Magic
Silver Magic

THE PROFIT LOGS
GlowGems for Profit
Thieves Profit
Profit Motives
Profit & Loss

ALUMINUM MAGIC

BRUCE DAVIS

Brick Cave Media
brickcavebooks.com

CHAPTER ONE

Lt. Simon Buckley swung the short-barreled PL44 bolt thrower to his right just as he was hit on his left side and slammed painfully to the concrete floor.

"You're dead, Loot," said the voice of First Sergeant Josen Taylor from somewhere above him. "Stand down everyone. I have to tell the Lieutenant's Noble Lady he was killed because he was stupid. Just how were you stupid, Loot?"

Simon hated the nickname "Loot" for Lieutenant, but he'd agreed to forgo any privileges of rank for the purposes of this training. "I didn't clear the room to my left before turning away, Top."

"That's right," said the retired First Sergeant of Royal Marines. "Don't you trust Sergeant Steelhammer? The right side was his responsibility."

"But I saw movement, Top," Simon protested weakly.

"Steelhammer would have handled it. Instead, your man got by you and now you're both dead." He gave an exasperated sigh. "Everyone, take five. We'll set it up again."

The rest of the mercenary team as well as the volunteers playing the EC's, Marine talk for Enemy Combatants, moved to the staging area of the huge training facility. The building housed a firing range, gymnasium facilities, and hand-to-hand combat mats. The main open area had movable walls, doors, and partitions that could simulate any number of building plans, even a small village. Catwalks and platforms above allowed trainers to evaluate a team's performance.

A private security firm ran the whole operation and rented it out to Peacekeepers, other security forces, and even the military. Hal had called in several favors and rented the building for a week at the cost of a single day.

Taylor slid lightly down a ladder just to the right of the door and grabbed Simon by the arm. "Over here, Loot. We need to talk."

Simon followed, expecting a thorough dressing down from the big ex-Marine. Instead, Taylor laid a hand on his shoulder and spoke softly. "I'm not sure bringing you on this mission is a good idea, Loot." He held up a hand as Simon started to protest. "I understand why you feel you need to go. Aside from your personal relationship, Lady Graystorm is a squad mate. You've been in action together. It might be easier if you were just a civilian, an advocate or account manager or some such. I could treat you like baggage, relegate you to the rear and teach you a few moves like a wind-up toy. But you're not a civilian, you're a trained Peacekeeper. The trouble is, Peacekeeper training isn't the same as Marine Special Arms training. What you think you know, what you do automatically as a Keeper will get you killed in this arena."

"I'll try to do better, Top," Simon said, his voice contrite.

"I know you're trying, Loot," Taylor answered. "Your unarmed skills are acceptable at Marine basic standard, you're in great physical condition, and you're a crack shot on the range. But none of that means horseshit in close quarters combat, or in stealth infiltration. We're on a short timeline here. Your foster father is paying me and my men some heavy coin, but I won't risk someone getting killed because you can't lift your load. Understood?"

"Yes, Top."

"All good. We'll do one more run-through, same scenario, then stand down for the day."

The final practice run of the day went better. Simon was slow on taking a shot but got the EC before he could harm the team. Taylor pronounced his performance 'acceptable.'

Simon stripped off his gear and carefully cleaned the PL44 and his Gowron sidearm before turning both over to Special Operator Gillis, the team's armorer. The PL44 was the next generation of his familiar D'Stang tactical weapon. Despite the PL's nearly solid aluminum body and inlaid ebony stock, it's shorter barrel and distributed cinnabar rather than the solid rod of the D'Stang, made it a lighter, more maneuverable weapon. The Gowron, on the other hand, was the same squat, heavy slug pistol it had always been. The only thing it had in common with the PL44 was the use of an Air spell to power its projectiles and even that was like the difference between an ax and a rapier. The real advantage to the PL44 was its tunable spell interface. A skilled armorer with basic Air talent could adjust the power of the spell to handle any projectile from low-velocity sleeper needles to armor-piercing fire bolts.

Simon stood for a long time in the showers, well

after the rest of the team had finished, and worked the kinks out of his aching muscles as he thought about Taylor's words. Was it love or just vanity that made him so determined to be part of the mission to rescue Sylvie from the Graystorm compound in Tintagel, where she was held prisoner? Held by her own father, no less, because she opposed the Traditionalist coup that had taken over the Gray Havens two months earlier. As her fiancé, he, of course, wanted to ride to her rescue. As a Peacekeeper, he felt a duty to a fellow Keeper to bring her home. But as a man out of his depth, he knew Taylor was right. His presence put the mercenary team at risk.

Simon had turned in his badge, effectively ending his career in order to do this. The whole operation wasn't just off-book, it was illegal, amounting to an act of war against a nominally friendly nation. No one doubted that the Havens and the Commonwealth were on dangerous ground right now. A small spark could ignite a wider war.

His older foster brother, Willston, had talked to Bendict Hammersmith in the Antiterrorism office of the Justice Ministry. Hammersmith had given them a name and a location, a bar in the West End. Simon and Haldron Stonebender, his foster father, were there at a back table at precisely 18th hour when Taylor had approached them. After a few words were exchanged to establish their identities and their connection to Hammersmith, they'd gotten down to business.

"Bendict Hammersmith tells me you're looking to hire a Special Arms team for a covert job," said Taylor. "Just what did you have in mind?"

"Hostage rescue," said Simon. "We need to get a high-value person out of the Graystorm Compound in Tintagel and bring her back here to the Commonwealth."

Taylor frowned, then looked to Hal. "If you weren't Haldron Stonebender, I'd be walking out of this bar right now." To Simon's surprised look, Taylor said, "I know who the both of you are. You've got solid reputations as honest Peacekeepers and capable operators. Hal here can tell you about some special services a few years back that left the Marines in his debt. But what you propose isn't just illegal, it could spark a war. Who's this high-value person you want to get out?"

"Sylvie Graystorm, youngest daughter of *Syr* Berland Graystorm, cousin to the Steward of Tintagel. She's also a Gray Ranger and my fiancé."

Taylor pursed his lips and said nothing for a long while.

"Can you get into the Compound?" Simon asked.

"Getting in isn't the problem," said Taylor. "Getting out again, and with Lady Graystorm, depending on her condition, is the problem. I assume you want a stealthy operation, no frontal assault or unnecessary gunbattles."

"As quick and quiet as possible," answered Simon.

Taylor rubbed his chin. "A half dozen men with personal flyers, seeing stones, and PL44's with sleeper rounds maybe could do it. But it needs serious operators and will cost some heavy coin in hazard pay."

"House Stonebender is good for it," said Hal.

"I know that, or I wouldn't have taken this meeting." He shifted his gaze from Simon to Hal and back. "What's the timeline?"

"Four weeks; twenty-three days to be exact," said Simon. "The Steward has announced a plan for public trials and executions of various 'traitors' to begin then. I don't know if Sylvie is on the docket but have to assume she will be."

"Not much time," grunted Taylor. "We'll need detailed plans of the compound and some idea of where the Lady is being held, as well as a map of possible infiltration and exfil routes. I can get the men together in a couple of days, but we'll need every bit of that time to simulate and practice the assault." Taylor paused and gave Hal a hard look. "And I'll need to see some coin."

"This should get you started," Hal said, passing across a purse heavy with gold Crowns. "There's a bank draft for twenty thousand drawn on the Dunharrow Trust inside the purse."

"My thanks." Taylor slid the purse into a breast pocket. "I'll call my guys right away."

"One other thing," said Simon. "I'm coming with you."

"The hells you are," said Taylor. "This isn't a game or some saga story where you get to rescue the Princess."

"Nevertheless, you need me," said Simon. "First, Sylvie isn't going to run off with you just because you say so. She'll want some proof of identity. What better proof than me as part of the team? Second, clearing the border on the way back could be difficult. I have contacts in West Faring who can facilitate that, but they won't likely deal with you. Finally, Sylvie's not just my fiancé, she's a fellow Keeper. I have a duty to her and all Peacekeepers to get her out."

Taylor shook his head. "This is a very bad idea."

CHAPTER TWO

Simon drove slowly, for him, back to Stonebender Hall in suburban Glenharrow. Before it had been consumed by the expanding city of Cymbeline, Glenharrow had been a Dwarven enclave, home to many of the ancestral homes of prominent Dwarf families, like the Stonebenders.

Stonebender Hall was modest by the ancient standard but still large enough to accommodate all of Hal and Molly's six children, plus Simon, and multiple grandchildren. It had been Simon's home since Hal had taken him in at the age of ten. He'd moved out to his own flat in the city when he joined the Peacekeepers, but he'd moved back into his old room since Sylvie's capture. It made it easier to coordinate the efforts of the family as they planned her escape.

He parked his Oxley Tornado in the stables adjacent to the main Hall and entered through the postern door to the side. This led him directly into the kitchen, the true heart of the Hall. His foster mother, Molly, stood by the huge stove, adding spices to a bubbling pot. Hal sat at the pine worktable with Willston sipping ale and talking in low tones. They all looked up as Simon walked in.

"Gods, brother," said Wills, "You look knackered. Training going well?"

"Don't ask, Wills." Simon sat heavily in a chair and poured a mug of ale from the flagon in the middle of the table.

"You're determined to go through with the sheep-brained scheme?" Wills asked. "I still think you should leave this to the professionals."

"And how will they get across the border and even close to Tintagel without help from the Cabal? And you know Kermal won't deal with anyone but me."

Wills shrugged. "So, you and Brackenville get them across the border and within striking distance. But there's no reason for you to go along on the actual rescue. They'll bring Sylvie out and link up with you and Kermal in the countryside."

Simon drank his ale and didn't answer. They'd covered this ground before and he knew he had no words that would persuade Willston. Hal stayed silent as well. Simon thought he understood but couldn't articulate it in a way Wills would understand.

"Will you be ready?" Hal asked instead.

"I think so," said Simon. "Of course, Top has his doubts."

"If Taylor says you're fit, fine." Hal sipped ale. "But if not, promise me you'll stay in the woods with Kermal and the Orcs and let the professionals do their job."

"I will," said Simon, wondering if he really would.

"All good, then," said Wills. "I heard from Katya today. Hamil Fairborn got in touch with her a few days ago. She was able to facilitate his crossing into the Free States. Liam and Becky were standing by with funds and transportation to the northern border of the Havens. Hamil has contacts that can get him to Tintagel, but getting out again may be hard. Katya and the Justice Ministry were able to forge convincing identity papers, and he's changed his hair color, but it won't fool anyone who knows him."

"We need him to get the latest disposition of guards around the Graystorm compound. We have a pretty good map and building plans but still don't know where Sylvie is being held," said Simon.

"That depends on whether she's under house arrest or in a cell," said Hal. "I favor the former. I'm betting she has enough good will from the rest of the family and retainers that her father won't treat her like a common prisoner."

"What news from Brackenville?" asked Wills.

"Kermal and the Cabal have pledged to get us into the Havens via West Faring." Simon took a pull on his mug of ale. "Once across the frontier, the Clans have a network of smugglers and resistance organizers that can get us close to Tintagel through the swamps and back roads. From there we'll wait until night and take flyers into the compound. If we can get in place by the next new moon, we should be able to get in and out before dawn."

"A lot of moving parts," observed Hal.

"Aye," said Simon. "It's a bit slapdash, but we haven't much time for detailed planning."

"How will Fairborn get his information to you, assuming he isn't captured?" Hal asked.

Simon smiled and finished his ale. "I needed that," he sighed. "An ordinary mirror summons to Liam, with a prearranged series of innocent phrases that will tell us where Sylvie is being held and the guard strength around her."

"Enough war talk, for now," announced Molly. "Supper is ready. Hal, get some crockery from the pantry; bowls and small plates will do. Willston, set the table. Simon, come help me with this cauldron."

They all jumped to Molly's commands, although Simon wondered about why she needed help with a cauldron she'd been lifting for as long as he could remember.

She spoke softly to him when he got to her side. "When was the last time you slept through the night?"

"I don't know. Not since Sylvie was taken, truth be told."

She reached up and touched his cheek. "We'll get her back. Hal and the family are behind you. But you'll do her no good if you don't have the strength to lift your load when the time comes. Let me make you a sleeping draught tonight. Get some sleep."

"I will," said Simon. "I promise."

They ate the meal, mutton stew and greens, in the companionable silence of family. Simon knew there were things Willston wanted to say, but he was too exhausted to deal with them. Hal may have talked with his third son, because Willston kept his doubts to himself, for which Simon was grateful. He wiped the last of his stew from the bowl with a piece of flat bread, ate it and thanked Molly for the meal.

"If it's all the same to everyone," he said. "I think I'll turn in. As Wills said, I'm exhausted, and Top wants an early start tomorrow."

"Of course," said Molly. She came around the table and squeezed his neck in a hug before he could stand up. "Get ready for bed. I'll bring the draught in directly."

Simon had already pulled back the covers and climbed into bed when Molly appeared with a small cup of green liquid.

"Drink this." She handed him the cup and watched as he swallowed it. She reached out and took his hand. "You know you and Sylvie are as much our children as Wills and the rest. I worry about you, my son. You burn hotter than a Dwarf and don't have the endurance of an Elf. Take care you don't get consumed."

"I won't, Molly," said Simon sleepily, the draught already taking effect. "It's just that I need her so. I don't know how to slow down."

She cupped his neck as he lay back in the pillows. "I know, Son. I know."

CHAPTER THREE

Simon awoke just before dawn, feeling refreshed. That is until he tried to get out of bed. Every muscle in his body protested. With a groan he heaved himself to his feet. He'd considered himself physically fit, but Taylor's standards were more demanding than anything he'd ever imagined. The fact that the rest of the team seemed unfazed by the physical training made him feel even more unprepared.

By the time he dressed and made his way to the kitchen, he felt better, refreshed but still stiff. He spooned porridge into a bowl and poured coffee into a mug. Molly was already up, bustling about the kitchen, humming softly.

"I'm boiling some eggs, Simon," she said. "Would you like one?"

"No, thanks, Molly. Top starts early and we're training hard. Just some porridge and coffee." He ate quickly, bent, and kissed the top of her head. "I'll see you tonight."

Twenty minutes later, he parked his sled next to the nondescript warehouse that housed the training facility. As he approached the door, he heard heavy footsteps behind him and turned to see three of his teammates jogging toward him running in formation.

Simon smiled. Taylor had made it clear that physical training was an individual responsibility, and Simon took that seriously. He had his own workout routine, as did Taylor and Steelhammer. The three others, Gillis, Falkes, and Herin, seemed to enjoy running in formation. They reached the door and fell out with good natured nods to Simon and jibes to each other. Simon held the door for them, and they all stepped inside.

"Listen up," Taylor shouted down to them from the overhead catwalk. "Briefing room, ten minutes. We have information from Fairborn."

Simon made his way directly to the spacious conference room. Unlike most of the 'rooms' in the building, which were constructed of movable partitions, the briefing room was a permanent space at the back of the building. A large conference table filled the center of the room with a series of slates and magic mirrors mounted on the walls around it. Front and center, opposite the entrance, a podium and large-screen mirror commanded the room.

Taylor stood at the podium and Georg Steelhammer, his Dwarf Second in Command, sat in the nearest chair. Simon nodded to each and took his own place, third back on the left. The rest of the team trickled in. First was Steron Gillis, the armorer, who Simon suspected was a half-Elf. He had a modest amount of Air Talent, a plus for an armorer, but not essential. Behind him came Christon Herin, the team's medic and communications specialist. A big man with a ready grin and easy nature, he still could be ruthless in a fight. Even in training, Simon saw and respected an intensity that would be intimidating in someone less approachable. Finally came Bran Falkes, Fire Mage and demolitions specialist. Falkes got on well with Herin but said little to anyone else. Simon didn't sense hostility in him, just an extreme reserve. The team poured mugs of coffee from a large pot set near the door and took their seats around the table.

"All right," said Taylor. "Time to get serious. The Loot's man Fairborn really came through. We have detailed intel on guard strength, schedules, and disposition in the residential part of the Compound. He confirmed that Lady Graystorm is under house arrest, confined to a suite of rooms near the North wall and not locked in the tower or some deep jail cell. All good for our purposes."

"Now tell 'em the bad news, Top," muttered Steelhammer.

"The bad news is that the North wall is right next to the main gate to the High Tower, the residence of the Steward and the most heavily guarded area in Tintagel," said Taylor. The big mirror screen behind him lit up, showing an aerial view of a formidable-looking fortification around a tall central spire. Just to the left of the tower, a second, lower wall enclosed a wide-open compound containing pavilions, fountains, and a few small elegant looking buildings.

Taylor used a pointer and indicated the compound and an area near the upper wall. "This is the Graystorm compound, and this is where the Lady is being held. As you can see, direct entry over the North Wall isn't viable. We'd be in full view of the High Tower the whole time. Entry over the South Wall—especially this Southeast corner—might be possible, assuming we can get close enough to just hop the flyers over. Crossing the open compound by air, even under Veil, doesn't seem doable."

"Agreed," said Steelhammer. "We have to assume

their security spells will detect any Veiled traffic. We'll need to get weapons in there and I don't see how that won't set off the alarms as well. It's a lot of open ground to cover, Top."

"What if we go around the perimeter?" asked Simon. Steelhammer turned slightly to look at him. "How is that better, Loot?"

"Well, Top said we have good intel on the guard schedules and dispositions. What if we time our entry to catch the guard team as they pass the Southeast corner?" Seeing puzzled looks around the table, he continued quickly. "We either stay close to them or take them out and assume their patrol pattern. The alarms must be set to ignore or at least account for their weapons, so the spell won't know if it's us or them."

Top nodded. "That's not bad, Loot. What do you think, Steron? If you were monitoring the area for weapons, how would you do it?"

The armorer grinned. "Loot's right. Wide area security spells can't distinguish between individual weapons like a door spell can. The simplest way is to designate certain areas as weapons-free so that any weapon will set off the alarm. Other areas can be set to ignore general alerts and alarm only at specific times." He stood and approached the image of the compound and pointed to various areas. "What I'd do is make the central courtyard, the residential areas, and the official chambers weapons-free. I'd alarm all the entrances with door spells but leave the guard patrol areas and a reasonable distance around them open." He thought for a moment. "You know, there's another area that would need to be unalarmed. The kitchens. A security spell can't tell the difference between a dagger and a paring knife. A blade's a blade."

"Right," said Taylor. "That gives us two possible options for infil and initial set up. Loot, how close can your Orc friends get us to that Southeast corner?"

"I don't know, Top," said Simon. "Kermal Brackenville assures me he can get us into Tintagel undetected but hasn't told me the actual location of any base or safehouse they may have."

"We'll need that information," said Taylor. The image changed on the main mirror and two of the side screens lit up with lines of text. "This is what Fairborn found out about the guard strength and disposition. As you can see, the emphasis is on keeping people in. It seems *Syr* Berland is more concerned with preventing his daughter from escaping than keeping us out. I suspect he has other important persons in the compound as his involuntary guests. The guard strength and patrol patterns suggest at least half a dozen people under guard."

"We can use that to our advantage," said Steelhammer. "A few diversions and they won't know who to cover."

"Some pyrotechnics maybe?" asked Gillis, looking at Falkes.

Falkes nodded. "Not difficult. Just a question of timing and location."

"All good then," said Taylor. "Put your heads together and come up with an op plan based on infil over the Southeast wall. Loot, I want you and Steron to take a look at the kitchens as well, both as an infil and possible exfil location. We'll reconvene at 13th hour and then set up some practice scenarios."

The group broke up and Gillis sat down next to Simon. "That was good thinking on the guards, Loot. What's your take on the kitchens?"

"Maybe as a way out, but not for infil," Simon said. "There's usually traffic in and out of kitchens at all hours, especially in a Great House. We'd get bogged down with civilians."

"You've had experience with this sort of thing?"

Gillis asked. "You didn't strike me as a Noble."

Simon laughed. "Far from it. I'm a ship chandler's son. But House Stonebender was a Great House once and they took me in when I was orphaned. The trappings are still there."

"Exfil it is then," said Gillis. "We need some good maps of the surrounding streets."

Over the next hour they poured over street maps and images coming up with several potential routes out of the city. They had little information on traffic patterns, but the routes avoided main thoroughfares and shopping areas. By 13th hour, they were ready to report to the rest of the team.

Taylor greeted everyone as they took their seats. "We'll get to the primary op plan in a minute. Loot, Steron, what are the possibilities with the kitchens?"

Simon looked at Gillis, but he waved for him to continue. "May be an option for exfil, but not practical for entry. Too high a risk of encountering civilians."

"Figured as much," said Steelhammer. "Write it up as a back-up. Top, take us through the primary plan."

Top went through the infiltration plan with Veiled flyers popping over the Southeast wall and landing in an open walkway close to a corner room labeled as a guard post. After securing the room, they planned to move down the east side of the center courtyard to secure a second room at the far end. From there, it was a short distance to the residential apartments. Top had marked the second suite as their target based on Fairborn's information. After securing Sylvie, they'd exfil quickly straight across the courtyard, sacrificing stealth for speed. Rally points were the guardrooms, the central pavilion, and the entrance to the kitchens along the South wall.

Over the next hour, they designated Farspeaker codes, assigned team numbers, Top being One and Simon Six. The team verbally drilled the route and the likely choke points, designated callsigns and code words for changes in movement. Then they broke, kitted up, and ran practice scenarios. The big open center of the facility was the courtyard and partitions simulated the passages, guardrooms, and apartments.

The team finally broke at 20th hour because Top said they were getting tired and sloppy. "Go home, get some rest. We'll run this again tomorrow. That's our last shot. New moon is in five days, and we need to get on the road." He pointed to Simon. "Loot, I'll need rendezvous points and transport capabilities of your Orc friends. I don't want to get to the border and find nothing but empty air."

"Brackenville will be there, Top. I'll have time and coordinates by tomorrow."

"Right," said Taylor. "We'll convene at 8th tomorrow, run through infil and exfil a couple of times, then prep weapons, the flyers, and individual load outs. Bare minimums, people. We may be humping gear through the bush on a short timeline."

Simon filed out with the rest of the team, wondering how he could reach Kermal. The half-Orc enforcer for the Cabal of Clans, and former Peacekeeper, didn't keep a regular mirror locus but shifted through several at random. Just as Simon reached his Oxley, the problem resolved itself when the summoning tone on his own hand-held mirror sounded. He swiped across it and Kermal's face appeared.

"Good meeting," said Simon. "I was wondering how I'd get in touch with you."

"Meet me at Lily's Place, one hour," replied his former teammate tersely.

"On my way. What's happening? Trouble?"

Kermal shook his head. "Just be there."

Simon drove rapidly across the Hanford Bridge over the Great Cut and turned south into the Orc slums known as the Hollows. On the corner of Canal and

Knacker, Lily Ponsaka's tavern occupied almost half of the Western side of the block facing Canal. Simon parked the Oxley in the lot behind the tavern, set the Warding spells, and approached the rear door that led to the kitchens.

Lily herself opened the door when he knocked. She was short and stocky, even for an Orc, with Azeri Fish Clan tattoos climbing up powerful forearms to disappear under a short-sleeved blouse.

"Why can't you use the front door like a normal person," she demanded by way of greeting.

"And good meeting to you too, Lily. I wouldn't want your patrons to think it was some sort of Peacekeeper raid if I showed up out in the common room," said Simon with a short laugh.

"Let me worry about that, Simon Buckley," Lily scolded. "Besides, you ain't a Peacekeeper anymore now." She stepped back and waved him in. "Come on in. Brackenville and the others are already here, in the alcove next to the bar."

The others? thought Simon as he crossed the steam-filled kitchen and went through the double doors to the common room. The long bar ended just to his right. To the left, a small alcove held a table and chairs half hidden in shadow.

Kermal rose as Simon turned toward the alcove and advanced with his hand extended. Simon took it but froze when he saw the other two people seated at the table. One was a huge Orc Simon had encountered before, known muscle for Kalmish Forsaka, Chieftain of the Azeri Wind Clan and de facto head of the Cabal of Clans, the organization that ran organized Orc crime in Cymbeline. The other person was Forsaka himself. He regarded Simon with a steady eye and a wry smile.

"What's going on, Kermal," asked Simon. "I thought this was just between us."

"Please, Lieutenant Buckley," said Forsaka. "Come

and sit. Have some tea and apricots. We have a few matters to discuss before you and Kermal get on with your mission planning."

Simon recognized the formula for a formal Orc parley, open hands, and invitation to share food and drink, essentially a guarantee of safety. He glared at Kermal, who only shrugged. Simon took the proffered seat and allowed the big Orc to pour tea for the two of them. Neither Kermal nor the bodyguard were offered any.

Simon sipped the cardamom-scented tea and ate a dried apricot; food, offered and received, it was permissible to discuss business. "What do you want, Chief Forsaka?" asked Simon. "I thought I made it clear through Kermal that, while I appreciate the Cabal's assistance in the matter, this was a business arrangement. You aren't buying your own pet Peacekeeper Lieutenant."

Forsaka laughed, a deep throaty sound. "I'm well aware of your ethical standards, Lieutenant. What I have in mind is a business arrangement. I have a task I wish you to perform as part of your mission to free Lady Graystorm. The Cabal is willing to go to considerable risk to get your team in and out of Tintagel. Surely you didn't expect that to happen without some payment."

Simon sipped tea. "What do you want me to do?"

Forsaka slid a heavy envelope sealed with an embossed wax crest across the table. "That is a bank draft for fifty thousand Crowns that you will deliver to the Hansiatic Bank in West Faring. Once it is confirmed, the bank will turn over to you ten thousand Crowns in cash. You will take the money across the border and see that it reaches Chief Kaldan Barca, the leader of the group that will guide you to Tintagel."

Simon swallowed tea and almost choked. "Ten thousand. In cash. Coin or scrip?"

"Coin. I'm afraid nothing else will work north of the Borderlands." Forsaka finished his tea and set the cup down upside down, signaling the end of the meeting. "I'll take my leave. You and Kermal have much to discuss."

He rose, bowed deeply to Lily and walked across the common room followed by his bodyguard. Most of the Orcs in the room ignored him. A few, those who had enough steel or prestige, nodded or waved at him. He acknowledged a few, and Simon marked those for future reference. Once a Keeper, always a Keeper.

CHAPTER FOUR

"I knew I'd have to pay for his help," said Simon as he stared down at the envelope. "I suppose it's too much to hope that this will be the end of it."

"Forsaka knows he can't expect you to do anything that would harm your family or the Peacekeepers. Moving cash across the border may be illegal, but no worse than this mission in the first place." Kermal pulled out a mirror and activated it. "Speaking of which, I have the rendezvous points outside West Faring and specs on transportation. The flyers are the concern. They need a lot of space, even if they don't weigh much. It means bigger cargo beds and wider sledge profiles."

"Maybe not. Top has access to some top-of-the-line gear. The flyers are collapsable. I'm told they fold down to a box about as tall and wide as this table." Simon tapped on the tabletop. "I'm more worried about this money transfer. Ten thousand Crowns, all in gold, will have to weigh at least a couple hundred weight. It'll be compact but heavy and hard to shift around quickly if something goes sideways."

"Hopefully that will be Barca's problem once we link up with him." Kermal looked at his mirror. "So, if you're right about these flyers, two should fit in a single cargo bed. Two men, two flyers per that's three sledges. What about weapons and ammo?"

"We'll need a fourth sledge for weapons and extra ammo as well as specialty gear and pyrotechnics," said Simon "Probably won't amount to a full load so maybe we can put the money there. I'll feel better if I stay with the cash until we turn it over. What's with all that money, Kermal? I've hired a full team of trained Special Arms operators for not much more."

"Do you really want to know, Simon?" Kermal kept his voice low.

"Look, it's one thing to pay off a crime boss who's acting out of simple greed. I get the feeling this is more than that. I've no love for the Gray Havens, but I don't want to face a charge of financing terrorists if this all goes bad."

Kermal shook his head. "Terrorism is a bit strong, but it's defined by those in power. Barca and his people are working for Orcish rights in the Havens. They have a political wing that negotiates with the major landowners and progressives on the High Council. They have a charitable trust that helps displaced Orcs find housing and work."

"Right, all sweetness and light," said Simon.

"There are rumors of a direct-action group," admitted Kermal. "There have been some unexplained arson and weapons thefts, but nothing solid. Nothing that rises above ordinary criminality."

"But what if this money is what finances them to expand operations?" asked Simon.

"And what if it helps a few thousand Orc families find food and shelter?" Kermal shot back.

Simon held up a hand in surrender. "I give in, we just can't know what the money will buy."

Kermal rechecked his mirror. "So, four cargo sledges and at least two escort sleds to run interference. Where do we pick up the gear?"

Simon gave him the address of the training facility. "Where do we meet your people at the border?"

Kermal brought up a map image on his mirror. "Here, about a league north of West Faring, there's an old logging road that runs to the border." He sent Simon the image. "Barca's people will meet us there."

"How far into Tintagel can they get us?" asked Simon. "Our planning depends on a short flyer hop over the compound wall."

"I don't know," said Kermal. "They were just asked to get you to the city, not into it."

"I know, but Taylor thinks it's our best shot. We'll need to plan something on the fly. Top is gonna hate it." Simon checked his timepiece. "It's just after 22nd now. Top wants to do a final run through at 8th tomorrow, followed by weapons check and individual load outs. Unless you hear differently from me, have your sledges at the facility by 16th. We should be able to load up and be on the road by 18th. I need a mirror locus where I can reach you."

"Tagged to the map I sent you." Kermal rose and extended his hand. "See you tomorrow, Simon."

Stonebender Hall was dark when Simon got home just before 23rd hour. He started up the stairs to his room but noticed a faint light coming from the left. He crossed the large reception room and entered Hal's private study. The old Dwarf sat behind an ancient oak table that served as his desk. He held a glass of brandy and didn't look up when Simon entered.

"Portalis brandy on the sideboard," said Hal. "Pour yourself some and sit."

"I'm really tired, Hal. I didn't expect anyone to be

awake. I was planning on going to bed."

"Too tired to have a drink with your foster father?" said Hal. "Sit. I have a few things to say."

Simon poured brandy into the cut crystal glass that matched Hal's and sat opposite him. "What is it, Hal?"

Hal stared into his glass. "You're my son, and Sylvie is going to be your wife. Plus, she has Rights of the Hall. House Stonebender will use all its resources to help the two of you." Hal sipped brandy. "That said, are you sure this is the best way to get Sylvie back?"

"Meaning?"

"Meaning you've given up your career over this." Hal held up a hand when Simon began to speak. "I know, you can't do what you think you must do and carry the badge. Just be sure that's the real reason you gave it up. If this goes badly, if you're caught North of the line, or in Tintagel itself, there will be no coming back, not to the Peacekeepers, maybe not even to the Commonwealth. The King may be in your debt, but not to the extent he'd risk war to save your ass."

"What choice do we have?" said Simon. "The Steward is planning to start show trials for treason in a few days. Sylvie is sure to be on the docket. She's too high profile to keep under polite house arrest. They'll want to make an example, show that even Noble Family connections won't protect 'traitors.' I doubt they'll execute her, but she'll be locked away in a maximum-security cell where we'll never get her out." He drained his brandy. "We go tomorrow evening. With luck we'll be in Tintagel by the new moon."

"Wish I was going with you," said Hal, finishing his own brandy.

"We talked about this. I need you and Wills to help Hammersmith run interference with Justice. If word gets out about this, even rumors, before we cross the border, it'll all be for nothing." Simon set his glass on

Hal's desk. "I'm off to bed. Good night, Father."

Simon rarely called Hal 'father.' Hal stood and embraced his foster son in a bear hug. "Gods be with you, Son."

CHAPTER FIVE

The small convoy of four sledges and two nondescript, four-seat Hilten sleds crossed the Great Cut over the Hanford Bridge and headed west along Tanner. They picked up the W205 at Westport and crossed the Ring Road in moderate evening traffic just before 19th hour. The covered sledges were well used and bore the sigil of an Orc-owned shipping company based in Fernhill, near the Southern Orc Reservation. The sleds were the economy model Hilten's, marketed to Orcs and working-class Humans who wanted the cache of the Hilten name without the expense of the brand's luxury models. No one paid them any notice.

Simon and Falkes were paired in the second sledge with an Orc driver, who gave his name as Merl but said nothing else. He drove steadily, eyes on the road and the sledge in front of them. Falkes leaned against the doorframe with his eyes closed, asleep or just not interested in conversation. Simon stared straight ahead as the miles slid by.

The convoy reached the outskirts of West Faring just after 2nd hour. They pulled off the highway into a shipping yard marked with the same company sigil and parked. Merl climbed down and walked over to where the other drivers congregated around a fire someone had started in a barrel. Simon climbed out and stretched the kinks out of his back as Kermal approached from the lead sled.

"There's cots, coffee, water, and snacks inside." He pointed toward a low building a few yards to their right. "The bank won't be open for another five hours or so. You should get some sleep."

"What about you?" Simon gently punched his friend's arm. "I'm counting on you to be my getaway driver or at least help me lift all that gold."

"I'll be along," said Kermal. He nodded toward the cluster of Orc drivers gathered around the fire. "I need to have a talk with the boyos over there. We'll be heading into rough country tomorrow, and I need to be sure they're up to it."

"You don't know them?" asked Simon, surprised.

Kermal shook his head. "They're Forsaka's boys; mixed bag of Clans, but Azeri's all. They may be accustomed to off track driving. I hope they are, but I don't know them."

Kermal strolled off toward the fire, and Simon turned toward the low building. He wasn't surprised that the drivers worked for Forsaka, only that Kermal hadn't been involved in selecting them. As promised, the building had a row of cots and long tables with coffee urns, tea canisters and piles of snack foods. Simon chose a cot near the far wall, rolled into a blanket, and fell asleep.

Kermal shook him awake just after 6th hour. "Awake and alert, Simon. Top wants us all on the parking pad before the day starts."

Simon struggled off the cot and stood, swayed for

a moment, then shook his head clear. His mouth felt full of dust and his eyes burned. He grabbed a cup of water from the table, drank most of it and splashed the rest on his face.

"What did you find out about our drivers?" he asked Kermal softly as they crossed the pad to where the sledges were parked.

"All Cabal soldiers, but country boys who can handle themselves in the bush," said Kermal with a smile. "Not a bad lot, but Azeri refugees They don't talk much because, where they come from, talking can get you dead."

The team and the Azeris assembled in front of Taylor, Simon, and the rest of the team in their usual line by numbers, the drivers in a knot.

"All good, then," said Taylor when the last of the drivers drifted over. "Loot, Brackenville, what's your timeline for your mission for the Cabal?"

"Leave here at 9th, back by 11th, if the bank cooperates," said Simon

"Brackenville, what's our best time to the border?"

Kermal turned and said a few words in Azeri to the drivers. They mumbled among themselves before Merl said, "Five hours."

"That puts us there before sunset," said Taylor. "When can we expect Chief Barca?"

"I can't say exactly," said Kermal. "The general plan is for us to cross and continue Northwest on the logging road until Barca declares himself."

"Not sure I like that," said Taylor. "We could drive straight into a Gray Ranger patrol or get bogged down in a swamp without a guide."

"I get that, Top," said Simon before Kermal could answer. "But he's got a vested interest in keeping us safe, at least until he gets the special cargo Kermal and I will be hauling."

"The drivers are all good with off-road travel?"

Taylor asked Kermal.

"They're all country boys," said Kermal with a nod. "They'll be good."

"Right then. Everyone get some food and rest while Brackenville and the Loot attend to their business," said Taylor. "Triple check weapons and gear. Any personal stuff, mirrors, ID, images of your grandma, coach tickets, anything that could lead back to the Commonwealth, gets purged and left here. I'm told there's a lockbox in the depot there where all that stuff can be left if you hope to retrieve it later."

Just before 9th hour, Kermal and Simon stripped off their travel clothes to shower, shave and dress the part of important Cymbeline businessmen. Simon pulled on silk hose, soft Glenharrow wool breaches and a matched jacket. He tied on a red cravat and added a gold stickpin. Kermal dressed all in black, but the breaches and jacket were obviously bespoke, and his soft calf-length boots were polished to a mirror sheen.

Gillis whistled as they exited the building and walked toward one of the Hilten sleds, and Herin turned around and said in his best South Dundarian accent, "Gor, ain't you two pretty!"

"That's enough," said Top with a smile. "Good hunting, gents. We'll be waiting for you."

Traffic was surprisingly light, and they arrived at the Hansiatic Bank in central West Faring in only twenty minutes. The bank occupied an imposing stone building on the South side of Temple Square in the heart of the old walled town. Kermal parked the sled in a space marked with a 'Bank Customers Only' sign and they climbed out.

"They certainly try to look solid, don't they?" Kermal leaned back slightly as he took in the tall Magisterium era façade of the building. "One has to wonder about why they'd do business with the Cabal."

"Bankers don't care where the money comes from," replied Simon with a bitter edge to his voice, "as long as it's gold."

Kermal gave him a sidelong glance but said nothing as they entered the bank lobby. The space was every bit as impressive as the façade with a double row of marble columns, polished limestone floor and high-top desks for filling out paperwork or deposit requests. Across the middle of the lobby stretched a row of brass teller cages behind which were the desks and offices of the various officers and managers. The entire back wall was a huge steel vault, its partially open door showing concentric rings of warding spells and glyphs as well as sturdy locking bars.

Simon approached the nearest teller, drew out the envelope and said, "I'm here as a representative of Kalmish Forsaka. My colleague and I wish to speak to your senior manager."

"Mr. Halber is in a meeting right now," replied the woman in her best customer service voice. "Perhaps I can help you?"

"I doubt that," replied Simon, striving for the right tone of arrogance, as would be expected from a wealthy customer. "I'll need to speak to a more senior bank officer immediately."

Before the woman could reply, an older man in a well-cut business suit stepped up behind her. "May I be of assistance? I'm Harold Vilson, Senior Teller."

"As I told your woman here, I am here as a representative of Kalmish Forsaka, and I need to speak to a senior bank officer. Now, if your Mr. Halber is too busy, perhaps I can deal with some other officer." Simon folded his arms and looked about impatiently.

Vilson stiffened at the mention of Forsaka. "Of course, sir. If you'll step to the gate just over there, I'll show you to a private office and get Mr. Halber straight away."

Simon and Kermal walked the few feet to the gap in the cages that Vilson had indicated and followed him to a cubicle that reminded Simon of his old office at Wycliffe house, wood and frosted glass in a small square giving the illusion of privacy. The small office contained a round ebony table and three leather-covered chairs. Simon sat down and placed the heavy envelope on the table where Vilson could see the wax embossed seal. It seemed to agitate him even more, and he excused himself with a slight bow.

"Wonder what that's all about?" mused Kermal as he took the other seat. "Good act, by the way. Even I believed you were a rich crime boss."

Simon looked up as a pair of vague shapes approached. The frosted glass door opened to reveal Vilson and a plump man in a dark gray business suit. He had a round face and a shock of white hair above a high forehead.

"Mr. Halber, I assume?" Simon nodded to the man but didn't rise.

"You're a day early," said Halber without acknowledging Simon's greeting.

Simon frowned. "I am never early. I arrive precisely when I plan to." He indicated the envelope on the table with a wave of his hand. "That is for you. You were told to expect it and were told what I expect to collect from this bank."

Halber seemed to deflate. He pulled a white handkerchief from his back pocket and wiped his high forehead. "You must understand. We rarely have that amount in cash on hand, at least not in coin. It's taken us three days to collect the sum. The last shipment just came in last night. We were still counting and verifying it by opening time today."

"Which is your problem, not mine," said Simon. He took a chance and went on, "You're being well paid to deliver what we require, not to make excuses."

Halber paled. "Of course. The coin is ready and being packed for transport as we speak."

Simon reached out and picked up the envelope, holding it out to Halber, who accepted it. "I believe that completes our business today. Now, I'd like to see Mr. Forsaka's gold for myself before we load it onto my sled."

"Of course," stammered Halber. "Where are you parked?"

"In front of your lobby, in the spot you so conveniently reserved for customers."

Halber shook his head. "Oh no, that will never do. We can't move that much gold through the lobby. It must go from the secure loading dock."

"And where is that?" asked Simon sharply.

"Just around the corner, on the East side of the building. We'll ensure there's no traffic or delay, if you will just move the sled to that side." Halber backed away a step as he spoke.

"Kermal?" said Simon absently.

"On it, boss," replied Kermal, playing the loyal retainer.

"Right this way, Mr., uh," Halber stammered. "Forgive me. I don't believe I caught your name."

Simon gave him a hard look. "I don't believe I gave it. Lead on, Mr. Halber."

Halber led him to the vault area as Kermal crossed the lobby toward the front of the bank. They stepped through the vault door to where two slightly oversized metal briefcases rested on a metal table. At a signal from Halber, a guard stepped forward and opened the cases. Simon had to struggle to keep his expression neutral. Nestled in neat rows side by side were hundreds of gold coins, more than he'd ever seen in one place. He managed to simply nod and motioned to the guard to close the cases.

The guards stacked them on a hand truck and

started out of the vault. Halber and Simon followed close behind, Simon's eyes on the cases. They turned left through a set of double doors and into a long hallway lined with small offices, breakrooms and storage areas. It ended at a warded security door and a guardroom with windows looking both onto the hallway and onto an area outside the building.

The guard behind the window looked them over and, at a nod from Halber, unlocked the wards on the door. It opened with a subtle crackle, and they wheeled out onto a small platform a few feet above street level. The guard guided the hand truck down a ramp just as Kermal pulled up in the Hilten. Simon watched as they loaded the cases into the rear seat. He leaned in and rechecked the contents. Satisfied, he nodded curtly to Halber, climbed in next to Kermal, and they pulled away. As soon as they rounded the corner and were out of sight, they burst out laughing.

"I always arrive precisely when I intend to," intoned Kermal.

"What about you?" said Simon, laughing. "'On it, boss,' just like a good henchman." They both laughed again.

The drive back to the shipping yard was uneventful, and they arrived just before 11th hour. Taylor was waiting for them on the pad. "Welcome back, gents," he said. "Business done?"

"Aye, Top," said Simon. "Give us a few minutes to transfer the goods to the tactical sledge, and we can be on the road."

"I'll alert the team. We slide out in ten."

CHAPTER SIX

They reached the logging road before 14th hour and stopped for a brief regrouping. They kitted up in tactical vests, helmets and Farspeaker receivers. After a quick communications check, they reboarded the sledges and moved out.

Simon again found himself between Merl and Bran Falkes. They crept along the rough track, sometimes paved with crushed gravel, other times marked only by a wide spot between the trees. Falkes sat forward and watched the tree line on either side as Merl concentrated on following the track. Simon looked straight ahead, watching the rear of the Hilten sled that acted as their lead scout.

Falkes had never been talkative, so Simon was surprised when he spoke. "How do you know Brackenville, Loot?" he asked without taking his eyes off the tree line. "What I hear, he's an enforcer for the Clans. How's a Peacekeeper Lieutenant on the same dig with an Orc like that?"

"Half-Orc," said Simon.

"Eh?"

"Kermal's mother was human," said Simon. "His father was the head enforcer for the Cabal but hid that from Kermal and his mother. When Kermal realized who Hasfal Brackenville was, after the man died, he became a Keeper, one of my team when I was a sergeant."

"But now he's the enforcer," said Falkes, half as a question.

"We had a case that involved the Cabal. The Force thought one of them was guilty, but it was actually a crooked Keeper. It convinced Kermal he'd do more good working with his own people, since the Keepers would never see him as anything but an Orc."

Falkes nodded once and resumed his watch on the trees. At half past 16th, the logging track suddenly widened into a clearing fronting a rough fence line. The lead Hilten was pulled up in front of a small shed built of corrugated iron next to a gate. The gate sagged, half of it already twisted on the ground. Kermal stood next to the sled, talking with his driver.

Merl pulled the sledge in behind the Hilten, extended the skids, and shut down the Air spell. The other sledges fanned out behind it. Simon climbed down and looked around. The clearing was longer than it was wide, and he could now see the burned-out skeletons of old buildings, stone foundations, and rusting machinery.

Merl and the other drivers walked over and joined Kermal. The conversation became more animated with the drivers clustered together and Kermal gesturing at them and the at the gate. Taylor stalked past muttering, "What the hells now?"

Simon fell in next to Taylor. "What's going on Top?"

"Some horseshit about the drivers refusing to go on," growled Taylor.

"...the contract says you'll take us to Barca," Kermal said loudly.

"Wrong, cobber," said Merl. "Read the words. Says we take you to the border where Barca will take charge of you." He pointed to the half-collapsed gate. "There's the border. Not my problem if Barca ain't here."

"Barca isn't here, but you are," said Taylor as he joined the group. "You were supposed to turn the guide duty directly over to him."

"And who're you to tell us what to do," asked Merl, folding his arms, and facing the team leader.

"I'm the fellow holding all the weapons," said Taylor, shifting the PL44 from his back to the crook of his arm.

Merl laughed. "You gonna shoot us, soldier-man? Go ahead. You'll still end up driving yourself. It ain't worth our lives to cross that line." He pointed to the shed. "Read the sign, cobber. It was true twenty years ago, even more truth today."

Simon squinted at the battered sign hung from the doorframe of the shed.

Caution: Non-Elf personnel are warned that the writ of Commonwealth Law ends here. No legal guarantees of basic rights of search and seizure, arrest, representation, and trial by jury have been extended by the High Council of Lords.

Entry is at the risk of the individual and no adverse job action will be taken if any individual does not wish to enter.

"All of us got warrants in the Havens," said Merl to Simon. "Last thing we want is to run into a Gray Ranger patrol. We'll end up in a slave labor camp, if we're lucky; more likely just end up dead. We ain't crossing that line."

"Forsaka will hear about this," said Kermal. "And then you'll have to deal with me."

There was a flicker of fear in Merl's eyes, but it

passed quickly. "We know who you are, Brackenville. We also know you won't kill us without Forsaka's say so. And right now, he wants you over there with Barca. You survive and make it back, we'll see what Forsaka says."

Kermal's nostrils flared, and he reached out to grab Merl by the shirt. Simon put his hand on Kermal's shoulder. "Let them go. If we force them, we won't be able to trust them. We'll be watching our backs the whole time. Besides, we have about ten thousand reasons for Barca to want to contact us. We just follow the track until he reaches out."

Taylor shifted the PL44, so it hung from its tactical harness. "Loot's right, Brackenville. I can't watch them and watch the road as well." He turned and walked away. "Let 'em go."

In the end, the Azeris crammed themselves into the second Hilten sled and headed back the way they'd come. Taylor called the team together.

"Loot, you and Brackenville lead in the Hilten," he said. "Falkes, you and me in the first sledge, you drive. Gillis in sledge two; Herin in three; Georg, you drive drag. Stay sharp." He pointed to the fence. "Bran, I need that gate out of the way."

Falkes smiled. "On it, Top."

Five minutes later, the remaining hinges holding up the gate disappeared in a flash of blue flame. Falkes closed his fists and the Fire ball between his hands dissipated. Simon and Kermal dragged the remains of the gate away and reboarded the Hilten. They slid forward across the border.

Simon pointed to the sign. "You worried about that, too?"

Kermal laughed. "Barca and his people live here. I wouldn't be much of an enforcer if I let that scare me when they live it every day."

Simon drove, struggling to stay on the track as the

sun sank below the tree line. He debated turning on the headlights as the track fell deeper into shadow. He was about to flick them on when Kermal reached out his hand and stopped him.

"Stop the sled," said Kermal in a calm voice. "There are men all around us in the woods."

Simon looked around and nodded. He activated the Farspeaker tactical net. "One, this is Six."

"I see them Six," Taylor answered. "One to all numbers, weapons on safe, nobody move without my release." Simon tapped his Farspeaker stone twice in acknowledgement.

Kermal climbed out of the sled, hands at his side, palms outward and faced the tree line.

"Brackenville, what the hells are you doing." Simon heard Top over the tactical net.

"One, this is Six. He knows what he's doing. Give it a few minutes."

Kermal moved to the front of the grounded Hilten, maintaining the pose of peaceful intent. "I am Kermal Brackenville, son of Hasfal, born for Wind Clan by Sheila, daughter of George Willoughby." He spoke slowly and clearly.

He was answered by a loud bark of laughter. A light skinned Orc with a full blond beard stepped into view. He was tall and lithe with unmistakable Orcish features and powerful bare arms covered in silver bracelets.

Simon noted the garnet ring on his left hand. *Water Mage?* He wondered.

"I'm Kaldan Barca, son of some random Elf overseer who raped my mother Sayrd who never knew her clan or her father." He looked Kermal up and down. "You're Forsaka's man? You've got my money?"

"I have Forsaka's coin that can be released to you after you fulfill your agreement," said Kermal evenly.

Barca folded his arms, and Simon tensed as the

garnet ring took on a faint glow. "And what's to stop me from just taking the money and leaving you here?"

"One to all numbers," whispered Taylor over the net. "Weapons free, wait for my signal."

Kermal made a slight downward hand gesture.

"One, this is Six," said Simon. "Stand down, Top. Kermal's got this."

Kermal kept his hands in the peace position. "Because there's forty thousand reasons in the Hansiatic Bank in West Faring that will be part of an ongoing arrangement between your people and mine if this mission succeeds."

Barca laughed again and turned away. "Gendry, take the fancy Orc and his people in hand. We move out in five."

A dark-skinned Orc stepped forward, clearly a Southron with his almond eyes and skin tone. "Gendry Stubblefield, son of Galt, born for Serpent Clan by Hella, daughter of Talsta. I'll take you to the camp where you'll spend the night. We'll move on toward Tintagel in the morning."

"Thank you, Stubblefield," said Kermal.

The shorter Orc held out his hand. "Call me Gendry."

"I'm Kermal." He pointed to the Hilten. "That's my Lieutenant, Simon Buckley. You want to ride with us?"

"I'll sit up on the front," said Gendry. "The path to camp is hidden, just turn where I point and make sure the sledges stay close."

Kermal climbed back into the passenger seat. "Turn where Gendry points. Make sure the sledges stay close."

"One, this is Six," said Simon into the net. "Did you get that?"

"Aye, Loot. We'll stay close. One out."

Gendry motioned straight ahead as Barca, and the rest of his people seemed to melt into the trees.

Simon slid the Hilten forward. The sledges bunched up behind them. After about a hundred yards, Gendry pointed sharply to the right. Simon turned, even though he didn't see a path through the trees. At the last minute the overhanging branches lifted to reveal an opening. The Hilten and the sledges slipped through into a broad clearing filled with Orcs, and the branches closed behind them.

There were women and children scattered around tents and cookfires. Armed men guarded the perimeter. More sat near the fires, eating and drinking. All looked up and watched Gendry guide the vehicles to the far edge of the camp. Simon lowered the skids and canceled the Air spell. The sledges slid into position in a rough circle around the Hilten. Taylor and Gillis joined them as Steelhammer and the rest of the team secured their gear.

Gendry pointed to a fire ring and a pair of low wooden platforms off to their right. "You can set up here. There's a wood pile over there and the lads will bring some food in a little while. Barca wants a parley later tonight. And he'll want to see the coin."

"Loot, Brackenville, that's on you," said Taylor. "Steron, you and Chris start setting up the shelters. Georg and Bran will set security and get a fire going."

True to Gendry's word, a group of women and children approached them a short time later with covered baskets of flatbread, leeks, yoghurt and *hraska*, a savory Azeri paste made of ground beans, garlic, and oil. It was a simple fare but nutritious and filling.

Herin accepted the baskets and knelt next to a child and his mother. "Hello little one," he said to the little boy. "It looks like you've hurt yourself." The child had a crude bandage wrapped around his left arm, which he held away from his body with exaggerated care. The woman said something in Azeri. Herin looked puzzled until she pointed to the fire pit.

"Steron, get my kit," he said as he gently reached out and touched the boy's arm. As the woman hovered, Herin unwrapped the burn and examined it. He opened a moist cloth from his aid kit and cleaned it. Simon watched as the boy, at first tense, relaxed. Herin applied a thick green salve and rewrapped the burn.

"Very sweet," said a voice behind them. "But what will he do tomorrow? Or the next day?" They turned as Barca and another large blond Orc stepped into the space.

"He will heal," said Herin, standing up. "The burn is painful but not that bad. The salve will help the pain and prevent infection." He drew up to his full height. "What's your problem?"

"We have others here who are sick or injured. Will you stay to help them?" asked Barca.

Herin picked up his kit. "I'll do what I can."

Barca waved a hand. "Later. Sit. We'll eat, then talk."

Kermal stepped close to Herin. "Food offered and eaten," he said softly. "It's ritual; ensures peace and hospitality. You need to go along."

The women spread the food out on blankets and the team sat. Barca, Gendry and the blond Orc, who Barca called Jolof, sat with them. The *hraska* and yoghurt were passed along with the flatbread and eaten with leeks and strong ale. Conversation was limited, with Jolof and Gendry not speaking at all and Barca only commenting on the food and the ale.

Finally, Barca set down his mug and said, "So, we talk. You have my money?"

Taylor looked at Kermal who reached over and pulled a tarp away from the cases they'd carried from the Hansiatic Bank. Barca lifted the lids, and a deep silence fell on the group. After a second, Barca slammed the lids and replaced the tarp.

"Not a word," he said to Gendry and Jolof. "These cases don't leave your sight, hey?" He rounded on Kermal and the rest of the team. "This stays here, get me? There are men in this camp who'd slit your throat for a handful of these."

"Ten thousand was the amount we promised," said Kermal. "Now you don't want it?"

"Oh, we want it. Look around. We need it." He rubbed his face. "Gods know these people need it. But that much, here; it's hard to know what to do next."

"Next, you take us to Tintagel," said Taylor.

"Aye, that's the deal," said Barca. "Two days gets you there at the dark of the moon. We've got a hidey hole just outside the Ring Road where you can get set up. We'll wait twelve hours. You don't show by then, you find your own way back to the border."

Taylor shook his head. "Not good enough. We need to get closer to the Compound. Shortest time possible on the flyers if we're going to get in without alerting the guards."

"How close?" asked Barca.

"Right under the Southeast wall," said Taylor.

Barca laughed. "Not with them sledges you don't. And not with my people."

"You're being well paid to get us where we need to be." Kermal gestured to the cases. "Well paid."

"Ain't enough coin in the world to get that close to the High Tower with sledges," said Barca scornfully. "That's High Elf country. Nothing but fancy sleds and limousines on those streets. Ranger patrol will snap you up inside of ten blocks."

"Surely there must be commercial deliveries that go in and out," said Simon.

"Sure," nodded Barca. "Them as have the right passes to get by the checkpoints and security spells. Which we ain't got."

"How far out is this hide you're talking about?" asked Taylor.

"Ring Road's about five mile from the High Tower," said Barca. "Your Compound is a little over four-and-a-half mile as the bee flies."

Taylor looked at Steelhammer who shrugged. "Still a lot of open ground, Top. Even with Veils."

"What are the streets like?" asked Gillis.

"It's the old section of the city," said Kermal, looking at a map he'd called up on his mirror. "A couple of main shopping and commercial arteries head straight into city center, but mostly a maze of small streets and alleys."

Gillis spoke to Barca. "Do you have people in there who know the streets?"

"Plenty, but they ain't soldiers. They're messengers and watchers, ordinary cobbers just trying to get by."

"What are you thinking, Steron?" asked Taylor.

"High-speed, street-level run under Veil," said Gillis. "I can tune the Air spells in the flyers to override the usual speed limits at low level, but we'll need a good guide to show us the way. And some good driving. If we don't run into traffic or a Ranger patrol, we should be able to make the run in ten to fifteen minutes."

"Georg?" Taylor looked to Steelhammer.

"Could work," he said. "Depends on how good we are on those flyers. One wreck and it's over."

"Loot, how's your driving?" Taylor asked.

Simon grinned. "I've been racing flyers since I was twelve. Try and keep up with me."

Taylor polled the rest of the team. Only Herin expressed any reservation but said he thought he could keep up as long as he stayed in the pack. He picked up his med kit and said, "Never was one for racing, but I'll be all good. I'm gonna see what I can do for these folks in the meantime."

Barca called over a pair of men from one of the fires

and, between them and Jolof, they managed to move the cases to a large tent at the edge of the clearing. Gendry and Jolof took up guard positions and Barca entered the tent.

"Looks like our host is turning in for the night," said Taylor. "I want watches by twos, Georg, you and Chris first. Don't let him get carried away with sick call over there."

Steelhammer chuckled. "I'll do my best, but you know our Christon."

"The rest of you, get some sleep. We'll be ready to slide at first light."

CHAPTER SEVEN

They set out in the light of predawn, sliding slowly along a rough track. Simon rode in the first sledge with Gillis and Falkes. Kermal drove the scout sled with Gendry at his side pointing directions. They passed several burned-out homesteads, rickety stone chimneys and piles of blackened logs. The remnants of cleared fields occasionally followed the track, but none had produced anything for many seasons.

"Squatters," Kermal commented when they stopped for a brief rest and to regroup. "The Rangers sweep this area periodically. Can't have Orcs living free and not making money for the Syr's pockets."

Twice, Barca's people called a halt in small hidden clearings to drop off supplies and distribute a few of the Crowns provided by the Cabal. Once, a high-flying cluster of Ranger flyers passed overhead but showed no indication they'd spotted the convoy.

Gradually, the forest thinned out and they passed well-tended fields of paved roads. Field workers watched them go silently, making no effort to wave or acknowledge their passage. Simon had no doubt they'd be reported to overseers and managers, but hoped they'd be passed off as legitimate commercial operators. He began to breathe easier as they joined the main roads and merged with heavier traffic, finding anonymity in numbers.

Late in the afternoon of the second day, they reached Barca's 'hidey hole,' a commercial warehouse under the shadow of the Ring Road that encircled the modern city of Tintagel. Despite the High Elf aversion to modernity, some concessions to it were necessary if the Gray Havens wanted to be taken seriously as a great nation. The Traditionalists clung to their ancient architecture and the trappings of plantation society, but the real power lay in the commercial and military infrastructure they purchased or stole from the Commonwealth. While more pragmatic Elves maintained the illusion of tradition, they ruthlessly exploited the labor of Orcs and Humans to build great wealth and power. More liberal thinkers simply emigrated to the Commonwealth or the Free States.

The small convoy of sledges pulled up to the big roll-up doors just before 16th hour. Bills of lading were ostentatiously checked for the benefit of any watchers, and the sledges were driven into the cavernous interior.

"Georg, Christon, mount security," said Taylor as the Air spells wound down and the sledges settled onto their skids. "Steron, you and the Loot get to work on unpacking the flyers and tuning the speed limits. Bran, you're with me. I want a look around before we get too comfortable here."

"You don't trust my people?" demanded Barca.

"Trust but verify," said Taylor. "No offense intended."

"Ha! I like you, Josen Taylor," said Barca. "You think like a warrior." He waved to Jolof and Gendry. "You two, help with the sledges. I want to see these flyers."

With Kermal's help, Simon and Gillis wrestled the compact metal crates down from the cargo bed to Jolof and Gendry on the warehouse floor. Once they were all unloaded, Gillis showed them how to release the fasteners and lift the tops off the crates.

Simon's first look at one of the folded machines left him puzzled. It looked like a tightly packed jumble of flat surfaces and random parts bound together with twine.

Gillis grinned as he stepped forward and cut the first cord. "If you like racing flyers, you're gonna love these babies," he said to Simon. He reached out and unfolded two of the flat plates and they formed themselves into streamlined steering vanes. Gillis quickly snapped parts into place on a narrow but sleek-looking aluminum frame. Yoke, footrests, throttle and brake controls; Simon identified each as Gillis smoothly attached them. He stepped back and Simon took in the entire machine. Half the length of his own Faleron Street Racer, the flyer looked like it was already moving. The saddle was low and slim, the footrests set back behind it pushing the rider into a low, almost prone position. The tiny windscreen seemed an afterthought until Gillis activated a mirror spell and a heads-up display showing speed, altitude and position lit up. Simon gave a low whistle and Gillis laughed.

"What about range?" asked Simon. "And where's the cinnabar?"

"Cinnabar is impregnated in the steering veins. It does limit the weight these things can carry, but the range is determined by the spell tuning and the altitude. Flying at street level with only a short hop over the walls, we should have plenty of range to get in." He paused. "Truth be told, Christon pushes the weight limit, and on the way out I assume Lady Graystorm will be riding with you. We're going to be cutting it close on the way out, and I won't have the time or the wood to recharge them." Simon knew Steron was referring to the ebony that was the final component of Air spells.

"How much Talent do you have?" asked Simon.

Gillis looked wary. "I'm not a Mage, if that's what you're asking. Just a very good armorer."

Simon sensed he was hiding something but didn't want to push. *As long as he gets the job done, I don't care if his Talent is registered. He's ex-military, after all. His aura must be on record somewhere.*

Under Gillis's instruction, they quickly unpacked the other flyers and grouped them in a circle behind the parked sledges. Gillis then moved to each one and spent a few minutes drawing symbols in the air and touching various parts of the machines.

Taylor and Falkes returned and pronounced the area secure. Taylor still wanted two team members on watch at all times, in addition to Barca's people, which seemed to amuse the big Orc. Barca was seriously impressed with the flyers, minutely examining one and asking Gillis questions about range, speed, carrying capacity, and recharge times and spell requirements. Gillis seemed reluctant to go into the latter but answered after a nod from Kermal.

"We don't have the time or the wood to recharge here," said Kermal to Simon's questioning look. "We always intended to abandon the flyers once we reached the forests. No harm in Barca getting some use out of them."

"How deep does the Cabal plan to get with these people?" asked Simon.

"Chief Forsaka doesn't discuss his goals with me, but he seems committed to some sort of serious action here in the Havens. This coup by the Traditionalists must have pushed him into action. I've never seen him so angry." Kermal shrugged. "I'm just a soldier. Not my call."

The reply did little to reassure Simon. *This is going to get out of control. We may be helping to set up a terrorist network that will make the Azeri Liberation Front look like a social club.*

He kept his reservations to himself as Gendry, Barca and Taylor approached, accompanied by a small orc with unmistakable Southron features. He was dressed in bright colored but mismatched hose and breeches, high faux-leather boots and an oversized striped jacket with puffed sleeves. As he drew close, Simon realized he was very young, hardly a teenager.

"This is Kaster Stubblefield, son of Garon, born for Serpent Clan by Horu daughter of Astra," said Gendry, following the formula for introductions.

"Good meeting, Kaster," said Simon.

"Yeah, whatever, Cuz," said the youth. "Call me Kas. I don't hold much with Cousin Gendry's ways. Chief Barca tells me you need a guide."

"We need to fly low and fast from here to city center near the High Tower," said Simon.

"Right, cobber," said Kas. "And you need to avoid the Grays and the checkpoints, too. What makes you think the good Elves who live along those streets won't report you in a heartbeat? You'll never make it, no matter how fast you fly. No, I'm not getting stuck in with this."

"We'll be flying dark, no lights, and under Veil," said Simon. "We don't need a guide, just a route."

Kas stood open mouthed for a half second, then laughed. "You people are crazy."

"Maybe, but we're on a tight timeline here so, one way or another, we have to make this run." Simon gestured to Kermal. "My friend here has a detailed map on his mirror. We'll find a way. So, thanks for coming. It was good meeting you."

Kas sighed. "Show me."

Kermal held out the mirror and Kas took it. "Not bad," he said. "But this street is closed at the second intersection and there are roving patrols here and here." He handed the mirror back. "You'll never make it without me."

"I thought you weren't going to get stuck in," said Gendry.

"I still think it's crazy, Cuz," answered Kas. "But it sounds like a real jolt hit. And I got nothing else on for tonight." He turned to Kermal. "Dark, and under Veil? Flamboyant! Absolutely flamboyant!"

"It is, but I'm not going." Kermal waved at Simon and the rest of the team. "These folks are."

Kas looked them over scornfully. "You look like a bunch of soldiers, not street racers. Any of you done street running before?"

"I've been street racing since I was younger than you," said Simon. "The rest of the team has different skills that we need, but they'll keep up. Are you sure you want to do this? How old are you, anyway?"

"Old enough to have had my head kicked more than once by a Gray with a hard spot for Orcs. Old enough to have seen my best mate beaten to death for mouthing off to a Gray Seargent who rousted him from a park bench." Kas looked away. "You want my help or not?"

Simon held up his hands in surrender. "Your call. We appreciate the help."

Taylor pointed to the flyers. "We only have six of these and riding double isn't an option. How will you guide us?"

"Don't need your shiny flyer, mate," said Kas. "Got my own. Just try to keep up. I ain't stopping if you smack a wall."

Taylor smiled at that. "All good, then. Steron, finish tuning the flyers. Everyone else, final gear check. It's almost 18th. Final brief at 22nd, slide out at 23rd."

They assembled in the circle of flyers at 22nd hour, and Taylor ran through the final briefing of the operation once they cleared the Southeast wall. Call signs were reconfirmed, assignments reinforced and the exfil plan reviewed. Simon and Sylvie would ride double on his flyer, not because of their relationship, but because they represented the lowest combined weight. The plan was to retrace their inbound route on the way out after creating some distractions within the compound. Left unsaid, was the knowledge that planning only went so far once the operation began.

As Taylor finished and asked if there were questions, Kas approached pushing a flyer on a wheeled dolly. It was as angular and ugly as the team's machines were sleek and refined. Simon looked it over. He recognized parts from at least three separate models of street racers, as well as what appeared to be custom construction on the saddle and steering vanes. The cinnabar rods in the undercarriage were twice the size of those on Simon's Faleron. This machine would be fast and agile with range to spare.

"We have a seeing stone and Veil emitter for you," said Taylor.

"Keep 'em," said Kas. "Just follow my lights, close enough to stay with me but not so close you stack up if I stop."

"Won't you just attract attention on that thing?" asked Simon.

"If I do, I'll just be another Orc gangster running the streets, a nuisance, Orc trash. I get off with a beating and a fine. Get caught with a seeing stone and a Veil and suddenly I'm a subversive. I'll end up dead or in a labor camp." Kas turned to Taylor. "Ready when you are, Top. Stay on my lights, twenty yards back, no closer."

The big roll-up door opened at 23rd hour, and Kas

led the way into the street. Simon followed the orange taillight on Kas's flyer. The world had the greenish hue of augmented light from the seeing stone in front of his right eye. Details were sharp enough, but depth perception was distorted. Simon was accustomed to operating with a stone, but that didn't make it easier to guide the flyer through the twisting streets. The Veil created its own distortion, a slight blurring at the edges of his vision.

Kas started slowly at first but, after a few turns, increased his speed until Simon found it challenging to stay close. He hoped the others were keeping up, but imagined he'd hear over the tactical net if there was a problem.

He almost missed the flair in Kas's taillight as he braked sharply. He slowed down until he was only about ten yards behind the young Orc.

"One, this is Six, slow at the next intersection and hold," said Simon. "Kas is scouting ahead."

Meanwhile, Kas had lowered his skids and dismounted from his flyer. He made a palm down motion with his hand, indicating for Simon to hold where he was. Kas walked forward to the edge of the building to their right and leaned carefully around the corner. He pulled back and walked quickly toward Simon.

"Roving patrol up ahead," he said softly. "Stay still, keep up the Veil. If they see me, I'll try to talk my way through. If they head down this street, you're gonna have to deal with them." He turned and walked back to his flyer.

"Six, this is One, what's going on?" asked Taylor over the Farspeaker.

"Roving patrol ahead, Top," said Simon. "Everyone hold. If they head down this street we're blown and may have to take action."

"Understood," Taylor double tapped his Farspeaker.

"One to all numbers, weapons out, sleepers only. Wait for my signal."

Kas sat comfortably on his flyer, watching the street ahead. Simon fingered the trigger guard of his PL44, watching Kas. After five minutes, Kas slid his flyer slowly forward to the next street. He paused for a few seconds before waving Simon forward and accelerating across the intersection.

"Six to all numbers," Simon spoke into the Farspeaker net. "Clear, moving."

Simon sped up to keep Kas in sight as the orange taillight rounded a corner. They raced down a long narrow alley that ran behind a street of large townhouses, city homes of wealthy High Elves. As the end of the alley neared, Kas held up a hand for them to slow down. The alley opened into an open space where three streets converged on a circle with a small fountain in the center. On the far side loomed the blank South wall of the Graystorm Compound.

Kas pulled forward and made a slow circuit of the fountain. He waved the rest of the team forward and they crossed quickly to the wall. A narrow access lane ran along the wall behind an official looking building that faced the circle. They reached the Southeast corner as a group.

Taylor dropped the Veil on his flyer and extended a hand to Kas. As the Orc took it, Taylor said, "Thank you. You're free to go. We'll find our own way back."

"Sure, you will," Kas said with a laugh. "I'll wait at the top of the alley until first light. It's not worth my life to be caught in this district after that." He turned his flyer and sped across the circle and up the alley.

CHAPTER EIGHT

"Rookery, this is Crow One," Taylor said into the Farspeaker.

"One, this is Rookery," came Kermal's reply.

"At the insertion point," said Taylor. "Status?"

"Clear, no unusual comms traffic, no alerts. You are good for insertion."

"Understood, Rookery, Crow One clear." He nodded to the rest of the team and reactivated his Veil.

Simon lifted his flyer straight up, just high enough to clear the wall. A sideways slide and he was over and descending into the dark courtyard. There were lights at intervals along the wide walkway that circled the open yard, enough that the seeing stone was more of a hinderance than help. Simon flipped it up with a practiced toss of his head and canceled the Air spell as his flyer settled to the ground. He dismounted and the rest of the team gathered.

They drew into a circle around the flyers, facing outward but saw no guards or any other sign of activity.

Close by, to their right, light spilled from the doorway of what they had designated as a guardroom in the mission plan. With hand gestures, Taylor detailed Falkes and Gillis to check it.

They moved quicky, sighting over their PL44's, Falkes high and Gillis low. They reached the door frame and edged close to it. Falkes tapped Gillis on his tactical helmet, and they rushed into the room. Simon could hear the hissing spit of sleeper rounds being fired, four in all.

"Clear," came Falkes's voice over the net.

The team filed into the room. Simon saw three Elves in green livery sprawled across a table where they had been sharing a meal. A fourth Elf lay in a heap near the far wall, a mug still clutched in his hand and a spill of liquid across the floor beside him.

Taylor surveyed the room, which was bare except for the table and four chairs. Weapons lockers and racks lined the walls, neat and well ordered. There was no other entrance and no windows.

"Move these people aside," he said. "Secure them well. We can't afford anyone raising a fuss. Then we move the flyers in here. It'll be tight, but the Veil emitters won't last long enough to conceal them outside and anyone walking the path will trip over them."

Simon understood the problem. Veils didn't render objects invisible. Instead, the spell compelled anyone looking in its direction to either look away or not pay attention to what the Veil covered. You could still touch an object through a Veil, and if one knew it was there, a strong-willed person could override the compulsion.

It only took a few minutes to bind the guards with flex ties and gag them. The table was upended against the far wall and the flyers moved into the room. Top was right. It was a tight fit and Simon hoped they wouldn't have to move them out again in a hurry, or worse, under fire.

They formed up in a combat stack outside the guard room and advanced down the walkway along the East wall toward the second guardroom at the far corner. Top led and Steelhammer brought up the rear. Simon, in the third position, sighted along his PL44 covering the forward right flank, his assigned field of fire. He avoided the temptation to look ahead, trusting Top to cover that sector.

The central courtyard stayed quiet and mostly dark. Here and there, paths wound through plantings and low hedges, leading between pavilions and small covered benches. The paths were illuminated by soft lights set low to the ground. Overhead, glowglobes set at intervals lighted the wide walkway the team moved along. Under different circumstances, the place could have been tranquil and beautiful. Simon saw only potential threats.

They reached the far corner without seeing anyone. Top held up a hand to signal a stop, then pointed to Simon and Gillis and then to the door to the room. Simon moved up behind Gillis, crouching low as Gillis went high. The door was closed. Simon reached up and carefully tested the door handle. It moved slightly; not locked.

He glanced up at Gillis, holding up three fingers. The armorer nodded; Simon counted down. Three. Two. One. He turned the handle, pushed the door open and rushed forward in his crouch, moving to the right to give Gillis a clear field of fire.

A lone Elf in a uniform sat behind a desk facing the door, a paper in his hand. He looked up as the door crashed open and immediately lifted a Gowron pistol from the desktop. Simon's needle took him in the neck a half second before Gillis shot him in the chest. He slumped forward, the pistol clattering to the floor.

"Clear," said Gillis.

Simon rose from his crouch and looked around the

room. It appeared to be an office with file cabinets and charts along the walls. The desk was covered with papers and a small magic mirror. The coat of arms of House Graystorm turned slowly on its screen. Simon touched its activation sigil, but it asked for a password, so he left it alone. Top and the rest of the team entered, and the Elf officer was quickly secured.

"Top, you want to see this," said Gillis. He pointed to a chart and pegboard near the door. The chart listed names, each with a peg and a key hanging beneath it. There were eight names in two rows, none of which Simon recognized other than the third along the top. *Lady Graystorm,* the script read.

"So, we have a key," said Taylor. "Any way to tell which door it opens?"

"Third down from here," said Falkes, pointing to another chart attached to the wall with a clear sheet of glass bolted over it. This one was a schematic representation of the compound with labels on each door, room, and stairwell. The third set of rooms from their position was labeled *Graystorm,* handwritten in greasepaint on the clear glass cover. Other rooms had names from the pegboard written on them as well.

"Let's move," said Taylor. "Loot, tuck in behind me. You'll make first entry. Let her know we're coming."

They resumed the combat stack and glided along the wall to the third door. It was heavy oak, ornately carved, with a thick iron lock just above the door handle. Taylor took out the key and made to fit it in the lock, but Simon stopped him and reached into a pouch on his tactical vest. He drew out a Peacekeepers badge—Hal's, in fact—and rubbed it, muttering an incantation. A faint glow flashed around the edges of the door.

"Warding spell," said Simon. "Should be canceled now."

Taylor unlocked the door and pushed it open.

Nothing happened, no alarms, and Simon didn't feel the tingle of a spell triggering. He brought up the PL44 and stepped into a narrow hallway that opened into a larger room a few steps ahead. Just as he cleared the entrance to the room, he sensed motion to his left. He ducked and rolled to the side as a heavy iron bar came down where his head would have been. He came up with the PL44 pointed at the figure standing in the dark shadow beside the door.

"Simon?"

"Sylvie, is that you?" he asked.

"What in the seven hells are you doing here," Sylvie hissed. "I almost killed you."

He dropped the bolt thrower and let it hang from the harness on his vest. "I thought I'd come and take you home. If you want to go, that is."

She rushed forward and embraced him. "Of all the foolish..." She noticed the rest of the team crowding into the room, clearing it, checking corners. "You brought help, I see. Oh, Simon, it's so good to see you. I never gave up hope, but didn't see how anyone could help me."

Soft calls of 'Clear' came from around them, but Simon hardly noticed. He continued to hold Sylvie in his arms as waves of relief washed over him. She'd lost weight, and her face looked pale and drawn, but she otherwise seemed fit to travel.

Taylor stepped up, his weapon slung at his left hip. "Very touching, Loot," he said. He made a slight bow. "Lady Graystorm, I presume?"

Simon released Sylvie and took a half step back. "Sylvie Graystorm, meet First Sergeant Josen Taylor."

Sylvie extended her hand. "Ranger Lieutenant Sylvie Graystorm. I abdicated any titles long ago. Thank you, First Sergeant, for coming to get me."

Simon quickly introduced the rest of the team as they gathered around. Taylor waved for silence and spoke into the Farspeaker. "Rookery, this is Crow One. Status?"

"Crow One, Rookery," answered Kermal. "Still quiet. You have just over three hours until first light. What's your timeline?"

"Package retrieved intact, starting exfil now."

"Understood. Rookery clear."

"Lady Graystorm, Sylvie," he said. "Are you fit to travel? Is there anything you need to take with you?"

"Fit enough, First Sergeant. Give me half a minute." She crossed the room and reached behind an ornate screen. She pulled out a small backpack and slung it over her shoulder. She then went to a desk and removed a pouch that she tucked into the backpack and a signet ring that she placed on her left second finger. She came back to Simon's side.

"The backpack has files and papers in it that must get back to the Commonwealth," she said. "Whatever happens to me, Simon, promise me they'll get to the Keepers on the other side of the Border."

"What do they contain?" Simon asked.

"War plans," she answered. "The Steward is determined to launch an attack on the Free States to try to draw the Commonwealth into declaring war. That will be a signal for the Azeri's to move on the Lordiss Valley through Holdfast. The Commonwealth will be squeezed between two enemies, and the Havens will sit back and bleed us dry."

"I can't believe the Steward would have anything to do with Orcs," said Simon.

Taylor shrugged. "The enemy of my enemy is my friend. Old Azeri proverb." He lifted the PL44 and motioned to Steelhammer. "Clear the door, Georg. The rest of you, by the numbers. Lady Graystorm in the Three spot; Loot, you cover her back."

"Wait," said Sylvie. "Wait. We have to take Flandyrs."

"Flandyrs? Galen Flandyrs?" asked Taylor.

"He's here, in the suite at the Northwest corner," said Sylvie. "He's behind the war fever that's seized the Council. Him and his spell-proof, undetectable weapons. He's convinced the Steward that he can build enough of those weird weapons to turn the tide in any war with the Commonwealth."

"Sylvie, this operation is off books and slapdash as it is. We'll be lucky to make it out of the city, and that only if we move right now." Simon looked at Taylor. "Let's go, Top."

"Georg, all clear?" called Taylor.

"Aye, Top. We're good for exfil."

"Hold there, Georg. I'm sending Chris to you. I want the two of you to scout the Northwest corner of the compound, report back in two minutes." Taylor waved at Herin who hurried out to join Steelhammer.

"Top, what the hells?" said Simon.

"Loot, your family is paying me and my men some heavy coin to get Lady Graystorm out of the Havens, and we'll do that. But Flandyrs has a price on his head that could buy a small country. If there's a chance of taking him, we need to give it a go." He faced Sylvie. "What can you tell me about Flandyrs. What is the layout of his place? Where is he likely to be at this time?"

Before she could answer, Steelhammer called in over the Farspeaker. "One, this is Two."

"Go Two."

"No guards, but reinforced cold iron door and frame. No way to breach quietly."

"Understood, Two," said Taylor. "Regroup back here. We have a possible mission change."

"Flandyrs suite is on two floors. He sleeps in the upstairs bedroom," said Sylvie. "The bottom floor has four rooms—entry foyer, dining room, common room and kitchen. Stairwell at the back of the common room." She looked at Simon. "He had me dine with him several times, gloating about how he won, and I lost. I think he hoped I'd beg him to intercede on my behalf. I don't doubt what his price would have been."

Simon struggled to control his anger and said, "I want to see that bastard in a Commonwealth Court as much as you, but my first priority is getting you out. Top, as you once said to me, this is a bad idea."

"Noted, Loot," said Taylor. Steelhammer and Herin returned, and Taylor turned to his Second. "Georg, possible mission change. Snatch and extraction from that set of rooms at the Northwest corner."

"Hostile target?" asked Steelhammer.

"Decidedly so. The target is Galen Flandyrs. Lady Graystorm wants us to snatch him and take him back with us." Taylor grasped the Dwarf by the shoulder. "This could be the big one Georg. But I need your honest take. Can we pull this off?"

Steelhammer thought for a few seconds. "If we can get in, take him and get out in under ten minutes, without alarms, and keep him under sedation." He looked at Herin who nodded. "It's doable. Transport out will be a problem though. Don't know which flyer can take the double weight."

"Leave that to Steron," said Taylor. "What about that door?"

"That's a problem. Bran can breach it, but not quietly. We'll be under fire as soon as we exit, and I don't know how we'll get back to exfil, much less out of the city."

"The door isn't a problem if we can overcome the wards," said Sylvie.

"How's that?" asked Steelhammer.

Sylvie reached into the backpack and drew out the small pouch she'd retrieved. "I have a key."

Taylor grinned. "Loot, will that badge of yours work on the wards on Flandyrs' door?"

Simon winced. "It's not a universal cancelation

spell. It works on most common commercial wards and some of the higher-level wards used by the Cabal and bigger gangs."

"So, the wards on Lady Graystorm's door were over the counter commercial spells?" asked Taylor.

"No," Simon said reluctantly. "Since Flandyrs escaped, the Peacekeepers have added a number of Haven based warding spells, in case they were needed."

"So, there's a good chance it will work on Flandyrs's door, too," said Sylvie. Simon only nodded.

"Georg, you and Loot lead; Sylvie and I second," said Taylor. "Chris and Steron, hold the door. Bran, set some pyrotechnics along our exfil route, wherever you think they'll create the most chaos. Retrace our route and start moving the flyers out of the guard room. Our exfil is likely to be hot and we'll need to get over the wall in a hurry." Falkes nodded. He touched Herin on the shoulder before heading out.

"I still think this is a really bad idea," said Simon as the team lined up behind them.

"I'm with you, Loot," whispered Steelhammer. "But Top is team leader, and your Lady won't take no for an answer."

They turned left out of Sylvie's suite and moved rapidly along the walkway to the Northwest corner. The door to Flandyrs's apartments was heavy black iron, ornately embossed with the Graystorm coat of arms and various mythical creatures. A transom topped the door, framing a complex geometric pattern in stained glass. Simon and Steelhammer took position on either side of the door. Taylor and Sylvie faced it, Taylor holding his PL44 at shoulder level, Sylvie aiming low with a Gowron pistol borrowed from Gillis.

Simon rubbed the Peacekeeper badge and muttered a cancelation incantation. The door and the transom glowed with a faint green light. As soon as it faded, Sylvie stepped forward with the key. The lock turned smoothly. Taylor pushed the door open and entered, waving for Sylvie and Steelhammer to follow him, and pointing Simon into position just inside as rear guard. Herin and Gillis took up position outside, a few paces away from the open door.

Simon stood sighting along his PL44 and the other three climbed the stairs at the back of the common room. He flipped the seeing stone down in front of his right eye to penetrate the deep darkness of the ground floor. He saw no movement in the washed-out green glow of his augmented vision. Above him, he heard a scuffling, then the distinctive hissing spit of a needle round being loosed. Twenty seconds later, Sylvie descended the stairs followed by Steelhammer. Taylor came last, his bolt thrower hanging from its combat harness and a still form on his shoulders in an emergency evac carry.

Simon turned toward the doorway and caught sight of a blinking orange light on a metal panel set into the inner doorframe. "Shit!" he cursed. "Six to all numbers. Silent alarm. We're going to have company soon."

CHAPTER NINE

Steelhammer rushed past Simon and took up position next to Gillis. Sylvie followed and tucked in behind the forming combat stack. Taylor grunted as he turned slightly to get his burden through the door. "Loot, ahead of me," he said. "Chris, take Flandyrs. Give your PL to Lady Graystorm and tuck in behind her. I'm last man. Move."

"One, this is Four." Falkes's voice was tight over the Farspeaker net. "I'm at the exfil, moving the flyers. I'm seeing movement on the wall above your position and along the West walkway. You're about to be flanked."

"Understood," said Taylor. "Moving to exfil."

They moved out at a quick trot, Steelhammer in the lead followed by Gillis, Sylvie, Herin and then Simon. Taylor covered their rear a few paces behind. Simon kept his attention on his left flank, trusting the team to cover the front. He caught sight of shadows moving up the West walkway toward the Northwest corner of the compound. They moved swiftly but silently, still avoiding a general alarm as if they hoped to trap any intruders inside Flandyrs's apartment.

Steelhammer reached the guard office at the Northeast corner and peeled off, assuming a crouch and sighting over his bolt thrower along their rear flank. Simon trotted past him followed by Taylor.

Top tapped Steelhammer on the shoulder and said, "Last man." Steelhammer rose and fell in behind Taylor, assuming the rear-guard position. Just as he cleared the office door, a brilliant flash followed by a loud explosion lit up the wall above the door to Sylvie's suite of rooms.

Klaxons sounded followed by shouted commands and the sound of running feet as the approaching guard team increased their pace and ran toward the explosion. Meanwhile, Gillis increased his pace to a controlled run. Simon could hear Herin's breath coming in controlled gasps as he carried his inert burden.

"Keep moving. Loot," said Taylor moving up on his shoulder. "Chris can handle it. We need to get out of here."

Gillis reached the Southeast guardroom as Falkes dragged a flyer out onto the walkway. He turned and moved his arm in a rally motion, then helped Falkes wrestle the flyer out of the room. Simon was a half-dozen paces away when he felt rather than heard another explosion, this one directly behind him back at the Northeast guard room. The entire sky lit briefly with the brilliant white flash. Simon thanked the gods he wasn't looking at it or he would have been temporarily blinded. Lights came on all over the compound. Searchlights swept the North wall, and more shouts sounded behind them.

Gillis and Steelhammer were already mounting flyers. Gillis leaned forward for Herin to secure Flandyrs to the flyer on which he was mounted, then waved Simon and Sylvie to the third flyer in line. Herin tied Flandyrs to Gillis's back before dashing to his own machine. Just as he, Falkes, and Taylor settled onto the flyers, a searchlight swept across them and stopped. There was a loud shout from across the compound and cold iron bolts bracketed their position. Taylor grunted as a bolt struck his tactical vest but failed to penetrate.

"Get over the wall," he shouted to the team as his flyer rose from the ground. Simon pulled back hard on the yoke and Sylvie clung tightly to his back. Their flyer rose, sluggishly at first and then faster. Bolts whizzed past and smacked into the wall beside them, showering them with chips of masonry. Then they were above it, and Simon jerked them over and down on the other side. Herin, Steelhammer and Taylor were already on the ground below them and Falkes flashed past on his way down. Simon settled the flyer to the ground and looked around.

"Where's Gillis?" he shouted.

Top pointed up and Simon saw Gillis wobble his flyer over the wall and start his descent. He clutched at the man secured to his back and leaned heavily on the yolk struggling to stay in control. Herin dismounted and was at his teammate's side as soon as the flyer touched down.

"I'm all good," said Gillis breathlessly. "Took one in the vest; knocked the wind out of me. Flandyrs is hit, bolt in his thigh."

"I see it," said Herin, already opening his kit.

"Chris, stop. We don't have time for this," called Taylor.

"Thirty seconds, Top," said Herin through gritted teeth as he ripped away the loose trousers that Flandyrs wore to expose the iron bolt sticking out of his thigh. He quickly wrapped the bolt and the wound with a gauze roll, simultaneously securing the shaft so it didn't shift around and staunching the flow of blood from the wound. He reached up to help Gillis secure the Elf more tightly to the flyer.

"Come on, Chris, we gotta move," shouted Steelhammer as he swung his flyer out of the access passage into the circle around the fountain. Simon and Sylvie followed. Herin remounted and swung in behind them. Before Gillis and Taylor could follow, Steelhammer stopped at the foot of the alley.

"Veils up," he called. "Top, it looks like Kas has been pinched. I've got orange lights at the top of the alley."

"Damn," said Taylor as he pulled up next to the dwarf. "We're gonna have guards over that wall any second. Try to sneak by under Veil?"

"If that's a Ranger patrol, they'll have detectors," said Steelhammer.

"Simon," said Sylvie. "Go left, up Fountain Street." She raised her voice. "Everyone, follow us!"

"Sylvie," protested Simon. "That's a major street. The patrols are sure to cover it. We won't get three blocks."

"We won't need three. Trust me, go left," Sylvie insisted.

Simon did as she said, keeping the Veil up but flipping the seeing stone away from his eye. This street was well, if softly, lit by glowglobes spaced along the sidewalks at knee level. After only a hundred yards, Sylvie tapped Simon's helmet.

"Slow down, it's up here on the right," she said.

"What's up on the right?"

"That house right there," said Sylvie. "Stop here." She jumped off the flyer and ran to an ornate gate that closed a wide drive off from the street. Set back along the drive stood a grand home in the traditional Elf style, all curves and spires.

"Six, this is One. What the hells is she doing?"

"Don't know, Top," said Simon. "But what other option do we have?"

After a few seconds, the gate swung open, and Sylvie waved them forward. Simon pulled through and Sylvie climbed up behind him. "Follow the drive," she said. "It will take us to a stable around back."

"How do you know about this place?" Simon asked as he followed the drive. He glanced back to see Taylor step out from his Veil and close the gate.

"An old friend lives here but he spends most of his time at his country house," said Sylvie. "Tandril isn't a known Progressive, but he has no love for the Steward and hates the politics of the Council. The house is empty, and I know where he hides the spare key and how to cancel the Wards."

The stables backed up to a high wall that ran along the alley they'd used for the approach. The doors were open. Sylvie guided them into a wide empty space designed for multiple sleds but holding none. They dropped the Veils and circled the flyers.

"It'll be dawn in a couple of hours," said Taylor. "I assume we can hole up here through the day?"

Sylvie nodded. "The house is empty right now. We'll be safe here for the day. Besides, Flandyrs needs care, and we all need some rest."

"Agreed," said Taylor. "Georg, Bran, mount security. Steron, see what you can do to extend the range on these flyers. We may need it."

"Not much I can do without some wood, Top, but I'll give it a go."

"Do your best," said Taylor. "Chris, you know what to do."

"Aye, Top." Herin helped Gillis get the still inert form of Flandyrs off the flyer. Herin started to lay the Elf on the floor.

"Wait," said Sylvie. "Not here. I know where there's a key and I know the Warding spells. We can take him into the house and lay up there until dark."

Taylor shook his head. "Not worth the risk. We're safer out here."

"Not by much," said Sylvie. "And I for one need a toilet and a shower. Coming?"

Taylor and Simon followed her as she made her way to the back of the house, Taylor reluctantly. Sylvie stooped over a planter and after a second came up with a key. She approached the back door to the house and muttered a series of incantations. The door flashed green, and she fitted the key into the lock.

The door opened into a large, well-appointed kitchen with a center table, several chairs and a wide counter next to the stove and oven combination. Pantries lined the wall to the left along with an oversized chiller. A double swinging door to the right led to the rest of the house.

Sylvie crossed the kitchen with a familiarity borne of frequent visits. Through the double door lay a formal dining room and another arched opening leading to a wide hallway. She pointed to a room across the hallway.

"Library there. I suggest you make it your op center while we're here. You've seen the kitchen and pantries. Bathroom is in the back, behind the staircase." She and Simon headed in that direction.

"Thank you, Sylvie," said Taylor. "Any food you people take will be paid for, so keep track and take only what's necessary. Two-man guard rotations. I want someone on the back door at all times." Herin entered with Gillis. Between them they carried Flandyrs. "How is our guest, Chris?"

"Bolt in the thigh, hit the bone but missed anything vital. He won't be walking for a while, but he'll live." He and Gillis laid the Elf across a couch in the library. "I dosed him again with sleeper potion. He'll be out for another eight hours or so."

"All good. You and Steron take the first watch. I may need you to tend your patient later."

"Aye, Top," said Herin. He jerked a thumb at Gillis, and they left the library together.

Taylor activated his Farspeaker. "Rookery, this is Crow One."

"Crow One, Rookery, what is your status?"

"Holed up for the day Rookery," said Taylor. "We should be secure in this location. Will try to exfil to the rally point after dark."

"Crow One, be advised the Gray Rangers have mobilized additional teams to cover the city. Checkpoints at all major intersections and roving patrols in an arc from the High Tower to the River. That's right across your exfil path."

"Understood, Rookery," said Taylor, silently cursing to himself. "We have the package intact. Also, an additional high-value target for exfil. How is our guide? Did Kas make it back to the rally point?"

"Aye, he's safe. Dodged a Ranger patrol just before your fireworks started and got back here about ten minutes ago." Kermal paused. "How about you, Crow. All your options will be hot."

"We'll make do. Will call when we're setting out. Crow One clear."

Sylvie came into the room looking refreshed. Her white-blond hair, already short, was drawn up in a tight bun at the back of her head. She was dressed in a black shirt and charcoal gray trousers. She carried a tactical vest like the ones the team wore. She'd returned the PL44 to Herin, but the Gowron pistol she'd borrowed from Gillis hung from the vest's side holster. Her backpack was slung over her right shoulder.

"Simon's watching the back door," she said. "Herin is in the front watching the street. Gillis is clearing the rest of the house. The rest of the team is welcome anywhere on the ground floor. I'd ask that everyone stay down here. There are blankets in the closet next to the door."

"Thank you, Sylvie," said Taylor. "We'll try not to leave the place worse for wear."

"Gillis took over the back door," said Simon as he came into the room. "What do want me to do, Top?"

"Get some rest. I'll tell Georg and Bran to stand down as well. Chris and Steron have first watch. You and Bran relieve them in four hours."

"Aye, Top." Simon crossed the library to a large, padded armchair. He shucked off the tactical vest and set it on the floor next to the chair. Sylvie stepped up next to him and dropped her own vest.

"Is this seat taken?" she asked, putting an arm around his neck.

"I was going to take a nap," said Simon snaking his arm around her waist and pulling her close. "But maybe there's enough room for two."

The chair was indeed wide enough for two, if just barely. They snuggled together, not caring if the others were nearby.

"Whatever happens," whispered Sylvie. "I love you. I knew you'd come for me. No one has ever cared that much, to risk everything for me."

"Without you, there'd be nothing worth saving," Simon whispered back. She burrowed her face into his neck and they both fell asleep.

CHAPTER TEN

Four hours later, Taylor shook them awake. "You're up, Loot. Meet up with Bran at the front door. You two can split the watch as you see fit. Sorry to wake you, too, Sylvie."

They struggled out of the chair and Simon donned his tactical vest. Sylvie pulled on her own vest and smiled at Taylor. "I'll check on the stables while you get some rest." She gestured to the now empty chair.

As Taylor settled into the chair, Simon and Sylvie walked to the hallway where they separated with a quick kiss, Simon toward the front door and Sylvie toward the kitchen and the stables. Falkes was waiting at the door as Simon approached.

"Did you get some rest, Bran?" asked Simon.

"A bit," said Falkes. "Rolled up in a blanket in that big dining room." He indicated the door with a tilt of his head. "Front or back?"

Simon settled his tactical helmet on his head and said, "I'll take the front. Sylvie went out to check the stables, so watch for her coming in."

Falkes nodded, donned his own helmet, and headed for the back. Simon settled the PL44 onto his chest and stepped to the small window to the right of the doorframe. This gave him a clear view of the gate and the street but allowed him to remain in shadow and unseen from outside.

The four hours of his shift passed slowly. Sylvie checked on him a couple of times and reported that Taylor slept soundly in the chair in the library. Herin had checked on Flandyrs several times, and the rest of the team was snoring in various corners around the library. The street remained quiet, with little traffic, and that moving steadily past the gate without pause.

At a quarter to 8th hour, almost at the end of his shift, Simon's eyes were glazed and beginning to droop. He shook his head and refocused on the street. A large Hilten limousine that he had not seen approach was stopped in front of the gate.

"One, this is Six," said Simon into his Farspeaker. "Top, are you awake?"

"Go for One," said Taylor, his voice still thick with sleep.

"We're going to have company. A sled has stopped in front of the gate," said Simon. "Doesn't look official, no sigil or flashing lights." A tall Elf climbed out of the sled and stepped to the gate, unlocked it, and pushed it open. He got back into the big sled and guided it carefully through onto the drive. He stopped again, climbed out, and closed the gate.

"One, I think it may be the homeowner. Where's Sylvie?"

"I'm here." She stood close behind him. She leaned forward and looked through the small window. "Oh, seven hells, it's Tandril all right. Why is he here now?"

"Doesn't matter," said Simon. "What do we do?"

"One to all numbers," came Taylor's voice over the

Farspeaker net. "Everyone up. Get ready to move."

"Wait," said Sylvie. "Simon, tell them to wait. Let me talk to him first."

"Well, you'll get the chance now," said Simon. "He parked the sled in front of the door. He's getting out." He activated the Farspeaker. "All numbers, this is Six. The homeowner is coming up to the front door. Sylvie thinks she can parley. I'll be ready to take him if that fails."

Simon lifted his bolt thrower, checked the safety, and stepped out of sight behind the door. A key rattled in the lock. Sylvie stood a step back, head up, hands at her sides. The door opened and Simon sighted along the barrel of his weapon.

"What in...Sylvie Graystorm? What are you doing here?" said a deep voice.

"Hello Tandril," said Sylvie. "Forgive the intrusion. Can we talk? It's rather urgent."

"But I thought you were...How are you here?"

"Please, Tandril, close the door," said Sylvie urgently. "I can explain."

"All right."

The door swung shut to reveal a tall, heavily built Elf with salt white hair worn pulled back with a red ribbon. His deep-set eyes were lavender and widened at the sight of Simon. He was dressed in a stylish business suit of matching blue jacket and hose. He eyed the PL44 and raised his hands to shoulder level.

"Sylvie?" he asked. "What the hells is going on?"

"Simon, lower that thing," said Sylvie. "Tandril Misthaven, please meet Simon Buckley. Simon, *Syr* Tandril Misthaven, High Counselor and Lord of Manor Misthaven."

Simon had to give Misthaven credit. Despite being met by an armed man in his own home, he bowed deeply. "Mr. Buckley," he said. "How do you know Sylvie?"

Sylvie took Simon's arm. "Simon is my fiancé, Tandril. He and his team have just freed me from my father's compound. We were forced to find cover for the day and your house was nearby. I thought you were at the Manor. We'd have been gone at nightfall and hopefully you'd never have known we were here."

"Freed?" Misthaven looked troubled. "I'd heard you'd been arrested but could hardly believe it. Your father and the Steward were holding you prisoner?"

Sylvie nodded. "The Steward planned to put me on trial in a few days as an example to any other Nobles who might consider defying the Traditionalist coup. The charge was treason."

"Treason? That's preposterous. Your views are a bit radical, but hardly treasonous. Has it really come to this?" The big Elf shook his head. "What do you need of me?"

"Just sanctuary for the day," said Sylvie. "We'll leave after dark, and no one will be the wiser."

"You plan to leave the city, I presume," said Misthaven.

"We have a rally point and transport near the Ring Road," said Simon. "From there we'll get out of the Havens."

"You'll never make it." Misthaven shook his head, his voice grave. "There are checkpoints and patrols everywhere. I passed through three between here and the Ring Road. I passed at least three more roaming patrols." He looked at Sylvie. "You've stirred up the ant's nest, my dear. The Steward want's you back badly."

"Not just me, I fear," said Sylvie. There was a shuffling of feet as Falkes and Taylor appeared behind her, weapons up.

"Stand down, Top," said Simon. "We're all good, at least for now."

Taylor stepped forward, hand extended. "Josen

Taylor, First Sergeant, Royal Commonwealth Marines, retired. My apologies for violating your home, but extreme circumstances demanded it."

"Tandril Misthaven," said the Elf taking Taylor's hand. "If you are helping Lady Graystorm, no apologies are needed."

"What can you tell us about the situation on the street?" asked Taylor.

"Not good for your endeavors," said Misthaven. "The Rangers have checkpoints at every main intersection between the High Tower and the River Tam. I also saw at least three roving patrols on the lesser streets stopping any sled without diplomatic sigils. I fear you will have difficulty making your way out of the city."

"We were hoping to make a fast transit running dark on Veiled flyers," said Taylor. "If we can map those checkpoints, perhaps we can avoid detection."

"You'll have to get out of the local district first," said Misthaven. "There's almost a solid cordon within six blocks of the Graystorm compound." He looked at Sylvie. "I'm surprised the Steward wants you so badly. But you said it wasn't just you?"

"You'd better come into the library," said Sylvie.

Simon and Falkes turned the watch over to Taylor and Steelhammer. They followed Sylvie into the library. Herin sat next to the couch in a small wooden chair that didn't look strong enough to support his bulk. He tended the bandage on Flandyrs's thigh.

Misthaven crossed the room quickly. "But this is Galen Flandyrs. Is he alive?"

Herin looked up. "Of course. I've tended his wound. He's sedated but will live." He stood, larger even than the Elf. "And you are?"

"Christon Herin," said Sylvie. "May I introduce Tandril Misthaven, the Master of this house. Tandril Misthaven, this is Christon Herin, our medic and communications specialist."

Herin bowed. "My apologies, I spoke harshly."

"None needed," said Misthaven. "But Sylvie. Why is this man here?"

"He's being returned to the Commonwealth to face justice," she said. "He's responsible for at least five deaths and conspired to plunge the Commonwealth into a ruinous war. Even here, he's been spreading lies among the High Council and advocating war with the Commonwealth."

"I know well what he's done over the past few months." Misthaven's voice was bitter. "I returned from Misthaven today because the Steward has called a special meeting of the Council to authorize his treason trials."

"When is that meeting scheduled?" asked Sylvie.

Misthaven pulled his timepiece from a pocket in his hose. "Ninth hour, about thirty minutes from now."

"You must go," said Sylvie. "Do nothing to arouse suspicion."

"Sylvie, I have no desire to legitimize the Steward's crazy plan," said Misthaven. "I plan to vote against his show trials."

"Then do so," Sylvie answered. "Your views are well known. It would be out of character to support the Steward." She touched his arm. "But Tandril, don't put yourself at risk. If they try to pressure you, pretend to reconsider, ask for more time, 24 hours, if they'll grant it. By then we'll be gone, and it won't matter what they do."

"It would be out of character for me to drive myself to the High Tower as well. I'd intended to hire a chauffeur as soon as I arrived." Misthaven looked around. "I don't suppose you want a hired driver in this house."

"No," said Taylor. "Loot, you can drive. *Syr* Misthaven, can you outfit the Lieutenant as your chauffeur?"

"Of course." Misthaven nodded thoughtfully. "And most agencies here in Tintagel employ Human drivers. They don't trust Orcs, and wage work is beneath any Elf's dignity. That also gives me an idea about getting all of you out of the district."

"How's that?" asked Sylvie.

"We'll talk after I return," said Misthaven. "Meanwhile, there's a chauffeur's uniform and cap in a closet in the stables."

Fifteen minutes later, Simon found himself behind the steering yoke of a big Hilten limousine. The sled was a late model, only a year old, with seating for eight and an oversized storage compartment in the rear with both outside and inside access. He looked up as the front door opened and Misthaven walked slowly but purposefully to the passenger door. Simon opened it for him, and he climbed in. Simon crossed around to the yoke and got in behind it. Misthaven motioned for him to drive.

Simon exited the sled to close the gate, which he had opened before Misthaven had exited the townhouse. As he climbed back behind the yoke, Misthaven smiled.

"Well done, Mr. Buckley. You're no stranger to this game."

"Nor are you, it seems," answered Simon.

Misthaven sighed. "For the past two years, I've helped Sylvie's Commanding Officer, Rulanis Summerfield, by feeding him names of High Council members who have promised support to Galen Flandyrs or the Steward in their coup. Unfortunately, they acted before Summerfield could move against them. I fear Rulanis is being held in maximum security now." He saw the look in Simon's eyes and added, "No, Sylvie didn't know. It's one reason why I feel obligated to help her."

"So, where to, sir?" asked Simon. "And thank you for that."

Misthaven laughed. "That way, down Fountain Street to the circle, then right. The street will take you around the Graystorm compound. As the wall ends, there will be a lane leading to the Council entrance to the High Tower."

"Will they buy me as your driver? Won't I need some credentials?" asked Simon.

"You underestimate the power of High Elf arrogance," said Misthaven. "I have less than ten minutes to appear at an important Council meeting called by the Steward himself. I'll simply order the guards to open the gate immediately. They'll comply."

It went down just as Misthaven had predicted. The guards passed them through the gate. Simon stopped at an ornate door where Misthaven got out and Simon was peremptorily directed to a parking area to wait. He lowered the skids and canceled the air spell. He found a control near the yoke that opaqued all the windows except the windscreen. He folded his arms, pulled the borrowed cap down over his eyes, leaving a gap so he could see out, and pretended to sleep.

Several other high-end limos were parked around him, the chauffeurs standing in a cluster, smoking pipes, and talking. They glanced Simon's way but ignored him, assuming he was asleep.

Simon saw the approaching guard a half hour later but made no move until he tapped on the window. Simon jerked slightly as if being awakened and lowered the window.

"Wake up lazy," said the guard. "Your master needs you. Pull around the circle and stop at the door."

Simon nodded and tugged his cap deferentially. He activated the Air spell and slid around the circular drive under the guard's critical eye. He stopped where directed, near the door. One of the guards stepped forward and opened the door. Misthaven walked out and climbed into the passenger seat. A second guard waved Simon forward, and they passed through the gate and onto the street.

Ten minutes later, Simon opened the gate to Misthaven's townhouse and pulled through. He jumped out, closed the gate, and pulled the sled around the back to the stables. He stopped near the rear door. He and Misthaven climbed out. The Elf looked toward the stables, but Simon shook his head.

"The less you see and know the better, *Syr* Tandril," he said.

"More games?" asked Misthaven.

"Just making sure you can deny knowledge of our transportation and not have to lie," said Simon. "The tech is new and advanced."

"I see. Your way. I need to talk with your team leader. I think I know how to get you out."

Simon pointed to the limo. "The windows. But we'll still need either you and your High Elf arrogance, or proper credentials."

"That's not all we need to speak about," said Misthaven. "Come."

Simon followed the Elf into the kitchen. Sylvie was there. Simon shed the chauffeur's cap and jacket and embraced her. "*Syr* Tandril and I may have a way to get the team out."

"I need to speak with First Sergeant Taylor," said Misthaven. "The Steward has authorized a kill on sight order for the 'criminals who killed four Graystorm security officers and kidnapped Lady Graystorm and Galen Flandyrs.' He's locking down the entire city."

"Top's in the library," said Sylvie. "Let's go."

Taylor looked up from a map spread on the library table as the three of them entered. "*Syr* Tandril," he said. "Did all go well?"

"With the meeting, and Lieutenant Buckley's impersonation of a chauffeur, yes. But the meeting was very disturbing. The Steward claims, and will soon issue a news release, saying that your team killed four security officers while kidnapping Lady Graystorm and Galen Flandyrs. He's locking down the entire city. He doesn't have the manpower right now, but he's ordered in two battalions of Border Patrol troops from the frontier. They'll be in position by 23rd hour. You must get past the Ring Road and into the countryside well before that."

"We won't have the cover of darkness, then. At least not full dark." Taylor looked at his timepiece. "Sunset is at 18:37. We'll be exposed most of the way on busy streets. We're stuck here."

"Maybe not, Top," said Simon. "*Syr* Tandril and I seem to have the same idea." He looked at Misthaven. "Would you like to tell him, or should I?"

"I can get you through in the Hilten with the windows blacked out." Misthaven pointed to Simon. "Lieutenant Buckley drives, with me in the passenger seat. The team hides on the floor of the sled and Flandyrs rides in the storage."

Taylor rubbed his chin. "Might work, but if it goes sideways, you'll be guilty of treason and the Steward won't hesitate to have you executed."

"Let me worry about that," said Misthaven.

"I still don't like it," said Taylor.

"I may have an idea," said Sylvie. "But it will need credentials for Simon and Flandyrs and will leave Tandril in a hard place for a while." Quickly she outlined her idea. By the time she was done, Taylor was nodding and Misthaven looked thoughtful.

"Four, this is One," said Taylor into the Farspeaker. "Bran, please come to the library."

A minute later Falkes appeared from the dining room. "What's up, Top?"

"How much pyrotechnic do you have left?" asked Taylor.

"Enough to take this house down." He shrugged at

their shocked looks. "I like to be prepared."

"If we clustered the flyers together, would it destroy enough so the Rangers couldn't trace it back to the Commonwealth or decipher the spell code?"

"There won't be anything left but some twisted metal," said Falkes. "But how will we get out without them?"

Taylor outlined Sylvie's plan.

"Nothing like putting it all on one throw of the bones," said Falkes. "I assume you'll want a delay on the fireworks when we leave?"

"Half hour should do it. By that time, we'll either be clear or in a melee." Taylor turned to Misthaven. "Are you all good with this *Syr* Tandril?"

"If it gets Sylvie and the documents she carries clear, then yes."

"I'd suggest you wait an hour or so after the fire brigade comes before reporting the Hilten stolen," said Falkes. "You wouldn't notice until you checked the stable."

Misthaven nodded. "Meanwhile, let me see what I can come up with as credentials for Lieutenant Buckley. And you'll need my papers as well."

At a quarter after 18th hour, they were ready. Simon wore the chauffeur's cap and jacket and carried a commercial sled license in the name of one Casmir Hansen of Talien. The image was wrong, as the license had been left behind by a fired former employee, but the hope was that with the cap pulled low, the Ranger at the checkpoint wouldn't notice.

"Sterilize these rooms," commanded Taylor. "No traces that can lead back to us or the Commonwealth." He knelt next to Misthaven, who was flex cuffed to one of the library chairs. "Sorry to leave you like this, *Syr* Tandril. I hope you're not too uncomfortable."

"All good, First Sergeant, or should I call you Top?" Misthaven smiled. "We must make this look good.

Just get Sylvie out. That's all I ask."

Sylvie knelt at his other side. "Thank you for this, Tandril. As soon as you can, get out of the city. I'm not even sure your own district will be safe. You may want to get to the Commonwealth or go north to the Free States."

"No, the Havens are my home, come what may." Misthaven's voice was tinged with sadness. "Someone has to voice opposition to the Steward and his cronies. Get yourself free and deliver those documents to the Commonwealth. Perhaps that will be leverage enough to reign in some of the worst of their excesses. Now go. Gods be with you."

Sylvie kissed him on the cheek and rose. Taylor grasped the Elf's hand. "You are a brave person, *Syr* Tandril. Gods be with you as well."

Herin scooped Flandyrs up in a medevac carry. They'd dressed him in one of Misthaven's best outfits and Gillis carried a formal bicorn hat they'd place on his head once he was in the limo.

They loaded up in the rear of the house. The flyers were stacked in a heap in the middle of the drive, as far from the house and stables as possible. Herin loaded Flandyrs into the passenger seat, slumped against the door. They set the hat on his head, pulled low. The rest of the team took their places. Simon slid in behind the steering yoke and opaqued the windows. Taylor, Falkes, Herin and Sylvie crawled onto the floor under the back seats and Gillis lay across the rear bench seat under a blanket. Steelhammer, with much grumbling, shut himself in the rear storage compartment.

They pulled out onto Fountain Street and headed East, toward the Ring Road, just as the sun disappeared below the horizon. They stopped at the first checkpoint in deep twilight with the darkening Western sky at their backs, further obscuring the inside of the limousine.

"Papers," said the Ranger Sergeant gruffly when he saw that Simon was a human servant. "Where are you going?"

"I'm taking my Master home to Misthaven," said Simon handing over *Syr* Tandril's identity papers and his own fake sled license. "He is unwell and wishes to be in more comfortable surroundings."

The Sergeant flashed a torch at Flandyrs but saw only the expensive clothes and formal hat. "What's wrong with him?"

Simon lowered his voice. "I fear he overindulged at the dinner after the Council meeting. It's not worth my job to disturb him before we reach Misthaven. He can be most disagreeable at times like these."

The Sergeant flashed his torch around the interior of the limo but apparently saw nothing amiss. "Slide on," he said with a wave of his hand. "Gods forbid we disturb an important Noble."

Simon thanked him profusely, having caught the hint of sarcasm in the Sergeant's voice. After clearing the Hightower district, Simon took lesser side streets they had mapped in their earlier exfil plan. He drove sedately, taking care to signal all turns, following a roundabout route that avoided the main streets. They saw a couple of roving patrols but managed to stop at corners and stay out of sight. Whether by luck or skillful driving, they managed to avoid contact with any other Rangers.

Twenty minutes after clearing the checkpoint, they heard the wailing klaxons of the Fire Brigade rushing into Fountain Street. Five minutes later, they slid into the warehouse under the Ring Road where Kas greeted them with a big smile, and Barca stood with arms folded, frowning. Kermal stood off to the side, his relief at seeing Simon evident on his face.

"Where are my flyers, Taylor," he said. "And what am I supposed to do with this fancy Elf car?"

"Sell it, abandon it, strip it for parts, I don't care," said Taylor. "By now the flyers are nothing but ash. Tell you what, keep three of the sledges as compensation. We'll move faster in one sledge and the small Hilten."

Barca nodded, still frowning. "Agreed. You'll need a guide to get you through the forest. He can bring the small sled back once you clear the border." He grinned now. "Compensation. You can get your own people to pick you up on the other side."

"I'll take 'em, Chief," said Kas. "These cobbers are the most flamboyant bunch I've ever seen. Major jolt hit."

"On you, Kas," said Barca, turning away.

"Load up, people," said Taylor. "Full kit but leave any unnecessary gear. Chris, you, Brackenville and Flandyrs in the back of the sledge. Georg, you, me and Bran in the front. Simon, you, Sylvie and Steron in the Hilten. Kas?"

"I'll ride my flyer," said the young Orc. "Any chance I can get a boost to the Air spell? Range is a little low."

"Any ebony around here?" asked Gillis. "I can boost all the spells if you have some wood."

"Got some ebony powder around here somewhere," said Kas. "Hey, Gendry, where's the box of wood powder?"

"I think it's under the workbench over there," answered Gendry.

Kas crossed the room, bent, and retrieved a battered box from a shelf. He presented it to Gillis who opened it. Inside were vials of wood powders, ebony, rowan, and willow as well as some small garnet and cinnabar fragments. Gillis scooped up the vial of ebony and the cinnabar.

"Bran," he called. "Do you need any rowan?" He held up the vial and tossed it to Falkes when the Fire mage nodded.

Gillis set to work with the ebony, first charging

up Kas's flyer, then the small Hilten and the sledge. Simon noticed that he pocketed the remaining ebony. He wasn't sure why he thought that important but filed it away in his memory.

"Get some rest," said Taylor. "We'll slide out at midnight. Kas tells me we can make the first camp before dawn."

CHAPTER ELEVEN

As they started to load up at half past 23rd, Herin gave a small cry of distress, then shouted. "Top, we've got a problem over here."

Taylor and Simon arrived at his side at the same time. He stood over the cot where they had placed Flandyrs, visibly shaken.

"He's dead, Top," said Herin. "He was fine just fifteen minutes ago when I checked him. Sleeping, breathing. I didn't even need to top up his sedation. The wound is clean and dry. It wasn't enough to kill him. I don't know what happened."

Simon touched Herin's arm. "Settle down, Chris. I'm sure it wasn't anything to do with you. Maybe there was a deeper problem that you couldn't know about with what you can do in the field."

Meanwhile, Taylor had bent over the Elf, checking for a pulse in several places and holding the shined surface of the aluminum stock of his PL44 up to his lips. He looked up at Simon and shook his head.

Simon bent over the body, examining it like he would a crime scene. He noted the blue tinge around Flandyrs's lips, checked his neck for bruising or instability. He pressed forcefully on the Elf's chest as he felt for air coming out of the mouth. There was none. He carefully checked the rest of the body for wounds or visible punctures. Again, nothing.

Simon pulled Taylor aside. "Top, this wasn't a natural death. I think he was killed by an Air spell that pulled all the breath out of his lungs. With the sedation, he wouldn't have struggled or shown any sign of distress."

"Are you sure, Loot?" Taylor whispered. He looked toward Gillis. "You're as much as accusing Steron of murder."

"Not necessarily," said Simon. "I'm pretty sure Barca has Water talent. There may be someone else here with Air talent. Kermal tells me that Orc magic is different, not limited to specific schools as Human magic is."

"What do we do, then?" asked Taylor.

"We take the body back to the Commonwealth." Simon shrugged. "With a little luck, a good forensics Mage may be able to get an aura from the spell and identify the caster."

"Explain it to Christon, but make sure you don't implicate Steron. We can't have suspicion in the team right now." Taylor turned away. "Mount up; we slide in ten."

Herin had already lifted Flandyrs's body and was walking heavily toward the sledge when Simon caught up to him. Before he could speak, Herin said quietly, "Somebody killed this man, Loot. His wound wasn't that bad. He was strangled or smothered somehow. I can see the blue around his lips."

Simon breathed a silent sigh of relief that Herin didn't suspect an Air spell. "I think so, too, Chris.

That's why we need to get the body back to the Commonwealth so the CSA mages can do a forensic exam. Meanwhile, keep this to yourself."

"Will do, Loot." He climbed into the rear of the sledge and covered Flandyrs with a tarp.

Kermal stood nearby. He grabbed Simon's hand and held it tightly. "I was worried. Good to see you, Simon." He inclined his head to the back of the sledge. "What's wrong?"

"We snatched Galen Flandyrs from the Graystorm compound," said Simon. "He was alive when we got here, but sometime in the past half hour, he was murdered."

"Damn. You took Flandyrs? No wonder the ant's nest is in an uproar. The Ranger coms are blowing up. We need to get out of here before the lock-down reaches this far out." He stopped, cocking his head and looking around. "Wait, murdered? By someone here?"

Simon grabbed his friend's arm. "Herin is upset, feels responsible because Flandyrs was his patient. Flandyrs took a bolt in the thigh on the way out, but Herin knows the injury wasn't bad enough to be fatal. He thinks someone smothered him. The Elf was sedated and wouldn't have struggled." Simon lowered his voice to a whisper. "He wasn't smothered or strangled. It was an Air spell, and the only person here with enough Air talent is Gillis. Unless there's some Orc with a latent talent we don't know about. Kermal, keep this close hold. Don't let Herin know."

"Holy shit, Simon," said Kermal. "What are we going to do?"

"Get the body back to the Commonwealth," answered Simon. "Maybe Kyle Evarts can pull an aura off the body and get us an identification."

Kermal nodded. "I'll keep it close hold. This trip will be sketchy enough without sowing suspicion in the team."

"Thanks, Kermal. See you at the next stop."

Simon walked over to the small Hilten and slid in behind the yoke. Sylvie was seated in the middle of the seat, leaving room for Steron by the window. The armorer was still over by the sledge, donning his tactical vest.

"Flandyrs is dead, Sylvie, murdered," whispered Simon. He inclined his head slightly toward Gillis. "I think it was an Air spell. Not sure without aural analysis. We need to get the body back to Kyle Evarts. If anyone can pull a casting aura off a three-day old corpse it'll be him."

"You think it was Steron? Not possible," she said.

"I don't know. I'm not making any accusations. Just keep this quiet."

Steron climbed into the sled without a word and settled against the door. The big roll-up door opened, and Kas lifted his flyer off the floor, leading the way out. Simon slid in behind him and the sledge followed.

Kas led them on a winding path through the quiet suburbs. Despite the lock-down, they encountered no patrols or checkpoints, the Rangers still concentrating inside the Ring Road. Soon they reached a more rural area and Kas turned down a wooded lane that eventually led to a dirt track. Three hours later, the small convoy turned into a tiny clearing in the thick wooded landscape. Overhead, a net of tree branches woven through cords and ropes completely concealed it from above. Kas dismounted. There was just enough room for the sledge and the small sled.

"There are some shelters under the trees," said Kas. "No fires though, can't risk the smoke."

"No problem," said Taylor. "We just need a place to rest up. How much farther to the border?"

"Another day and a half," said Kas. "Assuming no detours. If we leave this camp by early afternoon, we'll overnight about half-way to the first place you stayed on the way in. From there it's almost a full day to the fence."

"The fence will be the chokepoint." Taylor rubbed the back of his neck, working out a kink of tension. "If the Rangers even suspect this raid came from the Commonwealth, that's where they'll set up."

"There's another trail to the border," said Kas. "But the sledge won't make it through."

"We'll scout the main path once we're close to the fence," said Taylor. "Worst case, we send you back and shoot our way through after dark."

Kas shook his head. "Flamboyant."

The team crawled into shelters made of branches and natural materials, snug and nearly invisible with beds of soft bracken covered with blankets. Sylvie crawled in next to Simon and was soon breathing gently in the crook of his neck. For the first time in months, he slept dreamlessly.

Too soon, Steron shook them awake. "Time to get up, Loot, M'Lady. We're moving out in five."

"Thank you, Steron," said Sylvie. Simon managed a grunt but crawled out and adjusted his vest before donning his helmet and picking up his weapons. Sylvie had collected a PL44 from the spare gear as well as some extra magazines. In her black and gray trousers and shirt, she looked every inch the warrior.

Kas swung onto his flyer and led them down a narrow, barely visible track, with just enough clearance between the trees for the sledge if Taylor drove slowly. Simon guided the smaller sled easily behind the flyer. No one spoke. They were all in a state of fatigue but also heightened awareness, eyes often darting at shadows between bouts of trying to stay awake.

Simon almost missed Kas's desperate signal to stop. Just ahead, there was a break in the overhead cover of the trees, something Simon had come to welcome as a short break from the gloom of the dim forest light. This time, however, it seemed to offer a threat. How Kas had known, Simon wasn't sure, but just a few seconds later, a group of four military flyers glided almost silently overhead. They turned at a right angle and passed again, clearly executing a search pattern.

"Six, this is One," came Taylor's urgent whisper over the Farspeaker. "What's going on?"

"Ranger patrol, low overhead on flyers, Top," answered Simon. "I don't think they've seen us. Kas detected them somehow and got us stopped under cover."

They waited another fifteen minutes but saw no other flyers. Kas dismounted and came back to where Simon waited. "Don't think they spotted us. The next cover is about a hundred yards away. Best we move quick,"

Two hours later, Kas scooted between a small break in the tree line and disappeared. Simon stopped, looking about, but within a few seconds a curtain of green that had looked impenetrable rose high enough to allow the Hilten and the bigger sledge to slide into another clearing. Kas released the rope he'd been straining against, and the curtain fell back into place.

"We camp here tonight," Kas advised. "It'll be a full day to the fence. You'll be able to cross after dark like you said."

"All good," said Taylor. "Everyone bed down. Two-man watches, set your own rotations. Loot? A minute?"

Simon made his way over to Taylor. "Christon's worried that Flandyrs's body will start to decomp before we can get it back for forensics. Any suggestions?"

"Not unless someone here knows a master level stasis spell," said Simon. "All I can suggest is to keep it cool, maybe offload it from the sledge and cover it with some wet leaves or soak the tarp in some water.

Evaporation may cool it."

"Will do. I'll get Chris on it. Talk to Steron, work out your watch rotation." Taylor turned on his heel and walked away.

Simon and Gillis took the first watch, partly because Simon was fatigued from driving and wanted as much uninterrupted sleep as he was likely to get, and partly because Steron wanted to check the charge on the Air spells. Four hours later, Simon joined Sylvie on a blanket spread next to the sled. She was already asleep, and Simon drifted off soon after.

The Ranger kill team hit them just before first light. Their first warning was a shouted warning from Steelhammer followed by the snapping reports of bolt throwers. Both Simon and Sylvie struggled to their feet, grabbing their weapons and standing back-to-back, scanning for threats. Bolts whistled by Simon's head and Sylvie snapped off a couple of shots behind him.

Simon spun to his right and fired at a shadow moving up through the trees. His needles hit center of mass with no effect. The answering bolt struck him in the vest, nearly knocking him down. Sylvie dropped to her knees and loosed her needles low, taking the Ranger in his unarmored thighs and dropping him to the ground.

"All good?" asked Sylvie over her shoulder.

"All good, the vest took it." Just as he started to stand, the explosion of the Fire bolt hitting the sledge knocked him off his feet again.

All around him he heard sounds of combat, grunts and crashing undergrowth, the snapping of the PL44's and the thud of cold iron bolts hitting the trees. In the light of the burning sledge, Simon saw Steelhammer slash a Ranger across the groin with his combat knife sending a spray of arterial blood into the flames. The Elf fell with a scream that was cut short as the Dwarf slashed his throat. Simon knelt and put two needles into the thigh of a Ranger aiming at Steelhammer. Herin smashed the Ranger in the head with a heavy branch as he fell. Then all went quiet.

"All numbers, check in!" shouted Taylor over the net.

The team counted off. "Six clear, package is intact," said Simon when his turn came.

Taylor stepped into the firelight and circled his fist in a rally signal. They all gathered in a rough circle, every other man facing outward.

"The sledge is done," said Taylor. "We're on foot from here. Kas, is the trail to the fence clear enough that we can find it?"

"No problem, cobber. It's wide enough for the sledge so's you can't miss it. Just watch the overhead for gaps and stick to the trees."

"Good, because you're taking the small sled and going back to Tintagel." Taylor's voice brooked no argument. "You can strap your flyer to the back or the roof, but you're going back. I don't want to answer to your cousin if you get killed."

"Whatever you say, Top. This is too much heat for me. I think I'm allergic to cold iron." Kas grinned. "I guess I'm not flamboyant enough for your crew."

Taylor squeezed the young Orc's shoulder. "Wait a few years. Then we'll talk."

"Steron," Taylor turned to the armorer. "I want the PL44's retuned for lethal ammo, not sleepers. This was a kill team. The Rangers aren't going to give us a chance to surrender."

"About time," muttered Sylvie.

"Chris, get a shovel and bury that corpse." Taylor pointed at Flandyrs. "We at least can protect it from scavengers."

"No," said Simon. "Top, we need to get Flandyrs back, if at all possible. This was a murder. I can't let that slide."

"And I can't burden a man with carrying a dead body," snapped Taylor. "We don't leave our own behind, but Flandyrs is an EC, not one of us."

"So, I'll rig a drag litter from the tarp and pull him myself," answered Simon. "I can keep up and I'm probably the least combat effective here, anyway."

Taylor looked like he wanted to explode, but he turned. "Have it your way. You've got thirty minutes. After that we move out. And if you fall behind, I won't wait."

Between Simon, Sylvie, and to Simon's surprise, Herin, they managed to make a litter from a couple of sturdy branches and ropes wound tightly around the body. Herin managed to rig clips to attach the litter to Simon's tactical vest leaving his arms and hands free.

The team moved out in a double line, one on each side of the trail with Top leading one side and Georg the other. Simon walked next to last on the right, behind Kermal and followed by Herin.

After an hour, Simon's lower back ached, and his thighs burned, but he'd be damned if he'd let it show. *You insisted on this,* he told himself. *Warrior up and pull the load.*

"I can take it a while, Loot," said Herin softly from behind him.

"I've got it, Chris," said Simon, controlling his breathing. "But thanks, I'll let you know if I need help."

Herin slapped his shoulder softly in encouragement. "Good man."

Taylor called a halt just before midday and Simon gratefully unhooked the rig. He stretched the kinks out of his back and drank deeply from his water bottle.

Sylvie stepped across the trail from her place in the opposite line. "Are you all good, love?"

"Sore, but I'll be good after a bit of a rest."

"I'll take the litter, Loot," said Herin. "Top may not

like it, but I want to know what happened as much as you do. He was my patient."

They moved out fifteen minutes later, with Herin dragging the litter and Simon bringing up the rear. At the second rest break, Herin refused to let Simon take the litter back.

"I'm twice your size and in better shape, Loot. I got this."

Twice on the next leg, they faded back into the trees as flyers passed overhead. As the daylight began to fade, Taylor called a halt and circled them up well back into the forest. He gave Simon and Christon a hard look but said nothing as the big medic unhooked the litter from his vest.

"We hold here until full dark," said Taylor. "Then we scout forward in two lines. Seeing stones and weapons up. We aren't facing some Azeri shitheads this time. These are hardened operators. Probably as good as some of us, so stay sharp."

"They know we're coming, Top," said Steelhammer. "They've been tracking us with those flyers."

"I suspect so," Taylor agreed. "Suggestions?"

"Kas said there was another trail. Maybe we could find it," suggested Simon.

"Too much chance of getting lost, Loot. We're now on a schedule."

"Red Castle?" asked Steelhammer.

"Aye," said Taylor. "We need to make the fence by 3rd hour or we're on our own."

"Wait," said Simon. "Red Castle?"

"Quick reaction force," said Taylor. "Pre-staged before we started the mission, but on a timeline and not flexible once we called them. I messaged them just after the kill team hit us." He checked his timepiece. "It's almost 20th. Full dark. Kit up, nothing but weapons, seeing stones and water. Chris, you and the Loot need to make a hard choice on that corpse.

I'll back you, but we can't afford any slowdown in a melee."

"All good, Top," said Herin. "If it was one of us, it wouldn't be a problem. We'll get through."

Taylor turned away without another word. They formed up in two groups spread loosely through the forest within sight of the trail and each other. Gillis and Steelhammer ranged ahead, scouting for the Rangers they knew were looking for them.

The going was slow, both because of the need for stealth and the deep underbrush. The scouts ranged ahead, checking in periodically. Three hours passed and Simon recognized some of the turns of the trail from their trip in. They were getting close.

"One, this is Two," Steelhammer called softly over the net. "Contact. Looks like a sniper and spotter in a tree hide to the left and a pair of shooters set up on the right with a good view down the trail."

"Can you take them out, Two?"

"Not quietly. We'll be engaged as soon as we hit them."

"Fall back, Two," said Taylor. "We'll move up together, hit them and push through as fast as possible, try to link up with Red Castle."

"Understood. Two coming in."

Two minutes later, Steelhammer and Gillis crept into where Taylor had circled the team. They took a knee and Steelhammer brushed the sticks and leaves away from a patch of ground. He drew with a fingertip, quickly sketching the trail, a tree, and a circular spot on the opposite side of the straight portion of the trail. "The sniper is here in the tree hide, about ten feet up. High enough for a good sight line, low enough for a quick exit after taking his best shots. The two-man shooter team has good visuals on the trail and can provide cover for the sniper team. All in all, a professional ambush. These are trained operators, not a bunch of stupid cobbers."

"Any idea of strength further up the trail?" asked Taylor.

Gillis shook his head. "I couldn't see beyond the shooter team. Don't figure they're on their own though. We've seen four flyers. Eight men at least, probably more like a dozen."

Taylor thought for a moment. "Right. We need the sniper team down first. Bran, I'll want Fire on their position, don't give them a chance to take a shot." He turned to Steelhammer. "As soon as Bran strikes, I want you and Steron to hit the shooters. The rest of us will push up the trail in two lines, attack through the ambush. We'll try for the gate and a link up with Red Castle, if he's there."

"Top," said Bran softly. "Are you sure about the Fire? The Accords."

"This is a kill team, Bran. And we're an unsanctioned Special Arms force on a kidnap mission." Taylor's laugh was grim. "We're so far outside the Accords it isn't worth another thought."

"Just hope we don't start a war," muttered Steelhammer.

"If I get these documents to the Commonwealth, they may stop one." said Sylvie. "Now, First Sergeant, where do you want me?"

"By your man," said Taylor. "Loot, you, Chris, Brackenville and Sylvie on the left. Gillis, Bran, and me down the right. Georg, you're point, up the middle. Once the shooters are down, we drive hard for the gate. Red Castle will be waiting on the other side."

"You hope," said Steelhammer.

Taylor ignored the jibe. "Warrior up. Check mags, shoot first, keep moving. Everybody into position, wait for my 'Go.'"

The two groups split to their staging points. Simon and Herin lifted the sides of the drag litter, pulling it between them, keeping their shooting arms free. Sylvie moved ahead, despite Simon's protest, and Kermal fell in behind.

They crept forward, a foot or two at a time, making no more noise than the rustle of leaves in the wind. The seeing stones let them see ahead in the green glow of light augmented vision, but they had no doubt that the Rangers were as well quipped.

"One, this is Two," Steelhammer said over the Farspeaker. "In position."

"Four, make ready," said Taylor.

"Ready," said Bran.

"Stones up," said Taylor. "It'll be bright for a second. Go!"

Simon flipped his stone away from his eye and ducked his head as the tree in front of him exploded into fire. He glanced up to see the flaming body of the sniper, or his spotter, tumble to the ground. Off to his right came shouts of alarm followed by four soft reports of PL44's, two double shots taking down the shooter team.

"Go, Go, Go!" said Taylor over the net, his voice urgent but calm.

Sylvie moved forward at a quick step, sweeping from side to side, sighting along the bolt thrower. She loosed two into the darkness and Simon heard a man drop. Herin dropped another to his right as the Ranger struggled to clear his vision from the blast of Bran's fire bolt. Simon scanned to the left but saw nothing. He strained at the litter, trying to keep place with Herin.

Then they were past the glare of the fire and into darkness. Simon flipped his seeing stone down and immediately marked three dark-clad Rangers moving up on their left. Sylvie shifted her aim that way and Simon loosed two bolts at the nearest Ranger. One elicited a grunt as it hit center of mass, embedding in body armor. The second went higher and slashed through the Elf's neck. He clutched his throat and fell with a wet gurgle.

Simon glanced in alarm at Sylvie as she grunted in pain. She paused for a half second before putting a cold iron bolt through the eye of the Ranger who'd shot her. She glanced back over her shoulder.

"I'm all good. The vest stopped it. Watch to your right."

Herin had paused and was shooting steadily into the dark. Simon dropped to his knee and sighted under Herin's arm. A four-man Ranger team crouched behind some brush and began pouring bolts through the air around them. Herin and Sylvie both dropped prone and returned the favor. Kermal knelt behind Simon, shooting over his shoulder. Most of their bolts stuck harmlessly in the brushy cover, but it did force the Rangers' heads down.

"Four, this is Five," Herin said urgently.

"Go for Four," Falkes answered.

"Need a little help here, Bran. Four EC's under cover. They've got us pinned. Twenty yards right."

"On it," said Falkes. "Fire on the way."

"Heads down," shouted Herin. A second later the brush to their right exploded into flame. Simon didn't see anyone hit, but no more bolts came their way from there. They stood, lifted the sides of the litter, and started forward at a run. The clearing in front of the gate was visible now, about a hundred yards ahead.

Off to their left came the sounds of a struggle as Steelhammer got in close with a Ranger. Simon and Sylvie both swung that way but had no clear shot. They ran on. Steelhammer dispatched the Ranger with a head shot under the chin and pushed the body away. Simon faced forward and took up some slack on his side of the litter.

A bolt whistled past Simon's head from behind and

he glanced back. "Chris, Kermal," he shouted. "EC's behind, watch out." He tried to swivel and find a target but almost stumbled under the weight of the litter. Sylvie and Kermal turned fully around and sent bolts into the darkness.

Sylvie spun around to run forward again, but Kermal paused to aim. He got off two shots before a bolt stuck him in the thigh just below his vest. He fell with a cry, his bolt thrower falling to the ground.

"Chris, Kermal's hit!"

"Go," shouted Herin. "I've got this." The big medic took the full load of the drag litter and ran on, following Sylvie.

Simon loosed bolts blindly and took three steps back to Kermal's side. Blood spurted between the Half-Orc's fingers where he clutched at his thigh.

"Get out of here, Simon," Kermal gasped. "I can't walk. They'll get us both."

"Shut up," said Simon. "Let me see, damn it, let me see." He let his PL44 swing down on its harness as he pried Kermal's hands away. More blood spurted. Simon groped in the side pouch of his tactical vest for the tourniquet and clotting gauze that he knew were there.

Too slow, too slow, too slow. The mantra ran through his brain as he struggled to get the band of the tourniquet around Kermal. He shut it down and let his training take over, pulling the strap through the loop, tightening the windless and securing the sturdy rod to the now tight band around his friend's upper thigh. Kermal winced as the strap cut into his leg.

"Gods that hurts," he hissed through his gritted teeth.

If the tourniquet doesn't hurt worse than the wound, it isn't tight enough. The phrase from his training ran through his head. "Good, that means it's working. Give me your arm."

Kermal reached up, set his face, knew what was coming. He groaned as Simon ducked under his arm and lifted him across his shoulders in an evac carry. He grabbed the PL44 but couldn't maneuver it in his position across Simon's back. He managed to get it clipped to his harness. Simon set off at a run, shooting forward. Kermal pulled the Gowron from his thigh harness and lifted it, shooting at the Rangers behind them.

Simon ran on, now pacing just behind Herin and the litter. Sylvie moved smoothly and efficiently ahead, shooting, changing magazines, laying down cover for Steelhammer and Herin, all seamlessly. The tumbled down gate was in sight now.

"Red Castle, Red Castle, this is Crow one," said Taylor over the net. "Status."

"Five minutes out, sliding hot, can you hold?" The reply was calm.

"We'll be at the gate in two," said Taylor. "We need support, expedite."

"On the way, Crow One."

Sylvie slowed as the trail widened near the gate. The fires were behind them, the gate, and the old logging camp beyond, were dark. Simon tried to flip his seeing stone back down, but with Kermal's weight pressed against his helmet it didn't fall properly, only partially over his eye, obscuring his vision. He heard rather than saw the flyer rise out of the darkness next to the old checkpoint shed. There was no mistaking the heavy bolts from the repeating air-to-ground thrower mounted in its nose. Fire bolts struck the ground around him, and he fell to his knees with the concussion. The seeing stone dropped completely past his chin, hanging around his neck now.

Sylvie lay prone, shooting cold iron bolts at the flyer, hoping to bring down the pilot. Herin stood upright doing the same. Simon struggled to get his footing, lifting Kermal and groping forward. The Fire bolt struck Herin full on in the chest, smashing into his vest and lifting him into the air before exploding, tearing through his back and showering Simon with blood and seared flesh. The medic's body spun and fell on the litter.

Across the trail a roar of pain and anger erupted from Falkes. A solid lance of flame shot out of his left hand, dissolving the flyer in a flash of harsh blue light. The Fire mage raised his hands, gathering all the flames he could conjure into a blinding white ball above his head. Fire erupted from a dozen places along the fence line, spreading rapidly into the trees. Simon thought he saw shadows running and dancing in the flames.

Steelhammer rushed over, grabbed Herin by the collar of his tactical harness and dragged him toward the gate. Simon followed, but Kermal slapped him on the back.

"Flandyrs," Kermal shouted. "We need him. Take a knee."

Simon groaned as he lowered himself to the ground. Kermal grabbed a handful of the tarp around Flandyr's corpse and tapped Simon again. Standing was even harder, but Simon managed it and began to stagger forward under the combined weight of Kermal and the drag litter.

Then Sylvie and Gillis were by his side, taking the litter and pulling it forward. Taylor had reached the gate. Falkes still stood with his arms raised, Fire swirling above his head, but the Rangers had recovered from some of the shock of the Fire attack. Bolts began to strike all around Falkes, one staggering him as it struck his vest. Simon feared the mage would lose his containment and for a second, tongues of fire began to lick down toward the ground. Falkes recovered and began to collapse the fireball so he could move forward.

"Everyone to the gate," shouted Taylor. "Red Castle inbound."

Simon looked up as the heavy Armored Personnel Sledge that was Red Castle smashed through the trees on the other side of the border. Armor piercing bolts from the turret on the top of the sledge, every third one a Fire bolt, smashed through the fence. A secondary weapon shot smaller caliber Fire bolts skyward, arching across the path of three flyers, sending two of them spinning into the forest. The third withdrew to the north.

Somehow, Simon and Kermal made it through the gate. The heavy sledge spun sideways across the opening, still sending bolts into the forest. A rear ramp dropped, and Steelhammer and Taylor dragged Herin up and into the machine. Gillis and Sylvie hefted the litter in, then stood to the side covering the rear. Falkes walked heavily up the ramp and Simon staggered after him. He eased Kermal onto a bench seat and leaned against the armored bulkhead above him. Bolts clanging against the hull as the Rangers again regrouped and renewed the attack.

Sylvie and Steron rushed up the ramp, Steron shouting, "Last man."

Taylor tapped the driver on the shoulder. "All clear, get us the hells out of here."

Simon felt the APS slew sideways, then it turned and began to accelerate. Iron bolts rattled off the hull as the vehicle's turret spun and launched fire into the darkness. Simon sank down onto the seat next to Kermal and leaned over to check the tourniquet. It was still tight, the bleeding now stopped. The bolt had fallen out somewhere along the way and the wound gaped like an open red mouth.

"Still hurts like all seven hells," said Kermal through gritted teeth. "Thanks for getting me out."

Simon gripped his friend's shoulder but said nothing, too exhausted to speak.

"Red Base, this is Red Castle," said the driver.

"Go for Base," came the reply.

"Package recovered, no pursuit. Inbound with two dead, one wounded. ETA two hours."

"Understood Red Castle. Base clear."

Sylvie came and sat next to him, laying her head on his shoulder. Her face was streaked with dirt; there was a deep scratch down her cheek and a small gash on her forehead. Her hair was limp and sweat stained from the helmet she had just removed. Simon thought she looked lovely and told her so.

"You're sweet to say so, but you're lying through your teeth," she said. "Gods, I'm done in. Are you all good?"

"Tired, sore, worried about Kermal," Simon answered. "And I never lie to you."

"Kermal is just fine," the Half-Orc said, not opening his eyes. "You two take care of each other."

CHAPTER TWELVE

The low rumble of the APS as it made its way down the logging road nearly lulled Simon to sleep. Kermal breathed softly next to him, his sleep punctuated by an occasional soft moan. On the bench seat across from him, Falkes sat slumped with his head down, one hand resting on Christon Herin's shoulder.

Simon let his head fall back against the bulkhead and closed his eyes but opened them again when he felt movement nearby. Taylor stood over him, gripping a railing on the overhead of the APS to steady himself.

"How's your man?" Taylor inclined his head toward Kermal.

"He'll live, but I'm worried about his leg." Simon answered softly.

"Red Base has medics, and we'll call ahead for an evac." Taylor shifted, bent slightly to speak closer to Simon's ear. "What about Flandyrs?"

"Once we take care of Kermal, and Christon, I'd appreciate transport to the Peacekeeper station at

West Faring. There's a Sergeant there I know who'll expedite sending the body to Wycliffe House for forensics. I'll call the head CSA mage myself from the station." Simon looked up at Taylor. "That's not really what you wanted to know, is it Top?"

"What about this Air spell business and Steron? Are you sure that's what killed the Elf?" Taylor's voice was still soft, but his eyes were hard.

"As sure as I can be without aural analysis," answered Simon. "Look, Top, this is what I do. I was head of the Magic Enforcement Squad. It's my job to recognize illegal magic. If there is some other explanation, or if this was some weird Orc spell, forensics will tell us and clear Steron." Simon's look was equally hard as he held Taylor's eye. "But I can't let this go. Murder is murder."

Taylor stood upright. "All good. But I won't let my man be set up. Do your job right." He smiled grimly. "Besides, the bounty on Flandyrs reads dead or alive. If I can't turn over a prisoner, bringing in the corpse will still pay." He slapped Simon lightly on the shoulder. "You did good out there, Loot. Bringing you along on the mission was the right decision."

Taylor moved back to the rear of the compartment, still standing, but with eyes closed and a shoulder braced on the rear ramp.

"He doesn't trust you," Sylvie whispered, her eyes still closed.

"I thought you were asleep," said Simon.

"Tried. Still too jumpy." She shifted, and he put an arm around her. "Watch your back, love."

The APS halted two hours later, and the rear ramp slowly descended. Taylor walked down it with a shouted greeting to someone out of sight. The driver rose from his seat and moved through the compartment.

"Last stop," he said. "All out." He walked down the ramp as the gunner climbed down from the turret and followed him.

Simon and Sylvie watched as Herin's body was gently carried off by Falkes and Steelhammer. Gillis unceremoniously dragged Flandyrs down the ramp and dropped the corpse on the concrete pad outside.

Two men with a stretcher rushed in and Simon helped them get Kermal loaded. Simon gripped his friend's hand before he was whisked away. Sylvie took his arm, and they walked down the ramp. In the predawn light, Simon looked over the heavy APS. He could see the scars where old insignia had been scrubbed off and there was a deep spall along one flank. The dark red paint had been patched with slightly different colors, and one of the headlights was shattered. Clearly, this was a surplus or salvaged machine, not military grade.

Red Base proved to be the warehouse and transport yard they'd used as a rest stop on the trip in. The interior was unchanged, except for a table full of communications gear near the door and three more men in gray utility suits talking with Taylor. The team stood about, stripping off gear and stowing weapons in the hard-sided cases they'd left behind. Steron called first shower and was already heading to the back, stripping off his shirt.

Simon walked over to Taylor. "What is all this, Top? I don't remember Hal contracting for this kind of support."

"He didn't," said Taylor. "But he will get a bill. I called in a favor and put these guys on contingency pay only if called. You'd rather I hadn't called them?"

"No." Simon grinned. "Glad you did." He extended a hand to the man standing next to Taylor. "Simon Buckley. Thanks for coming to get us."

"I'm Grayson Melke." The man's grip was firm and his smile ready. "Glad to help out. The boys are always ready for a scrap. And some coin."

"House Stonebender is good for it," said Simon.

"Oh, I know it," said Melke. "And I can always take it out of Josen's hide if he tries to stiff us."

The arrival of a sled outside the open door interrupted any reply. Simon stepped out and was relieved to see Kermal being loaded into an ambulance. The medic noticed and stepped over.

"They're taking him to Reverend Mother Hospital in West Faring. He's stable thanks to that tourniquet." He put a hand on Simon's shoulder. "The bolt took out the big artery in his thigh. They may not be able to save his leg. Thought you should know."

Kermal gave a small wave as the ambulance door closed, and Simon turned away. Back in the warehouse Sylvie saw him and came to his side. She had managed to change and shower and was toweling her wet hair. "What's wrong. Simon?"

"Kermal's on his way to the hospital in West Faring. He'll live, but the medic says they may not be able to save his leg."

She embraced him. "I'm sorry, love. But he's alive and there still may be hope."

He held her for a moment then pushed away. "I need a shower. See when we can get out of here and back to West Faring. I need to get Flandyrs to Sergeant Utzler. He'll make sure the body gets to Wycliffe right away."

Ten minutes later, he was showered and dressed in a clean set of uniform trousers and dark blue shirt. It wasn't a full Keeper uniform, but it gave the impression that he wanted. He packed his vest and PL44 into a hard-shell case but kept the Gowron and hip holster.

The rest of the team had gathered outside, and Simon joined them. Two cargo sledges had arrived from somewhere, and Taylor began calling orders to load the gear and get aboard. Simon took hold of the drag litter and hauled it over to the nearest sledge. Taylor helped him load it.

"We need to make a stop at the West Faring Central Keeper station, Top. I want Flandyrs sent to Wycliffe House ASAP, and the station can register you and your team for the bounty. Should be a big payday for the lot of you."

"You and your Lady deserve a share, too," said Taylor as they climbed into the cargo bed. "It was a team effort."

"No need," said Simon. "All I wanted was to get Sylvie back."

Gillis climbed in beside Taylor, and they settled onto the flat bed. Sylvie and Falkes rode in the cab with Steelhammer driving. One of Melke's men drove the other sledge with the gear, and they set out down the paved road toward West Faring.

It was full daylight when they slid up in front of the Peacekeeper station near the Old Wall. Utzler and a trio of Keepers were on hand to meet the sledge. Simon had retrieved his handheld mirror from the lockers in the warehouse and made a call before boarding the sledge. All of the Keepers were armed and had their badge lanyards slung.

"Good meeting, Sergeant Utzler," Simon called as he stood up in the cargo bed.

"Good meeting, Lieutenant Buckley," said the old Sergeant. "What have you got for us today?"

"Two things, Sergeant. First, meet Ranger Lieutenant Sylvie Graystorm. She has critical information that needs to get to Cymbeline. Can you arrange fast transport for her?"

"I've heard of you, M'Lady. Hamil Fairborn spoke highly of you. There's a courier sled leaving in ten minutes," said Utzler. "That quick enough?"

"It will be fine, Sergeant," said Sylvie. "Thank you." She looked at Simon. "See you in Glenharrow?"

Simon nodded." Don't know how long this will take. Give my love to Molly."

Sylvie walked into the station and Simon pointed to Flandyrs's bundled corpse. "Second, is this high value target. I need the body chilled and transported to Kyle Evarts, CSA at Wycliffe House ASAP."

"High value, as in bounty?" asked Utzler, now taking in the rest of the team.

"Aye, Sergeant," said Taylor. "That there is none other than Galen Flandyrs. The Loot here and my team took him and brought him out. Now where do we register his bounty?"

"Kandlis will take you inside." Utzler pointed to one of the Keepers. He caught Simon's eye as Taylor started to follow the man. Simon nodded.

Gillis jumped down from the cargo bed and looked around. Simon turned to him and took a step back, out of reach. Utzler and the other Keeper moved up on either side. Taylor sensed something was amiss and turned back but Kandlis stood in his way.

"Steron Gillis," said Simon in a firm voice. "I am placing you under lawful detention on suspicion of the murder of Galen Flandyrs. You are under caution that any statements you make may be recorded and used in evidence against you. You have the right to legal counsel before making any further statements to me or to any other King's Officer. Do you understand this caution."

"Loot, what the hells?" said Taylor.

"You ain't a keeper, Loot," said Gillis. "You got no power to do this."

"No," said Simon. "But Sergeant Utzler does."

Gillis looked to either side, then at Taylor. Simon saw the look and said, "Stand down everyone." He eyed Taylor. "You could probably take us all out Top. But then what? Run? Fight the whole station?"

"Leave it, Top," said Gillis. "You know who to call.

I'll go along quietly, Loot. But this ain't right."

"If I'm wrong, I'll be the first to admit it and apologize. But badge or no, I'm not letting this one go. Christon wanted to know the truth as well. That man was his responsibility. He took the death hard." Simon motioned to Utzler, who touched Gillis on the arm.

"Come along," Utzler said. "There's a good lad. No cuffs needed, eh?"

Gillis gave Utzler a wry smile and Simon a hard look. "This is for Chris, Loot, not you."

Simon felt the stares of Falkes, Steelhammer and Taylor as Gillis followed Utzler into the station. He ignored them, turned, and walked away toward the street. He didn't know where Reverend Mother Hospital was but expected any cab driver to be able to get him there, and he desperately wanted to know what was happening with Kermal.

The driver indeed knew the way. Twenty minutes later, Simon stood in front of the main entrance to a gleaming modern hospital with the statue of the Mother Goddess, welcoming arms outstretched in the traditional pose, standing in the open lobby. He hesitated, wondering what he could do or say to Kermal, if he would even be able to see him.

Stop stalling, he told himself. He pushed open the glass doors and walked to a reception desk. A pretty Dwarf receptionist looked up at him, waiting for him to speak.

"I'm trying to find someone?" said Simon tentatively.

"Is he a patient here?" she asked.

"Yes, he would have been brought in by ambulance a while ago with a leg injury."

"E&A case," said the receptionist, touching the mirror in front of her. "What is your friend's name?"

"Kermal Brackenville," said Simon.

She made a few hand motions across her screen

and frowned. "He's here, but he's in surgery. Are you a family member?"

"He's my brother," said Simon.

Her eyes narrowed. "It says here he's half-Orc. You don't look Orcish."

"Different fathers," said Simon, wishing he still had his badge. He'd left the one he'd borrowed from Hal with the rest of his gear, tucked into the pouch of his tactical vest.

The woman must have sensed some of his distress. Either that or she believed him. "One floor up, end of the South Hall, is the surgical waiting room. Let the person at the desk know you're waiting. They will inform his surgeon."

Simon found his way easily to the room. The clerk at the desk took his name and Kermal's and told him he could sit anywhere, that the coffee was complementary, and the mirror screen in the room could only be tuned by hospital staff. Simon found a reasonably comfortable chair next to the wall with a view of the entire room and settled in. He was asleep within two minutes.

Sometime later, he awoke to a gentle tap on his shoulder. "Mr. Buckley?" An older man, in the traditional sky-blue jacket of a Healer, leaned over him. The man wore a tight cap on his head and a cloth mask hung loosely around his neck. His face was lined, but his eyes were sharp and youthful. "You're waiting for word about Kermal Brackenville?"

Simon sat up rubbing his eyes. "Yes," he said. "Yes. Is he all good?"

"He's doing well," said the man. "I'm Healer Corton, Max Corton. I'm the surgeon who worked on your friend's leg."

"His leg, is it..." Simon couldn't finish the question.

"The wound was deep," said Corton. "It severed the artery in the middle of his thigh. Between that and the time it took to get to surgery, I'm afraid the damage to his tissue was too great." He reached out and gripped Simon's shoulder. "We had to amputate the leg. Mr. Brackenville should recover. He'll need help for a while, but he's young and can learn to walk again with an artificial leg."

Simon felt the tears. Blinked them back, cursed himself for being weak. *Kermal needs me. Warrior up.* He rubbed his eyes again, stood and shook Corton's hand. "Thank you," he said. "May I see him?"

"Not just yet," said Corton. "The staff will let you know when he's moved to his room. You can see him then."

Two hours later, Simon stood in the doorway to a small hospital room. Kermal lay back with his eyes closed, the head of his bed propped up and a pillow behind his head. The lower half of his body was covered by a sheet and blanket, the empty place where his left leg should have been was obvious.

Kermal took a deep breath and opened one eye. "Simon," he said hoarsely. "What the hells time is it?"

"Just after 18th," said Simon, finally stepping into the room and going to the bedside. "You've been napping all day."

"Give me some water, will you?" Kermal croaked.

Simon poured water from a bedside pitcher into a small cup and handed it to Kermal, who sipped slowly. "Thanks." Simon just nodded awkwardly. Kermal set the cup down. "I know about the leg, Simon. Shitty deal but beats being dead."

"I'm sorry, Kermal. If there's anything I can do, just say the word."

Kermal held up a hand. "Save it. I know. The people I work for have deep pockets. I'll be taken care of. You did your part getting me out of that melee. I owe you for that."

"You owe me nothing, Brother." To Kermal's

puzzled look, Simon grinned. "I think I convinced a receptionist we were brothers from different fathers. But I mean it."

Kermal reached out and gripped Simon's hand, nodding. Simon pulled up a chair and sat. They said nothing more. Kermal closed his eyes, and Simon watched his brother sleep.

CHAPTER THIRTEEN

"I'm sorry, Lieutenant," said the front desk Sergeant at Wycliffe House. "I can't let you up without authorization. Captain Axhart is in a meeting, and Mr. Evarts isn't answering his mirror. If you'll have a seat, I'll call you if anything changes."

Simon sat on a hard bench, struggling to control his frustration. In the three weeks since returning from the Havens, he'd tried every connection, every bureaucratic channel he knew to get some word on Steron Gillis. The detention had been dutifully logged by Sergeant Utzler in West Faring, Gillis had been checked into the cells, and transport to Wycliffe House for formal charging by the King's Prosecutors had been arranged. And then Gillis disappeared. Worse, no one Simon could reach seemed to even know of the man's existence.

The first week home had been a blur of activity as Sylvie was interviewed and debriefed by the Foreign Service, the Justice Ministry, the War Ministry, and a dozen other government agencies. She'd been sworn to secrecy, which Simon respected, but what she'd been able to say during their nights together told him enough.

The quiet resignation of the Deputy Finance Minister, the retirement of several high-ranking military officers, and the sudden change in the support for the Crown's legislative agenda in the House of Lords came as no surprise to him. The documents Sylvie had managed to gather, and the elimination of Galen Flandyrs, changed the landscape of politics and Foreign Relations in the Commonwealth, hopefully for the better.

Tensions with the Gray Havens and the Steward remained high, especially after the Steward started the promised treason trials. Sylvie was tried in absentia and sentenced to life in prison. Rulanis Summerfield as well. There were threats and accusations of illegal cross-border attacks, but troop movements in the Borderlands had been recalled, and the military exercises in the Lordiss Valley had been canceled. The Foreign Office position was that the internal affairs of another sovereign nation were none of the Commonwealth's concern, no matter how reprehensible, so little further action was taken regarding the treason trials.

Good news had arrived that morning from the Free States as well. Hamil Fairborn had reached the border and was safe with Liam and Becky Aster. An unexpected traveling companion had come with him, Tandril Misthaven, much to Sylvie's relief.

Sunk in his own thoughts, Simon started when he heard his name called.

"Simon Buckley, what are you doing here?" asked a Dwarf woman, standing in front of him with her hands on her hips.

"Oh. Good meeting, Mistress Cairns," said Simon.

"I was hoping for a chance to speak with Captain Axhart, but the desk Sergeant says the captain is in a meeting."

"He is," said Elvira Cairns, formidable Secretary to Gelbard Axhart. "But he'll be out shortly. Is this about your petition?"

"Yes. Mistress Cairns," said Simon.

"Well, best you come along. I won't have a Peacekeeper Lieutenant cooling his heels in the lobby like a street person." She gathered up the huge carpet bag she always carried and bustled toward the stairwell. Simon followed, ignoring the wave of protest from the desk Sergeant.

He followed her up to the Command level and waited as she unlocked Axhart's office. He dutifully sat where she directed in the anteroom as she opened the inner office. She returned, started brewing a pot of coffee and set her carpet bag beside her reception desk.

Gelbard Axhart swept in a few minutes later. He glanced at Simon and frowned but didn't speak to him. "Mistress Cairns, coffee please," he said as he stalked into the inner office.

She rose from behind her desk and poured coffee into two mugs, set the pot and one mug on a tray and handed the other mug to Simon. She opened the inner door and carried the tray in to her boss. She returned without a word and sat behind the desk. Simon sipped coffee and waited.

"Mistress Cairns," Axhart called from the office a few minutes later. "Send Buckley in."

Simon rose, looked about and finally set the mug on the small table next to his chair. He approached the door, uncertain if he should knock or simply walk in. In the end, Axhart settled the question by calling, "Get in here, Buckley."

Simon closed the door behind him and crossed the

green carpet that occupied the center of the room to stand in front of Axhart's wide desk. He drew himself to attention.

"Oh, at ease, Buckley," said Axhart. He signed a paper on the desk and placed it into a folder. He leaned back in his chair, folded his hands on the desktop and looked up at Simon. Despite being a Dwarf, Axhart had a presence that seemed to fill the room. "This is about your petition for reinstatement, I presume?"

"Yes, sir," said Simon, keeping his gaze on the wall just above Axhart's head. "I want to return to active Peacekeeper status."

Axhart chuckled. "You once told me you doubted your fitness for command, that you were used up and hadn't the heart for the job anymore. What changed?"

"I've reconsidered, sir. I'd like to resume my duties," said Simon carefully.

Axhart didn't answer. The silence stretched on until Simon looked down, meeting Axhart's eye for the first time. "Talk to me, Simon," said Axhart. "Convince me. What changed?"

Simon relaxed his posture slightly. "The past few weeks showed me some things about duty and the nature of command. I felt part of a team, worked with people I depended on and who depended on me. We lost people, but we accomplished the mission, got Sylvie and Flandyrs out." Simon paused. "Captain, I'm a good Keeper. It's what I do. Pretty much the only thing I'm really good at. I need to get back to the work, back to the teams that I built and ran."

Axhart took a long breath, let it out. He reached into the top drawer of his desk and took out a badge and lanyard. He set it on the desk. "So, you think you're ready to grab the wolf by the tail again?"

"I am, sir," said Simon.

Axhart slid the badge and lanyard and the folder across the desk to Simon. "Your signed commission is in the folder. Stop by the armory and draw a sidearm. Elvira will see to setting up your office. I want your teams up and running in 48 hours."

Simon picked up his badge, saluted and turned to go. "Thank you, Captain," he said, but Axhart didn't answer. Simon closed the door as he left the office.

"Welcome back, Lieutenant Buckley," said Elvira. "Your office is in the same place it was before. Captain Axhart wouldn't let maintenance change anything."

"Thank you, Mistress Cairns."

"Don't thank me," she said gruffly. "Thank the captain. Now get out of here and start doing your job."

Two hours later, after signing for a sidearm, a tactical vest, obtaining an updated image for records, checking in with payroll and taking care of a half-dozen administrative chores, he finally made his way to the office he'd left nearly two months earlier.

"Welcome back, sir," said Lessa Greenwater as he opened the door. Lessa had been his secretary before his leave; a young Orc woman personally selected by Elvira Cairns. She'd been the perfect complement to his management style, and he felt a surge of gratitude that she was here.

"Thank you, Lessa," answered Simon with a grin. "And don't call me sir. LT or Simon is fine."

"Right, LT," she said. "I took the liberty of telling the team sergeants you were back. Today's dispatches are on your desk. Would you like some coffee?"

"No thanks," Simon said. "I had some earlier. I'll meet with the teams in their spaces later."

He settled behind the desk, read the dispatches with a smile. He didn't know the specifics of the cases, the street reports, but the action was familiar, and he could fill in the blanks. *It's good to be back.*

He worked through most of the afternoon, reading files, acquainting himself with the cases his teams were following, and getting familiar once again with the way his team leaders worked.

Lessa opened the door just after 17th hour and asked, "Do you need anything else, LT? If not, I'll be leaving for the day."

"Nothing, thank you, Lessa. Have a good evening." He watched her go. Then he signed onto his desktop mirror. He opened a commercial search scroll and looked up the warehouse that housed the training facility the team had used. He wasn't surprised to find that it was listed only as a commercial facility. He tried the company name that Hal had paid the fee to and again found no listing. He sat staring at the mirror. *What in the seven hells is going on?*

He shut down the mirror and left the office, making his way down past the squad room. The day watch was leaving as the night teams took over. A number of the Keepers acknowledged him with smiles and nods. He returned the silent greetings but continued down the stone staircase to the lower levels. Kyle Evarts's office was on the lowest level, near the morgue. Simon hadn't called ahead, took a chance that the Forensics Mage would still be at work. He wasn't disappointed.

"Got a minute, Kyle?" Simon asked.

Evarts looked up from his desktop mirror. "Simon," he said with a smile. "You're back on full duty? Good. It's been too quiet around here lately." He stood and came around the desk to shake Simon's hand. The Half-Elf mage stood almost a head taller than Simon but was thin and lithe. He moved with the unconscious grace of those with Elf blood.

"Yes," said Simon. "Just today. I've been trying to catch up on the cases and my teams. I thought I'd stop down and see if there are any issues with the forensics."

"Nothing other than the usual delays in getting outside records," said Evarts. "Was there anything specific?"

Simon noticed the slight hesitation in his friend's voice. "Yes. I'm looking for a report on the aural analysis on Galen Flandyrs. There's nothing in the files."

"That's because there's nothing to put in the files," said Evarts.

"You couldn't get a reading from the body?" asked Simon.

Evarts frowned and looked around. He waved Simon into the office and closed the door. "Why are you asking, Simon? That case has been moved out to Justice. My involvement ended when they took possession of the body."

"But you did get an aura off of the body, right?" said Simon. "At least you confirmed that it was an Air spell that killed him?"

"Why do you care, Simon. Justice has taken the case. It's not our concern."

"Because it was murder, Kyle," said Simon. "Flandyrs was killed by someone on that team. The most likely person is a former Marine, an armorer with considerable Air talent. And he's someone I trusted with my life, who kept me from being killed by my own stupidity. I can't just accept that he committed cold-blooded murder."

Evarts looked around again, as if he expected someone to be watching. "It was an Air spell. And I did get a clear casting aura from the body. It wasn't in any of the usual registries, so I checked military and known criminal registries. I got a hit on the military search, but the name was redacted."

"And?" asked Simon, sensing there was more.

"So, I filed a request for information through the liaison office. I didn't hear anything for a few days, so I checked the registry again. The aural record had been removed. Not just redacted—but removed, as if it had never been there." He stopped and rubbed a hand across his face. "The next day I got a visit from a hard-looking Dwarf who said he was an Agent for the Justice Ministry, at least that's what his credentials said. He told me that Justice was handling all aspects of the Flandyrs case, and my 'meddling' was unwanted. Threatened me with an obstruction charge if I looked at it again."

"Seven hells, Kyle," whispered Simon. "Justice is covering up the whole case."

"Maybe," said Evarts. "Maybe they are investigating. I don't know. I'm willing to push the limits here in the House. But I like my career. It's not worth it to push back against the Justice Ministry, especially if they've warned me off."

"Sorry, Kyle," said Simon. "I won't ask for more. I appreciate you telling me this. Forewarned and all that."

"Watch yourself, Simon. This sounds serious and you've only been back for a day. Don't poke the wolf without a damned good reason." He opened the office door. "Meet up for a beer and a meal sometime soon? I'd love to hear more about how you brought Sylvie Graystorm home."

"I'd like that. I'll get in touch once I get my feet on the ground." He shook Evarts's hand again.

He'd parked his Oxley in a public stable near Tanner Street, since he didn't have a pass to the Wycliffe stables yet. He sat behind the yoke, going over what Evarts had said. It seemed clear that someone high in the government was covering up Flandyrs's murder. But why? He shook his head. He had other issues to deal with. *Go home. Spend time with Sylvie. Talk to Hal. You need to get back in the game and give the teams your best.*

CHAPTER FOURTEEN

Simon climbed out of his sled an hour later and walked toward the postern door. Traffic had snarled on the Westport Bridge and his commute was twice as long as usual. Sylvie met him at the door with a kiss and a mug of ale.

"Welcome home, Lieutenant," she said.

"You heard," said Simon after returning her kiss.

"Hal made the announcement as soon as he got home." Sylvie smiled. "He probably knew before you did."

Hal had been a Peacekeeper longer than most active Keepers had been alive. He had sources everywhere. Little went on at Wycliffe House without his knowledge.

They found Hal in the kitchen at his usual place sipping ale and watching Molly preparing dinner. The look on the old Dwarf's face spoke of pure contentment. He noticed Simon and Sylvie and banged his mug on the kitchen table.

"Well met, Lieutenant," he roared.

"Haldron Stonebender," scolded Molly. "This is my kitchen, not some tavern taproom."

"Yes, love," said Hal with mock meekness. He winked at Simon.

Molly gave both Simon and Sylvie quick hugs. "Sit. Now that you're home, dinner will be just a minute."

"So, you decided to get back in the game," said Hal as they sat and accepted refills on ale.

"Aye," said Simon. "I wasn't sure when I left. I made a hash of the Lieutenant's job my first outing. I wasn't sure I was up to the job."

"Dreck and tailings," said Molly, shaking a spoon at him. "You solved cases, took down a rogue Mage and stopped an attack on the Royal family. From what Hal says, your teams loved you. You, Simon Buckley, are the only one who doubts you can do the job."

"She's right, Simon," said Sylvie, taking his hand.

Hal was more serious. "There's many a great Keeper who isn't fit for command. What changed your mind?"

"First Sergeant Taylor," said Simon. "Top stayed in command but gave his people, including me, space to do what they did best. He stayed professional and focused in the face of changes and losses. I want to be like that."

"You already are, love," said Sylvie. "I've seen you in action, thinking on the run, staying focused but flexible. Top's only advantage was a team he'd drilled and trained with for years."

"That's what I want to build at Wycliffe House." He nodded at Hal. "With your help."

"Ha," said Hal. "So. you admit your foster father might know a thing or two."

"How are the teams, Hal?" asked Simon. "I went through the active files today and looked at the clearance rates, but how are they getting along?"

Hal sipped ale. "Gervis Birchfield is headstrong, brilliant and runs a tight team. He needs some seasoning and a dash of humility, but he's going to make a mark on the Force one day. Jason Hanks is quiet, methodical, follows procedure and has one of the highest clearance rates on the Force."

"And you, the reluctant Sergeant," asked Simon.

"Getting the job done," said Hal as he poured more ale. "Handel Brookstone is a solid armorer, good investigator, and has a wicked sense of humor. I like him, which is a big change for me." Brookstone was an Orc and, for as long as Simon could remember, Hal had voiced the typical Dwarf prejudice against Orcs. "Jack Ironhand is back. He finished his sobriety training and was cleared for duty by the Healers. He's sober, steady, but the old fire isn't there. We'll see if he finds his way back, but for now, the rest of the team is carrying him. Sonia Milhaven is the glue that's holding us together. She knows just the right tone to take with Jack, and she can laugh with Handel. She's a decent investigator, but her real talent is for interrogation. She gets in the subject's head and gets them to talk."

Before Simon could respond, Molly announced that dinner was ready and all 'Keeper talk' stopped. She set a platter of pork chops with mushroom sauce in the center of the table along with a large bowl of fresh peas and tiny onions and a loaf of fresh bread.

"So," said Molly, once everyone had helped themselves to food. "Sylvie and I were talking and think that the 15th of next month would be a good day for a wedding."

Simon coughed as he almost inhaled a mouthful of peas. Sylvie smiled shyly and nodded. "So soon? But Sylvie and I haven't even found a flat or a house yet."

"Oh, that's all decided." Molly waved her hand. "You'll live here in Willston and Meredith's old rooms. It's a large enough suite with its own door."

Simon looked at Sylvie, who cocked her head and gave him a wry smile. Clearly, she'd long since surrendered to Molly when it came to the wedding. Living at the Hall until the birth of the first child was the Dwarfish way. Wills and Mery had been the last to live there and had moved into their own suburban home shortly after Jasmine's birth.

"Yes, Molly," said Simon. "I hope Kermal will be well enough by then. I want him as my Second."

"How is Kermal doing?" asked Sylvie. "I heard he had left the hospital."

"He's in a recovery facility in East Wray, learning to use his artificial leg," said Simon. "I heard from him last week, but he hasn't replied to any of my messages."

Sylvie took his hand. "The date isn't firm, Simon. We'll make sure Kermal can be there. But I don't want to wait anymore. I want to be with you, whether in our own place or here at Stonebender Hall. And I like the idea of living here. I haven't felt like I had a family for many years. This feels right."

Simon squeezed her hand as Molly went on about wedding plans. He heard little of it but gathered that nothing was needed from him other than a list of people to be invited. Conversation turned to family news. Katya had been promoted and was returning to Cymbeline as a Kings Prosecutor in the Business Crimes division, Wren and her husband were expecting their second child sometime after the New Year, and Wills and Mery were finally finished with the renovations on the old house they'd bought two years earlier. Simon listened but all the while watched Sylvie's eyes light up with delight at each new revelation.

Later, after the dinner dishes were cleared away, they sat together in the room they shared. "You really do want this, don't you?" said Simon.

"I do, Simon." She held his hands, looked into his eyes. "To you, this is everyday life. To me, it's all new and exciting and vital. It's been many years since I left my father's house and, even then, it was never a place of love and safety. At least for now, this is what I need."

"Funny, when I first joined the Force, I thought it was my chance to get out on my own, to be my own man." He smiled. "But I always came back. Working with Hal made it impossible to ignore the family, but even so, this place grounded me. If it's what you want, then you'll have it."

The next few days passed quickly. Simon focused on the cases his teams were investigating and slowly felt comfortable once again with the way they worked. Sylvie started a three-week training course at the Peacekeeper Academy to familiarize her with Commonwealth law and procedures. Captain Axhart had enthusiastically endorsed her application to transfer from the Gray Rangers to the King's Peacekeepers at her same rank.

It was late afternoon and Simon and Hal sat in his office going over the active cases Hal's team was following. "How's Jack doing?" Simon asked.

"Coming along," Hal answered. "He's more engaged and, once in a while, a hint of the old Jack shines through. He'll be all good."

"How about you?" Simon cocked his head at the old Dwarf. "Adjusting to being in command of your own team?"

"Bah," scoffed Hal. "Never wanted it, but that doesn't mean I can't do the job. Taught you everything you know, didn't I?"

"That you did," laughed Simon. "Say, did you ever get a final bill from Taylor for the Havens rescue?"

"We paid full price up front, lad," said Hal. "That was the agreement. If there are other charges, I'll want a word with the First Sergeant."

Simon shrugged. "I guess the bounty on Flandyrs covered the extra costs. But when I searched for the corporation we sent the money to, I couldn't find any trace of them. And the warehouse where we trained is listed as a commercial property, no mention of Allegiant Security, the company that runs it."

"Maybe that's to keep a lower profile," said Hal. "Keep the neighbors from complaining."

"Maybe," said Simon. "But I can't find any listings for Allegiant Security either. That is the outfit that runs it, right?"

"Aye." Hal tugged at his beard. "I'm getting the impression that somebody doesn't want that place to be common knowledge."

"How did you hear about it?" asked Simon.

"A contact I know over at Justice sent me the address and mirror locus."

Simon grunted in frustration. "Justice again."

"What's that supposed to mean?" asked Hal.

"The Justice Ministry took over the Flandyrs investigation, sent an agent to shut down Kyle Evarts's efforts to trace the aural reading he got from Flandyrs's body. They've not responded to any of my inquiries about the case and there's no trace in any of the registries of Taylor or any of his team."

Hal sat back in his chair and didn't speak for a long moment. "I think you should let this go, Simon. Some tunnels are best left dark."

"Not you, too, Hal," Simon said with a frown. "Kyle said the same thing. This is a case of murder by magic. Isn't that exactly what I'm supposed to investigate?"

Hal shrugged. "And Justice has taken over the case. Your job is done."

"It doesn't feel right, Hal." Simon stood and paced. "It feels like they're covering it up. Other than a brief announcement that Galen Flandyrs was dead, there's been nothing more; no action by the King's Prosecutors, no arrests, no investigation as far as I can see."

"And that's the way of the Justice Ministry," said

Hal. "They're a bunch of arrogant bastards who play by their own rules and can't be bothered with 'low level' Keepers like us. Best you mark this down as experience and move on."

Simon stopped pacing and sighed. "You're probably right. All good. I'll see you at home. I've got a couple of things to clear up here."

"Don't be late. Your foster mother wants to talk about wedding plans." Hal rolled his eyes.

Hal took his leave and Simon checked the time. *15:45. If I leave now, I can get to the East End and still be home in time for dinner.*

He drove across the Hanford Bridge on Tanner and turned south. He reached the warehouse by 16:15 and was surprised to see the big rollup doors open and sledges in the front being unloaded. He parked his Oxley across the street and approached the regular doorway near the parking area. It was open and a burly man with a short beard checked bills of lading and shouted an occasional order toward the sledges.

Simon flashed his badge and asked, "Excuse me, are you in charge here?"

"Aye." He looked at Simon's badge and asked, "What can I do for you, Agent Buckley."

"How long have you been at this location?" asked Simon.

"Two weeks now," said the man. "We outgrew our old warehouse and got lucky with this one. The estate agent we hired found it just as it went on the market, and we were able to snap it up before the price got bid up." He cocked his head. "Why do you ask?"

"You haven't heard about the rash of thefts in the area then," said Simon. "We're warning businesses to make sure they lock up properly and have an up-to-date warding system installed."

The man looked relieved. "No worries there, the system that came with the building is top branch.

Haven't seen anything like it since I managed a bank. We're all good."

"Glad to hear it," said Simon. "Is it monitored?"

"Aye, with SafeGuard."

"Not Allegiant?" asked Simon.

"Never heard of them." The man looked puzzled. "We had SafeGuard on our last location. Stayed with them."

"All good," said Simon. "Some of the other buildings are on Allegiant. I figured they had the local market locked up. Glad to hear you're well covered. Don't hesitate to call the local station if you see anything suspicious."

"Will do, Agent Buckley," said the man. "Thanks for stopping by."

Simon walked back to his sled, thoughts spinning. Allegiant Security was either a front or had shut down and sold the training facility for what sounded like below market price. Why? He reached the Oxley and almost missed the slip of paper wedged in the door. He pulled it out and unfolded it. *Bankside Necropolis 3-b, 134,* it read.

He climbed in behind the steering yoke. He didn't know what the note meant, but he knew someone had followed him here and left it for him. He needed to find out who that was. He took out his handheld and opened a map scroll. Bankside Necropolis was out in West Wray, beyond Glenharrow. *Tomorrow, then. No time today.*

He rose early the next morning, in time to see Sylvie off to her Academy course and was in his office before 7th hour. As usual, Lessa was already there and had coffee ready. He took a mug and sat behind his desk to review the night's dispatches. Shortly after watch change, his team leaders reported in, and he reviewed the active cases and plans for the day. Then he tackled the paperwork—budget reports, watch schedules, known Mages on the crime watch lists, either because of prior offenses or active investigations. This was the part of the job he'd tried to forget.

He took a break at midday and walked up Tanner Road to a small café that served Dundarian style chicken, one of his favorites. When he returned to the office, Lessa greeted him.

"The captain asked to see you when you returned, LT." She looked concerned. "He didn't say why."

"Thanks, Lessa. I can't think of any toes I've stepped on recently, so maybe it's some new assignment for the teams."

Elvira Cairns barely acknowledged him as she waved him into Captain Axhart's office. Simon stood in front of the broad desk at ease but alert.

"You wanted to see me, Captain?"

Axhart looked up, settled into his chair and asked, "Is there some crime wave in the East End that I wasn't aware of?"

"No, sir," said Simon warily. "Why do you ask?"

"Because the Public Liaison received an inquiry from a citizen, a man named Hiram Woodly, who just purchased a warehouse in the industrial complex south of Tanner Road. His foreman expressed concern because a Peacekeeper, an Agent Buckley, warned him about criminal activity in the area. Asked questions about how long they'd been at the location and about their security system." Axhart sat forward, his voice taking on an edge. "What's going on, Simon? Do you have information about some planned heist in the area?"

"No, sir," said Simon. "Would you believe me if I said I was just fostering good relations with the community?"

"Don't show me horseshit and tell be it's fresh fruit, Simon," scoffed Axhart. "What the hells is going on?"

"I don't know, sir," said Simon. "But something isn't

right. Justice took over the Flandyrs investigation, their prerogative. But the man I detained on suspicion of Flandyrs's murder has disappeared from custody, the facility where our mercenary team trained has been sold, and the company that ran it has vanished from all the commercial registries. Kyle Evarts was warned in no uncertain terms to stop looking for the spell aura he got from Flandyrs's body by someone claiming to be from the Justice Ministry. Someone up there is covering up Flandyrs's murder; hells, covering up the whole damned mission that got him out. Why?"

Axhart waved Simon into a chair. "Sit down, Simon. Think about it for a second. I don't know all of the intelligence that Sylvie Graystorm managed to get out, but I saw enough to know how important it was. That entire operation of yours was off books and illegal. The fact that it succeeded and produced both Sylvie's documents and Flandyrs is probably the only reason you're wearing that uniform right not and not prison yellow. You could have started a war or been caught and paraded in front of the newsies as proof of Commonwealth duplicity."

"But a man was murdered with magic," protested Simon. "That's what I and my teams exist to investigate. Why would Justice take that case away?"

"I don't know, Lieutenant." Axhart's voice hardened, and Simon regretted his outburst. "The fact is that they did. Your involvement in the case ended there. Am I clear on this?"

"Yes, sir," said Simon. "I'll stick to the cases my teams are currently working."

"Good." Axhart seemed to relax. "Now get out of my office and get back to work."

Simon walked slowly down the hall to his own office. *He knows something. Either that or someone higher up ordered him to shut me down. High brass jingle.* Simon smiled grimly at that last thought, Keeper talk for politics interfering with regular investigations.

He leaned into the office and said to Lessa, "I'll be out for the rest of the day but available by mirror for anything urgent. Personal business."

"Aye, LT," she said smiling. "Wedding business?"

"Something like that."

As usual, traffic was heavy on the Westport Bridge, but he made better time on the A52 road that bypassed Glenharrow and East Wray. His mirror showed him the way to Bankside Necropolis, nestled in a wooded area on the northern side of the suburb. The necropolis wasn't large but had a feeling of permanence about it. It was bounded on one side by a tributary of the Wray River, from which the town drew its name, and on the other by a city park. All in all, it was a pleasant place for folk to remember their dead loved ones.

A directory at the front entrance showed him where the correct ossuary lay. He parked the sled and walked that way through well-tended plantings under shady trees. He easily found the drawer where the bones of Christon Herin were laid to rest. He read the name on the front of the sealed drawer, looked at the dates and frowned. Herin's date of death was all wrong, a date five years in the past. He reached out to touch it, assuring himself that he had read it correctly. *Something is very wrong here.*

"Did you know Chris?" asked a female voice from behind him.

He started and spun around, a hand going to the small of his back where his needler was holstered.

A large woman with short dark hair and green eyes held up her hands, palms out. "Sorry," she said in a calm voice. "I didn't mean to startle you."

Simon relaxed and looked at her more carefully. She was tall with broad shoulders and hips, probably a few years older than he. Her face was round and pleasant, and she stood with her feet apart and her hands in plain sight.

"I'm Sara Braxton," she said. "I'm Christon's sister. Did you serve with him?" She shook her head. "Of course you did. I should know better than to come up behind someone from the Teams."

Simon held out a hand, "I'm Simon Buckley. Lieutenant Simon Buckley, King's Peacekeepers. And yes, I knew Chris, served with him once on a difficult mission."

If Sara thought it unusual that Simon was a Keeper, she didn't show it. She stepped past him, and he now saw that she held a small bunch of daisies. She slid them into the tiny vase attached to the side of the drawer.

"They were Chris's favorite," she said. "When did you serve?"

"Years ago," said Simon distantly. It seemed years in that moment. "Has it really been five years since Chris passed?"

"I know," she said. "It doesn't seem that long, and yet some days it seems forever." She looked at him earnestly. "Do you know anything about his last mission?"

Simon closed his eyes, seeing the vision of Herin's body tossed in the air by the fire bolt. He shuddered. "What have you been told?" he asked.

"They said it was a training exercise, that the boat he and his team were in capsized in heavy surf and the entire team drowned. But Chris was strong, a good swimmer, it just doesn't sound right."

"I wasn't there. I was in the Peacekeepers by then," said Simon. "But I can tell you that Chris died protecting others, both team members and innocents. I can't say more, and if anyone asks, we never met."

Her eyes filled with tears, but she wiped them away. "I knew he didn't die for no reason. And I was around Chris and his mates enough to know there are some things you just can't talk about." She reached out and squeezed his hand. "Thank you, Lieutenant. And I'll keep this meeting to myself."

He watched her walk away, any regret he might have felt about telling her a partial truth wiped away by the set of her shoulders, the lightness of her step. *No, he didn't die for nothing. But why would he let her think he was dead for five years?* He looked again at the date on the ossuary drawer. *Something is definitely not right.*

CHAPTER FIFTEEN

Simon walked slowly back to his sled. This was far deeper than he'd suspected. Officially, Christon Hernin had been dead for five years. Almost certainly, the same was true of the rest of the team. Sara had said that the entire team drowned, and Simon had no doubt that meant Taylor and his people.

He activated the Air spell and pulled back on the yoke, intending to go back to the office and start a search for any other surviving relative of the mercenary team. It was a long shot, he knew, since all he had was their names, but figured it was worth a try. As he passed through the town of Wray, he remembered that Kermal was in a facility nearby. He got off the highway at the exit his mirror showed him and soon pulled up in front of a low-lying building. The front entrance looked more like a hotel or resort than a medical facility.

He parked the Oxley and walked up to the entrance. He was surprised to find a security door with a mirror and a buzzer. He pressed it and a voice said. "May I help you?"

"I'd like to see Kermal Brackenville. I understand he's staying here?"

"Are you family?" the voice asked.

"I'm his brother," said Simon.

"Mr. Brackenville has no living relatives," said the voice. "Have a good day."

"Wait," shouted Simon holding up his badge in front of the mirror. "I'm Lieutenant Simon Buckley, King's Peacekeepers. I need to speak to Brackenville about an important matter."

A few seconds later the lock buzzed, and the door opened. Simon stepped through into an opulent entryway with a marble floor, walls draped in muted colors with artfully placed statuary on low tables. Directly ahead, a reception desk sat in the middle of a wide lobby furnished with comfortable chairs and tasteful artwork on the walls. A tall man stood from behind the desk and approached him.

"Lieutenant Buckley," he said. "I'm Lucas Heiss. I'm the medical director here. What is your business with Mr. Brackenville?"

"It's personal," said Simon. "He's my former teammate, and I was the one who pulled him out when he was shot. If you'll tell him I'm here, he'll want to see me."

"Wait here." Heiss turned and walked past the desk into the rear of the facility.

Simon found a chair with a view of the door and settled in to wait. He didn't wait very long. He looked up to see Kermal rolling toward him, pushing the wheels of a wheelchair. Simon stood and Kermal stopped a few feet away. Simon noticed the artificial leg where Kermal's left leg had been.

"Simon," he said with a smile. "I wasn't expecting you. Is everything all good? Mr. Heiss said you had something important to say."

"Aye," said Simon. "How are you doing?"

"Well enough," said Kermal. "Getting stronger, getting used to the new leg. The only problem is that my foot, which isn't there, itches abominably." He laughed at Simon's expression. "Ease up, Simon. I'm fine. Now, what did you need to see me about?"

"Sylvie and I have set a date for the wedding," said Simon. "It will be at Stonebender Hall on the fifteenth of next month." Simon smiled at his friend's wide grin. "If you're able, I would like to have you stand by my side as my Second."

By way of answer, Kermal locked the wheels of the chair and pushed himself to his feet, standing free of the chair. "Simon, I would be honored." He extended his hand and Simon gripped it.

"Thank you, Brother," said Simon.

Kermal leaned into him, embracing him as well as supporting himself. "No thanks needed, Brother."

Simon helped Kermal ease back into the chair and stepped back. "Nice place, this."

Kermal nodded. "And exclusive. They have a number of important folk here. And then there's me. They know who's paying the bill. They're happy to take the coin, but don't want the other guests to know who I am."

"The mysterious Mr. Brackenville," said Simon.

"Something like that." Kermal looked up at Simon. "There's something else bothering you. Out with it."

"Steron Gillis has disappeared," said Simon. "I placed him under detention after you were taken to the hospital in West Faring. Turned him over to Sergeant Utzler for holding until he could be transferred to Wycliffe House. Utzler swears he was picked up twelve hours later with all the proper paperwork, but there's no record of it and he never arrived at the House."

"Sounds like someone with more steel than you

wants him," said Kermal.

"That's not all," said Simon. "The warehouse where we trained has been sold and now is just a warehouse. The security company, Allegiant, that ran it has vanished as if it never existed."

"So, they were a front for something else. The Cabal has dozens of fake companies like that."

"Kermal, you were there when Christon Herin died." Simon lowered his voice. "You saw it, right?"

"Yes, I saw. Why?" asked Kermal.

"Because I found his ossuary in a necropolis in West Wray. The date of death on the drawer is five years ago."

Kermal shrugged. "The engraver must have made a mistake."

Simon shook his head. "No. I met his sister at the ossuary. Her name is Sara. She was told Chris died in a training accident five years ago. She's believed him dead for all that time."

"Now that is strange," said Kermal. "Why would Chris want his family to think he was dead?"

"I don't know," said Simon. "But I suspect if we could access their service records, we'd find that all of our mercenary team was listed as dead, killed in action of some kind or in unfortunate training accidents."

"But why?"

"I don't know." Simon shook his head. "It would take a lot of steel, very high up, to make that happen."

Kermal reached up and grasped Simon's arm. "My advice, drop whatever you're investigating. Just let it go."

"That's what Hal advised, too." Simon looked away, not meeting his friend's eye. "I guess I should take that advice."

Kermal pulled at his arm. "Like I believe you. Look at me when you say that."

Simon looked at him, finally. "I don't know if I can

just drop it. This was murder, Kermal."

"Yes," said Kermal. "With a heavy dose of what you Keepers call 'high brass jingle.' You need to pick your battles, Brother."

Simon gave him a wry smile. "Don't I know it. You're right. I'll drop it for now."

"I mean it, Simon. You wouldn't look good at your wedding in prison yellow."

As he guided the Oxley onto the A52, Simon thought about Sara Braxton and Chris Herin. *Sara clearly cared about her brother. What could induce a person to cut all ties with family, let them believe you were dead? And the rest of the team, did they have families, people who would miss them?* Despite his friend's advice, he resolved to look.

CHAPTER SIXTEEN

Simon slammed his hand on the desk, frustrated. He knew that searching for relatives based solely on the names of the mercenary team was a long shot, but repeated searches on multiple registries turned up nothing. He'd initially tried the military records, but any reference to Taylor, Steelhammer or any of the other names also came up negative, as if they'd never existed.

He'd gone home after seeing Kermal and spent a pleasant evening with Sylvie. First thing in the morning, after meeting with his team leaders and going through their reports, he'd started searching. Three frustrating hours later, he was ready to admit defeat.

Lessa opened the door to the inner office and stepped in, carrying a tray. She set it on the desk in front of him. "Coffee and a fresh meat pie from the cart on the Greenway, the one you like."

"Thank you, Lessa," said Simon, picking up the wrapped pie. The Dwarf who ran the cart was from

Halting, in the Northwest Territories, and his pies were full of venison, leeks and rich gravy. He took a bite and looked up at Lessa who lingered in front of his desk. He swallowed, washed the mouthful down with a sip of coffee. "Was there something else?"

"It's a personal thing, LT," she said nervously. "You can tell me I'm out of place and I won't ask again."

"What is it?" Simon put down the pie and sat back.

"It's my Gran, LT," said Lessa. "Her pension payment. See, my gramps worked for the Peacekeeper station in Holdfast as an evidence clerk, checking stuff into the evidence rooms and keeping the logbooks and all. He did that for twenty years. Retired with a pension. When he died a few years back, my Gran got a survivor's pension."

"So, what's the problem?" asked Simon.

"Six months ago, Gran moved here to the city to be with us, me and my husband," said Lessa. "She put in the form for a change of address, but it hasn't been paid, and the Pension Office says her address is invalid and the drafts have been returned. Both she and I have tried to fix the problem but, so far, nothing. The pension isn't that big, but it would help out a lot at home."

"Would you like me to call the Pension Office and check? Unofficially, of course. But an inquiry from a serving lieutenant might get some attention." Simon smiled.

"Could you, LT? Would you?"

He laughed. "Of course. I may even beg a favor from Mistress Cairns. I'm sure she could crack a few whips over those people."

"Thank you, LT," she said. "Thank you."

He waved her away and returned to his lunch. If he could enlist Elvira Cairns, he likely would have to do little more. He finished the pie and was sipping coffee when a thought struck him. *Survivor pensions.*

The military pays survivor benefits to the next of kin if a man dies on duty. I wonder who might be receiving a survivor's draft from any of the 'dead' team? Especially Steron Gillis.

He summoned Axhart's office locus and, as expected, Elvira Cairns answered. Simon explained his conversation with Lessa. As he hoped, Mistress Cairns was outraged.

"You leave this to me, Simon Buckley," she said. "I'll have this straightened out today or there'll be hells to pay."

"Thank you, Mistress Cairns," said Simon with a smile.

It turned out that access to the survivor benefit rolls was open to law enforcement. It only required his badge number. He hesitated. Giving his badge number would leave a trace that would lead back to him if Axhart or the Justice Ministry cared to look. But why would they? He wouldn't take any action, only check on the disbursements.

Within an hour, he'd found it. He first checked on Christon Herin and quickly found a disbursement to Sara Braxton, listed as sole next of kin. He checked on Josen Taylor. Again, a disbursement to an ex-wife and son in Holdfast. Bran Falkes, and Georg Steelhammer revealed nothing. Finally, he entered Steron Gillis, and the date of death listed on Herin's ossuary. *Ruthen Gillis, Grandmother, received a draft of 278 Crowns per month as the service member's listed next of kin.* He read the name, an address in Gilford on the North side of the city. He closed the registry and shut down his mirror.

He sat for a long while, staring at the whirling Peacekeeper logo in his inactive mirror. He should drop this, like Hal and Kermal had advised, like Axhart had as much as ordered him to do. He resolved to leave a little early, get home before Sylvie and surprise her with reservations at a nice restaurant in Glenharrow or East Wray, far away from Gilford.

He bade Lessa a good evening and assured her that Elvira Cairns was working on her Gran's case. He descended the broad central staircase to the stables and pulled the Oxley out onto Tanner Road. He should have turned West, toward the Westport Bridge and Glenharrow. Instead, he turned east as far as Canal, then went north crossing the Greenbelt, Kings Road, and the High Street, then turning farther east on side streets to bypass the congestion around Caledonia University. Gilford lay north of the University, a small village that had been overtaken by the expanding city of Cymbeline. Now a nearby suburb, it managed to retain a smaller feel due to the lack of tall buildings, the narrow winding streets and the small modest houses that lined them.

The older, central portion of the town looked more tired than quaint, and the address Simon had for Ruthen Gillis turned out to be a narrow, three-story building with a flat on each floor, what in his native Westport was called a three-flat. He parked a half block away and walked up to the entrance. Three mailboxes, each with a stenciled name on the top, were built into the entryway. The third in line belonged to Ruthen Gillis.

Simon climbed the stairs to the third floor and knocked on the green door fronting the landing. He was about to knock again when he heard a voice from the other side of the door.

"Who is it?" The voice was slightly querulous but strong.

"Mistress Gillis," said Simon. "My name is Simon Buckley. I'm a King's Peacekeeper. I'd like to ask you a few questions?"

"About what?"

"About your grandson, Steron Gillis."

Locks turned, and the door opened a crack. Simon could see part of the woman's face, blue-green eyes like Steron's, high cheekbones, pale skin and steel-gray hair pulled back from her forehead.

"Is Steron in trouble?" she asked. "I haven't seen him in some time."

Is Steron in trouble? Does she know he's still alive?

"If I could just come in?" said Simon.

She stood aside and opened the door, closing it behind him. She crossed the room at the center of the flat and sat on a brocade sofa that looked older than Hal. Simon looked about. There were several chairs, all covered with stacks of newspapers, books and assorted bric-a-brac. The walls were stained and everything, except the sofa and the small table next to it, was covered with a fine layer of dust.

"Are you a friend of my Steron?" she asked.

"I like to think so," said Simon. "We served together."

"Oh, in the Marines?" She looked him over. "But that's not a Marine uniform."

"No, Mistress," said Simon. "I'm a King's Peacekeeper now."

"Did Steron send you? Sometimes he sends people to check on me."

"When was the last time you saw Steron?" asked Simon.

"Oh, I don't know," she answered, her eyes looking past him to the wall. "It's been quite a while. But Steron is very busy working, you know."

"What kind of work does he do?" asked Simon.

"Oh, he's in the Marines," she said brightly. "Serving King and Country." She picked up a small, framed image from the table. It showed a much younger Gillis in Marine fatigues standing with a heavy D'stang bolt thrower. His collar pin showed he was an armorer second class.

"When was this taken?" Simon asked.

"Just a month ago," the old woman said with a nod. "Yes, a month ago. That's the last time Steron visited."

"Last month?" *She's not all there. She thinks Steron is still on active duty, still a young Marine.* "Don't you get a draft each month?" Simon asked. "In Steron's name?"

"Oh, yes," she said. "Steron sends me part of his pay every month. He told me it was to make sure I could stay here and be safe. The outside is a dangerous place, you know."

"Have you had any contact with Steron since he left the Marines?" asked Simon.

"But he hasn't." She looked confused and vaguely distressed. "The draft comes every month. It has his name and rank on it. I'm sure you're mistaken."

"And you say he was here just last month?" Simon repeated.

"Yes," she said with certainty. "He took me grocery shopping, and we bought some flowers. See?" She pointed across the room to a bunch of bright silk flowers in a small vase. Simon examined them. They looked real, they were so bright and fresh appearing. He spun around, seeing the rest of the room, the objects and surfaces covered in dust. *But the silk flowers are bright and fresh. Steron was here recently. His Gran may be doty, but some of the things she remembers are clear.*

"Does Steron talk about any of his other friends, his teammates?" Simon asked.

"No." She shook her head vigorously. "That's confidential. He never speaks of it."

"Thank you, Mistress Gillis," said Simon, hoping he sounded sincere. "Steron may contact you soon and he may be in some trouble. Here is my card. Would you give it to Steron and ask him to summon the locus on it."

"What sort of trouble," she asked, "Has he done

something illegal? Steron would never break the law."

"No, of course not, Mistress," said Simon. "But some bad people may want to cause him trouble. I'd like to talk to him before that happens."

"And you really are a Peacekeeper?" Her voice was doubtful and frightened, as if he was a threat.

Simon held out his badge and identity card. "Here's my badge. I'm a Keeper Lieutenant from Wycliffe House. I want to find Steron, to find out what happened and why these people want him."

"I don't know" she muttered, looking away. "I just don't know. Steron will tell me what to do." She looked at Simon. "I think I'd like you to leave now."

Simon made a small bow. "As you wish." He backed toward the door, making sure his card was on the small table next to her. "Good parting, Mistress Gillis."

Rather than try to cross the city in evening traffic, Simon headed North to the Ring Road and followed it West across the Chain Bridge and into North Glenharrow. *I shook the tree. Let's see what falls out.*

CHAPTER SEVENTEEN

Simon settled behind his desk. It was just before 7th hour, Lessa had delivered his morning mug of coffee and the night's dispatches, and Gervis Birchfield was due in about fifteen minutes to brief him on a case that was due to go before the King's Magistrate later that day. He flipped through the message flimsies, but nothing unusual caught his eye until he'd looked at about half of them. The message that stopped him was short, terse even. *Did you speak to Sara?* it said, followed by a mirror locus.

He summoned the locus, and a familiar voice answered immediately, sound only, no image. "Is Sara all good? Did you tell her about Chris?"

"I spoke to her, Bran," said Simon. "But she thinks Chris and the rest of you died five years ago. I couldn't let her know her brother had lied to her about something like that. I just told her Chris died defending his team and other innocent people."

"How did she take it?" asked Falkes.

"She knew the training accident story was a lie, but she seemed happy to know Chris didn't die for nothing." Simon paused, but when Falkes didn't say anything, he asked, "Why would Chris let his sister think he was dead?"

"The mission," said Falkes with an edge of bitterness. "She had her husband and her children. The team's operational schedule kept them from seeing each other more than once or twice a year, anyway. There wasn't anyone else to miss him. None of us have anyone who would miss us."

"What about Steron's Gran?" asked Simon. "What mission?"

"You did good, Loot," said Falkes. "Gave Sara some closure. She always loved her brother." His voice broke as he said it.

"You loved him too, Bran," said Simon. "What mission?"

"Best you drop it, Loot. Good parting." The mirror went dead.

Simon summoned it again but got only a black field on his mirror. *By all the gods, enough is enough. The more people tell me to drop this thing, the deeper it gets.* He resisted the urge to storm up to Axhart's office and demand to resume the search for Steron Gillis. He knew it would do no good and would tip Axhart that he'd done some unauthorized investigating already. *Justice has the case. So, I'll go to the Justice Ministry, see Bendict Hammersmith, demand some answers from him.*

He listened patiently to Birchfield outline the case the King's Prosecutor would present and the testimony the team would be called to give. It was fairly routine, and Simon felt his attention wandering. Finally, Birchfield finished, and Simon came back to attention.

"Well done, Gervis," said Simon. "Do you anticipate

any surprises?"

"Not unless the perp pleads guilty, LT. We're ready."

The morning seemed to drag after that. Reports from the rest of his teams were routine and, while showing progress, there were no breakthroughs. Even Hal had little to report, and they spent some time talking about Jack's progress. "One day at a time," Hal said.

Simon managed to control his impatience until midday. He stepped into the outer office and said, "Lessa, would you please call Bendict Hammersmith over at the Justice Ministry. Ask, no, tell him I need fifteen minutes of his time. I'm leaving now. He can see me right away or I'll wait in the lobby until he will see me."

10 West Tanner, the main headquarters of the Justice Ministry, was a comfortable walk from Wycliffe House. Simon made it in seventeen minutes. He flashed his badge to the gate guard.

"Lieutenant Buckley," said the guard with a smile. "It's good to see you again, sir. I was on the gate when those Orcs tried to blow the place up a few months ago. You probably saved my life." He pointed toward the East wall. "Go on in. Mr. Hammersmith told us to expect you."

Simon crossed the landscaped courtyard to the glass and iron East wall. The wall had been severely damaged by a terrorist attack several months earlier. Repairs were still ongoing, but the central portion had been rebuilt with modern techniques that mimicked the historical methods from a hundred years earlier. Simon opened the glass doors and entered a spacious lobby.

Bendict Hammersmith waited there for him, his face hard as granite. He said nothing, merely pointed to the lift doors. They entered and spent an uncomfortable minute as the loft slowly rose to Hammersmith's floor.

He led Simon down the narrow hall to his office, waved him inside and didn't quite close the door behind them. He walked to the glass wall and looked down on the courtyard.

"What the hells do you think you're playing at, Simon," growled Hammersmith. He spun around. "You were told by your boss to stand down on the Steron Gillis case, yet you continued to poke around and stir up trouble. Justice has the case. You're out."

"And what the hells has Justice done with the case?" Simon demanded. "Gillis was placed in detention in West Faring, logged into the cells there and then turned over to the prisoner transport service the next day. He disappeared, never logged into Wycliffe. Where is he, Bendict?"

"That's need to know," answered Hammersmith.

"What the hells, Bendict?" Simon felt his anger rising. "Need to know? Sara Braxton, Chris Heron's sister, thinks he died five years ago in a training accident. I saw Chris die. I didn't tell Sara that Chris lied to her, but did tell her he died a hero, defending his team. Doesn't she need to know the truth? Gran Gillis is convinced Steron visited her within the last month. She's a bit confused, but the fresh flowers in her apartment confirm it. I detain Gillis for murder and Justice releases him to go take his Gran shopping?"

"You're down a deep tunnel without a lamp here, Simon," said Hammersmith, his voice quiet and controlled. "This is bigger than any single man, way above our ranks. Drop it. If you value your career, maybe even your life, drop it."

"After all we've been through, explosions, political scandal, threats against the Royal family, you're threatening me?"

"Not a threat, Simon," said Hammersmith. "Advice to a friend. If Higher decides you're a liability, I can't protect you."

"Gods, Bendict," Simon whispered. "How high does this go?"

"Way above me," replied Hammersmith. "I'm not even sure the current Minister knows the whole story. Please, Simon, let it go."

"I don't know if I can do that," said Simon. "I need to know what you're going to do about Gillis. I know the man, fought with him. I need to know why he'd commit cold-blooded murder."

"Don't ask me that, Simon." Hammersmith turned away to look out through the glass wall. "I can't tell you. No matter our past relationship or how I might want to, I can't."

A horrible thought occurred to Simon. "Sanctioned killing?"

"Shut up, Simon. Don't go there." Hammersmith looked stricken. "I beg you as a friend, don't." He turned and pointed to the door. "You need to leave now."

"Bendict, talk to me."

"Leave now, Simon, before I call security." He folded his arms, face set.

Simon held up his hands in surrender. "All good, Bendict. I'll leave. But please, think; do the right thing here." He searched Hammersmith's face, thought he saw a flicker, but then it was gone. He turned and left the office.

As he reached the street and turned toward Wycliffe House, the summoning tone on his mirror chimed. He answered, but the image was blank, the connection, sound only.

"You shouldn't have tracked down my Gran, Loot. That crossed the line."

"Where are you Steron," asked Simon. "I know you're out; I just don't understand why you did it."

"Need to know, Loot," said Gillis. "You don't need to know. Leave my Gran out of this. I'm her only support and she's gone a bit senile. She needs me. Leave her out of this."

"Then talk to me," begged Simon. "I'll meet you anywhere you like. Let me hear your side of this."

"Good parting, Loot," said Gillis and broke the connection.

Simon returned to Wycliffe house only long enough to get into his sled and drive West along Tanner. He passed All Gods Square and made his way deep into the narrow streets and alleys of Westport. At a certain corner, where the street met a quay fronting a narrow canal, he stopped and parked at the top of the quay. He lowered the skids as he canceled the air spell and climbed out. The burned-out chandler's shop had been rebuilt under a new owner but looked much the same. Narrow mullioned windows displayed rope and tackle, thick braided metal cables, bundles of ebony and jars of ground cinnabar, willow wood and garnet. He leaned against a bollard and closed his eyes, inhaled deeply, taking in the smells of brine and seaweed and fish, All the smells of his childhood.

Bendict is truly frightened, not just for himself but for me, my safety. What in the name of all the gods have I gotten myself into? Maybe he's right. I should drop this. Justice is clearly protecting Gillis, on orders from the Minister, or maybe someone even higher. The First Minister? That thought frightened him. He shook his head. *Time to go home. I'll talk to Sylvie, see what she thinks.*

He took a last look at the site of his father's old shop, climbed into the Oxley, and headed for Glenharrow and home.

Sylvie was waiting for him in their room. She caught the look on his face and embraced him. "You smell of the waterfront. You've been in Westport. What's troubling you, love?"

She knew how he would roam Westport when he

was troubled or needed to think. He told her about his confrontation with Hammersmith, the Justice advocate's warning and the conversation with Gillis.

"He's out of detention," said Simon. "Justice is protecting him and has no intention of investigation Flandyrs's murder; Bendict as much as said it was a sanctioned killing. The antiterrorism branch has a lot of latitude, but sanctioned murder? That's not how the rule of law works. And how are we any better that the Azeri's or the Steward if we don't follow the law?"

Sylvie kissed him gently and stroked his cheek. "That's one of the reasons I love you, Simon. That dedication to doing what's right. But you're naïve if you think governments, any government, won't bend their own laws when their vital interest is at stake. The difference here is that the Commonwealth does it reluctantly and doesn't let it be known."

Simon lowered his eyes. "That doesn't excuse it."

"No, but this isn't a fight you can win," said Sylvie. "Let it go for now. When the time comes, you'll know when to bring it up again, either to the Ax or to Hammersmith. Wait, watch, see how this plays out. A lot of good has come from the information I brought back. Maybe good will come from Flandyrs's death as well."

"Maybe," said Simon softly. "You think I should let it go as well. I will. I'll wait and see what happens, concentrate on the active cases." He kissed her. "Thank you, my love."

CHAPTER EIGHTEEN

Over the next few days, Simon fell into the day-to-day managing of his teams. The cases were mainly routine, the usual insurance fraud schemes using Fire or Earth spells for arson or building collapses. One case involving use of a Water spell to cause drowning, a registered Mage killing his estranged wife. He didn't bother to hide his aural signature, nor mask his credit draft when he checked into a guest house near the Northwest border. It was almost as if he wanted to be caught. Simon approved the funds for Jack Ironhand and Sonia Milhaven to go up there and make the arrest. Hal approved, saying that the time together might do Jack some good.

His last meeting of the morning was with Jason Hanks. He'd developed an appreciation for Hanks's slow methodical style and enjoyed his report, concise, precise, and free from a lot of speculation. Just as Hanks rose to leave, Lessa peeked into the office.

"LT," she said tentatively. "The captain wants to

see you right away. He didn't sound happy."

Simon sighed. "On my way. Don't keep the lights on."

He walked slowly down the stone floored hallway to Axhart's office. Elvira Cairns waved him in immediately. He opened the inner door without knocking and stepped inside. He crossed the green carpet and drew himself up in front of Axhart's desk. Only then did he notice Bendict Hammersmith standing off to the side near the chairs facing the desk.

"At ease, Simon," said Axhart. "I'm not going to pull the shoring out from over you. I don't understand why, but Mr. Hammersmith is here with a Justice writ commanding you to accompany him. No detention, no charges, simply a command you accompany him. I don't like it, but I can't override it."

Simon turned to Hammersmith. "What's this all about, Bendict?"

"I can't say anything more, Simon. You just need to come with me," said Hammersmith, his voice flat. "Here's a copy of the writ."

"Captain?" Simon turned to look at Axhart.

"I don't know, Simon," he answered. "It's legitimate. Maybe it has to do with your insistence on looking for Steron Gillis, but no one at Justice will confirm it."

Simon sighed. "All good. Lead on, Bendict."

They made their way down to street level where a black Hilten six-seat sled waited. Hammersmith opened the rear door and held it for Simon. He climbed in after him. They crossed the Greenbelt and headed West along King's Road.

"What's this about, Bendict?" asked Simon. "I assume it has something to do with Steron Gillis. Where are we going?"

"You have questions. We're going to see people who will answer them, whether you like it or not." He turned his head to look at Simon. "This is the last stop,

Simon. You either accept the explanation you'll get here, or you'll lose your badge, your career, whatever reputation you have. Last chance." He lapsed into silence and Simon didn't push him.

They followed the King's Road to a nondescript street and turned North. After twenty minutes and several miles, the Hilten turned into a parking lot fronting a three-sided, low-rise office complex. The buildings had no real distinguishing features; modern construction built for the expanding service economy; rapidly built with no concession to style or beauty beyond some half-hearted shrubs and young trees around the entry.

The big sled pulled up in front of the far building and stopped. Hammersmith climbed out and motioned for Simon to follow. They approached the glass door. A hard-looking Dwarf opened it, making no attempt to conceal the D'Stang bolt thrower slung from his left shoulder. Simon and Hammersmith entered an empty lobby and faced the Dwarf. He lifted his hands in the universal command for Simon to raise his arms. He patted him down quickly and expertly, confiscating his Czeck and Hawley needler and his boot knife.

"He's clean," grunted the Dwarf. "Go on back. They're expecting you."

Hammersmith merely nodded, grasped Simon's elbow, and led him to a door at the far side of the lobby and entered a code into a small keypad. The door buzzed and Simon felt a slight pinging sensation at the base of his spine as the Warding spell canceled.

Simon followed Hammersmith into a long, narrow hallway. Hammersmith walked to the end and opened another door. He waved Simon through, followed, and closed the door.

"Hey, Loot," said Steron Gillis from the other side of the room. "Long time, no see."

"Steron, Top," said Simon, taking in his two former

teammates standing at the far side of the room across a wide conference table. *Of course, they're here.*

"Loot," said Taylor with a nod of his head.

Simon sensed motion to his left and turned his head. "Stenson? What are you doing here?"

Lieutenant, no, now Captain Stenson Harold, Head of Security for the Royal family smiled. "Hello, Simon," he said. He lifted a Farspeaker bracer to his lips and said, "Clear."

Behind Harold, a door opened and a Royal Guardsman in House Fangbern livery over full body armor entered, a D'Stang at his shoulder. He swept the room. "Clear," he repeated.

A large man stepped into the room and stood between the Guardsman and Harold. He was dressed in a simple business suit of green breeches and jacket, white shirt and hose, and a subdued gold silk cravat. His build was large and inclined to plumpness, but his broad shoulders carried it well. His face was round with the slightly hooked nose, full lips and prominent front teeth that ran in the family. He held Simon's eye with a wry smile. "Lieutenant Buckley, you are a lot of trouble."

Simon gasped and immediately took a knee. "Your Highness," he said.

Crown Prince Henrick Fangbern laughed. "Stand, Simon Buckley, you've more than earned that right."

Simon stood but still avoided the prince's eye. "I apologize, Highness, if I have caused offense."

Henrick reached out and grasped Simon's shoulder. "No, it is I who should have trusted you before now." He waved to all in the room. "Sit, we have things to discuss."

Taylor and Gillis sat across the table from Simon and Hammersmith. Prince Henrick sat at the head, to Simon's right. Harold and the guardsman remained standing behind the Prince, the Guardsman watching the doors.

"So, Lieutenant Buckley, what do you think you know about Steron Gillis and Galen Flandyrs?" asked the prince.

"I know that Galen Flandyrs didn't die of the wound he sustained getting out of the Graystorm Compound. He was murdered later by an Air spell that sucked all the breath out of his lungs." Simon turned to look at Gillis. "Steron Gillis was the only person in that warehouse with sufficient Talent to cast that spell. I know that Flandyrs's body retained enough of the caster's aura to identify, that the aura was in a military registry with the identity of the Mage redacted. When my CSA Mage sent a request for identity, the entire entry was removed, and he was warned off by a Dwarf claiming to be a Ministry of Justice agent.

"I detained Gillis for murder in West Faring and turned him over to a trusted Peacekeeper. Gillis was then remanded to Prisoner Transport but never reached Wycliffe House. Captain Axhart was told that the case against Gillis had been taken over by the Justice Ministry and I was to stand down. I know that Gillis was released soon after that and has been under the protection of Bendict Hammersmith by order of some higher authority." Simon paused and looked the prince in the eye. He then pointed toward Taylor and Gillis. "I know that a Special Arms team was reported killed in a training accident five years ago. I know both Steron Gillis and Christon Herin were on that team. I surmise Josen Taylor, Georg Steelhammer, and Bran Falkes were also on that team. The only man who is truly dead is Chris Herin, a good man who deserved better. What I don't know is why. Why are these men pretending to be dead, lying to their families and friends? Why did Steron Gillis, a man I trained with, fought with, came to see as a friend, commit cold-blooded murder by Magic?"

Gillis shrugged. "Orders Loot."

"First Sergeant Taylor," said the prince before Simon could speak. "I believe we should read Lieutenant Buckley in before this discussion continues."

Taylor nodded. "Agreed, Highness. Shall I?"

The prince waved a hand. "No, it's my responsibility. Lieutenant Buckley, what I'm about to tell you falls under the Official Secrets Act. This is one of the most closely kept secrets this nation holds. Nothing we say leaves this room. Any leak is punishable by death or such other penalty as a Military Tribunal may decide. Do you understand this?" Simon nodded. "I need a verbal acknowledgement, Lieutenant."

Simon swallowed hard. "I understand, Your Highness."

"Do you agree to these terms?"

"I do, Highness."

"Very well." The prince sighed. "As you may have surmised already, First Sergeant Taylor and his team are not ordinary mercenaries. They are still on active duty as one of a very few elite teams of Special Arms operators who report directly to the Crown, outside the normal chain of command. They work off books, undertake missions of the utmost sensitivity and secrecy, and are not connected in any way to this government. In short, they don't exist."

"We're ghosts, Loot," said Taylor. "Officially we're dead. We do take legitimate mercenary contracts as our cover, and to maintain contacts with other outfits for hire, like Red Castle. But the names we use for those contracts aren't our own."

"But you gave Hal and me, and Kermal Brackenville, real names," protested Simon.

"Because the mission to rescue Lady Graystorm was done on my orders," said the prince. "She's a valuable intelligence asset, and when word got out that you intended to go after her, it seemed a perfect opportunity to make an attempt to kill or capture Galen Flandyrs as well."

"Kill or capture?" asked Simon.

"Yes." The prince's voice was hard. "Either option suited our purpose."

"Actually, Highness," said Taylor "The original order stressed that Flandyrs dead was better than Flandyrs alive. Lady Graystorm's presence along with the Loot here, changed the mission profile to capture."

Simon was surprised at the familiar tone Taylor took with Prince Henrick as much as the prince's casual acceptance of it.

"It was my preference, Josen," said the prince. "And my direct order to Steron, if the opportunity arose." He must have noticed Simon's face, for he turned to hold Simon's eye. Simon struggled to control his reaction. The eyes of the Crown Prince were not those of a benign future monarch, but those of a warrior, someone accustomed to command and hard decisions.

"You object, Lieutenant?" The prince asked, not really expecting an answer. "Think about it. You know how deep the Flandyrs conspiracy ran. Hells, you uncovered most of it. Aspenwald, Alorton, the deep conspiracy with the Steward and the Azeri's. Can you imagine the political ramifications of a public trial where all that information would come out in open court? Bad enough that Tintagel could release it with Flandyrs alive to back it up. That we could try to undermine or discredit. But an open trial in a Commonwealth Court, with the various appeals and rules of evidence available to Flandyrs, would be a disaster. I gave the order. I stand by it; it was my sole responsibility."

"But your Highness," said Simon. "With utmost respect, extrajudicial execution? Assassinations? Secret Special Arms teams? How can you ask men to give up their names? Their past and families?"

Rather than the anger Simon expected to see from Prince Henrick, the man's face grew sad. "I wish it could be different, Lieutenant. Even my father is not aware of the extent of the Ghost Teams' operations. He knows they exist, but the operational decisions are all mine. He can deny any knowledge of my actions and condemn me if the need arises. We live in a world where such things are necessary, where nations compete behind a veil of secrecy in a deadly game of gambit and reprisal because open warfare has become far too dangerous and destructive." He smiled wryly. "You yourself know that the lines between right and wrong are sometimes blurred. Your special relationship with the Cabal of Clans, for instance. Would you want that common knowledge with the upper levels of the Peacekeeper Force?"

"No, your Highness," Simon admitted.

"No," agreed the prince. "I don't like the orders I am forced to give sometimes, but we all owe a debt to the men like Steron Gillis, who carry them out and then must carry the burden of the things they have done."

"And so, you need me to drop the case against Steron." Simon nodded. "Nothing personal, Steron. It was the law."

"Never was personal, Loot. And for what it's worth, I respect the hells out of you for sticking with your dig."

Simon sat quietly for a long moment, aware that the entire room was watching him. "I understand, Your Highness," he said quietly. "It ends now. Steron is clear as far as I'm concerned."

There was an awkward silence before the prince spoke again. "Thank you, Lieutenant. I think I understand what this is costing you. This country, and especially my family, owes you a tremendous debt, and not just on this matter."

"How so, your Highness?" asked Simon.

Prince Henrick laughed. "Seriously? You uncovered the Flandyrs conspiracy in the first place. You saved my sister the indignity of public condemnation for her actions as a Fire Latent until she could reveal them on her own terms. You handled the George Lathem detention and trial with respect for his sensitive position with the House of Fangbern. Seven Hells, you probably saved my life and the life of my mother, the Queen. Yes, the Royal Family owes you a life debt that we can hardly acknowledge or repay."

"Just doing my job, your Highness," Simon mumbled, not trusting his voice.

The prince smiled, then stood facing Simon. "Rise, Lieutenant Simon Bickley and take a knee."

Simon pushed out of the chair and knelt, not knowing what to expect next.

Henrick reached into his jacket and removed a gold chain hung with a disc bearing the coat of arms of House Fangbern. "Simon Buckley, for services rendered to the Crown, as set forth in the accompanying citation, you are by my hand and at the command of His Majesty King Thorston Fangbern awarded the Legion of Merit of the Commonwealth of Centralia and the Rank of Prince's Companion. Rise and never take a knee in my presence again." He hung the chain around Simon's neck, then took his hand in a firm handshake, pulling him to his feet.

Simon shook the prince's hand in a daze. "Thank you, your Highness, but this is too much."

"Nonsense," said Henrick in a low voice that only Simon could hear. "Learn to accept accolades when they are earned, Simon. And compromise those principles of yours when the greater good demands it." He gripped Simon's shoulder once, then stepped back. "Now, I have a request for you, Simon Buckley. I understand you will be marrying Lady Graystorm soon. Will you do me the honor of allowing me to officiate at your wedding? As Crown Prince I am empowered as a Magistrate to perform wedding ceremonies."

Simon managed a passable bow. "The honor would be all ours, your Highness."

"Good. Stenson, see to the arrangements. And now, I have other pressing matters that demand my attention. This meeting is ended; you men are dismissed. Stenson?"

The Guardsman opened the door and led the way out, followed by the prince. Harold took Simon's hand and gripped it warmly. "Congratulations, Simon. We'll be in touch soon." He followed the prince and closed the door.

Taylor and Gillis stood and walked toward the door. Taylor smiled and laid an arm across Simon's shoulder. "You did good, Loot. It takes a lot to impress Colonel Fangbern." To Simon's surprised look, Taylor said, "Oh yes, the Crown Prince is the real deal. Went through the Gauntlet like any other Marine and did Special Arms camp with the rest of us. None of the Ghost Teams would follow him if he hadn't. If you ever get tired of that Peacekeeper job, let me know. You may find a place on the teams."

"Don't think he'd likely leave that warrior woman of his, Top," said Gillis as he grasped Simon's hand. "Take care of yourself, Loot, and that Noble Lady of yours."

"I will, Steron." Simon returned the handshake. "Take care of your Gran. If there's anything I can do to help, let me know. And watch out for Bran. I'm not surprised Georg wasn't here, but it was Bran who tipped me to Sara Braxton. He truly loved Chris, and I worry about him."

"I will, Loot. We take care of our own."

The two of them walked out, leaving Simon and Hammersmith alone. Simon smiled, realizing he no longer disliked the name Loot, at least not from Taylor or Gillis.

"I guess you're my ride home, Bendict," said Simon. "Did you know?"

"About the Ghost Teams? No, but I've signed the Official Secrets Act, so I'm under the same restriction as you." He shrugged. "Not that either of us would talk about something that secret."

"And the extrajudicial executions?" asked Simon.

"Look, Simon, that's something that's not on our level. I was asked to take over the Gillis investigation. I did, fully expecting a routine but thorough case. Instead, I get a call from the Royal liaison who tells me the Crown wants the entire case dropped and Gillis released on his own hook immediately." Hammersmith looked away. "Did I like it? No, but I like my job, and you don't say no to the Crown."

Simon held up his hands. "Not judging, Bendict. I was ordered to stand down, too."

"It's done, Simon. Come on, I'll take you back to Wycliffe, maybe stop for a beer or two on the way to celebrate your new rank. Prince's Companion, no less." Hammersmith opened the door and Simon walked through.

CHAPTER NINETEEN

A beer or two turned into five or six as Hammersmith and Simon talked at length about the rescue mission. Simon was relieved to have someone with sufficient clearance to know the details of his actions. Just talking about it helped him put things in perspective. The citation that accompanied his medal made it clear that much of the action for which it was given was secret. Simon could wear the medal or ribbon openly but could not discuss the events involved without clearance.

"It was the most intense, frightening experience of my life, Bendict," said Simon. "I didn't think, didn't plan, just moved."

"I've never been in that situation," said Hammersmith. "But I've heard about it. What will you do now? Just go back to the office and manage investigations? I think you miss being in the field with your men. Seems to me, this latest adventure will make that even harder."

Simon smiled at that. "Actually, I welcome the routine. I'm not a warrior, not like Taylor and the others. Maybe not even like Sylvie. Truth be told, she frightens me sometimes."

"This isn't really what you wanted to talk about, is it Simon?" Hammersmith drank from his mug of beer and motioned toward Simon's. Simon finished and signaled the barmaid for another round. They sat at a rear table, well away from other patrons, and it was still early in the evening.

"Not really," Simon admitted. He lowered his voice. "I'm still disturbed at the idea of these Ghost Teams and their sanctions. I know the prince doesn't take the idea of eliminating our enemies lightly, but I'm troubled by it anyway."

"And yet you agreed to keep the program secret," said Hammersmith.

"What else could I do? Especially after getting this." Simon tapped the citation in his jacket pocket.

"I admire your principles, Simon, but this is pragmatic statecraft. Our enemies have never hesitated to come at us in secret. Just look at the last few months. We need to have the options the Ghost Teams offer, even if we don't like them."

"It's not just my principles, Bendict," said Simon. "It's what we're supposed to stand for as a Commonwealth. The Royal family has been weakened by enough scandal. What with Rebeka's abdication and confession, Latham's murder trial, Flandyrs's penetration of the Finance and Justice Ministries. What do you think would happen if it got out that the Crown Prince was authorizing secret extrajudicial executions?"

"Gods, Simon," whispered Hammersmith. "Don't even think that."

"We have to, even if the prince won't." Simon picked up his mug, thought better of it and set it down again.

"The King could disavow him, force him to abdicate, even detain him. But then what? Thorston would be isolated, without an heir, and would lose most of the political power he's managed to gather since taking the throne. The anti-Monarchists would sweep the Commons, and the Lords would have to go along."

"Who's going to know?" Hammersmith demanded. "I won't say anything. I trust you—and Sylvie, too. The Teams themselves are about as deep under cover as possible."

"I don't know, Bendict. But you know as well as I that no secret stays secure forever, no matter how well guarded."

"Well let's hope this one does, at least for the foreseeable future." He caught the look in Simon's eye. "What are you thinking, Simon?"

"I need to at least warn Prince Henrick." Simon shrugged. "I'm a Companion now. Maybe I can talk to him at the wedding, at least let him know why I'm worried."

"Always pushing the edge." Hammersmith finished his beer. "Come on. I'd better get you back to Wycliffe House before you're too drunk to make it home."

Simon rose and clapped the Dwarf on the shoulder. "Thanks for listening, Bendict. You'll be coming to the wedding?"

"Wouldn't miss it. I can't wait to see Hal's face when Prince Henrick shows up."

Simon ended up leaving his Oxley at Wycliffe House and begging a ride from a patrol sled headed for Glenharrow station. Dinner was over by the time he walked into the kitchen, much to Molly's displeasure.

"Where have you been, Simon?" She sniffed his breath. "Out drinking? You can't at least let someone know not to wait dinner for you?"

Sylvie noticed the slight smirk on his face and frowned. "Simon, what has happened?"

"Oh, not much," said Simon. "Just a summons from the Justice Ministry to meet with a higher authority about our adventure into the Havens and my concerns about Steron Gillis."

"How high?" Hal spoke up from his place at the table.

"The highest," said Simon. "Everyone sit down; I have an announcement. This afternoon I met with Crown Prince Henrick. He ordered me personally to drop the Gillis case. Steron and Top were at the meeting, and I'm convinced that I need to let it go." He shot Sylvie a sharp look and she nodded. "Also, I was awarded this by his Highness." He drew out the chain with the Legion of Merit on it and put it around his neck. "I'm now one of the Prince's Companions, entitled to stand in his presence. Not bad for a chandler's kid from Westport."

No one spoke for a second. Then Sylvie rushed to him and held him tightly. "Oh, Simon, I'm so happy for you," she cried. She whispered in his ear, "There's more, I can tell. We'll talk later."

Hal and Molly rushed up, Molly grabbing him about the waist and Hal pounding on his back. Molly wiped tears from her eyes as she steered him to the kitchen table and demanded a full accounting. Hal simply beamed at him.

Simon told them what he could about the meeting, leaving out the Ghost Teams and Prince Henrick's role. Instead, he emphasized the need to avoid further scandal and the Crown's personal request that Simon drop the case.

"What else can I do?" said Simon. "When the Crown Prince asks a favor, you don't say no."

"But the Legion of Merit." Molly shook her head.

Simon reached out and took her hands. "That's not all, Molly. Prince Henrick has asked to officiate at the wedding. His security team will be in touch soon to coordinate his visit."

Molly opened and closed her mouth, but no words came out. Simon gripped her hands and nodded, and she gulped and screamed, "Hal!"

The next few minutes were a bedlam of cries, gasps, exclamations, and Hal's gentle, "Yes love," repeated over and over. Molly fairly babbled about cleaning and the silver and decorations and the worthless caterer and a dozen other shortcomings of the Hall. Simon was taken aback. In all his years at Stonebender Hall, he'd never seen Molly in such a state. She was the rock that held the rest of them steady. Finally, she took a deep breath and seemed to regain control.

"Shame on you, Simon Buckley," she said. "You fair gave me a stroke. Prince Henrick, indeed."

"It's true, Molly. The prince himself is to preside on our ritual and vows. He's a Chief Magistrate, after all." Simon smiled and reached out to touch her cheek. Hal stood behind her holding her shoulders. "It'll be all good, you'll see."

After much reassurance that there would be plenty of room, plenty of time to coordinate the Royal visit, and a promise to have Stenson Harold summon Molly's private mirror as soon as possible, Simon and Sylvie were finally able to escape to their shared room.

Sylvie embraced him and kissed him as soon as they closed the door. "I am proud of you." She punched his arm lightly. "I give up a title and you gain one?"

"Not exactly in the same bracket," said Simon. "It's more of an honorific. You needn't address me formally or bow." He grabbed her hand with a laugh as she moved to smack him. She laughed as well.

After a moment, she said, "What's troubling you, Simon? I can tell there's more to your meeting with Prince Henrick than you told Molly and Hal."

"It's true that I agreed to stop pushing a murder charge against Gillis," said Simon. "It wasn't exactly voluntary. I could agree or fall afoul of the Official Secrets Act. Sylvie, Top and the rest of the team aren't mercenaries. They're a secret active-duty Special Arms team reporting exclusively to the Crown; specifically, to the Crown Prince. They don't officially exist. They're ghosts, listed as dead. Prince Henrick himself is a Marine Colonel with SpecArms training."

Sylvie just nodded. "That much at least isn't a secret. It's not well known, but in his younger days, Prince Henrick trained as a Marine. He's still on the Reserve lists. And these secret Special Arms Teams? Rumors in the Havens, never confirmed, but again I'm not surprised. Why does this bother you? The Commonwealth's enemies certainly have no reluctance to mount secret operations against you."

"Because they're off books," said Simon. "Hells, Chris Herin let his own sister believe he died five years ago. All contact cut off. Steron Gillis stays in touch with his Gran, but it's permitted only because she's half-senile and lives alone." He took a deep breath. "Who asks men to do things like that?"

"Maybe ask instead, what kind of men agree to a mission like that?" answered Sylvie. "You know these men, love. We fought with them, bled with them. They're patriots."

"The Crown sends them on kill missions, Sylvie." Simon's voice grew tight. "Henrick sends them out for extrajudicial executions, assassinations. Steron killed Flandyrs with an Air spell on direct orders from the Crown Prince."

Sylvie didn't speak. She reached up and cupped his neck, drew his head down to her shoulder and held him tightly. "I know this seems like a betrayal, Simon, but you need to breathe. Think about this. Talk it through with me."

He returned her embrace. "It's not that I feel betrayed, Sylvie. Oh, I know, I'm the one who's all about principles, the Law, but you said it yourself, our enemies don't balk at assassinations or terrorism. Hells, they tried to kill the King with secret weapons. The prince made it clear that we wouldn't be hamstrung in responding. I get the need to be pragmatic. But damn it, it still doesn't feel right."

"It wouldn't to you, no matter the justification," said Sylvie. "It's one of the things I love about you."

Simon waved a hand dismissively. "That's not what I mean, Sylvie. It's deeper than that. This feels wrong in a way I can't put my finger on. Like something basic is off center."

"Like what?"

"Like why Prince Henrick would be in this position in the first place." Simon shook his head. "The Teams may report to the Crown, but when have you ever heard of direct reporting to the Royal Family? This should go through at least a high military staffer or another of the Companions. A trusted aide who could give deniability and a degree of separation." Sylvie looked doubtful, so Simon went on. "Think about what would happen if it came out that the Crown Prince was personally ordering extrajudicial executions? King Thorston could deny him, even detain him but then what? Without an heir, without the legitimacy of the Accords, the Crown could be fatally damaged. I made the same point to Bendict Hammersmith earlier this evening. The prince has to be warned."

"Warned about what, love?" asked Sylvie.

"I don't know," said Simon. "I just have a bad feeling. There's something or someone behind all that's happened in the past few months, and it involves the Monarchy."

They talked far into the night, but Simon could get no closer to the root of his fears. Finally, they slept.

CHAPTER TWENTY

The next morning dawned gray and cold, which suited Simon's mood. He kissed Sylvie good-bye and rode with Hal to Wycliffe House, arriving just before change of watch. Despite Lessa's excellent coffee, he felt sluggish as he went through the morning routine. The first thing he did after his sergeants' reports were in was to find his own notes on the Hightower case from nearly a year ago. He sent down to the Archives to have the official reports sent up as well. The raid on the farmhouse where Glendowyn Hightower died had been the catalyst that had opened the whole Flandyrs conspiracy with Joby Blackpool and the Azeri Liberation Brigades. Flandyrs's mad plan to use the Brigades to start a war with the Azeri Empire and supply Blackpool with the deaths he'd need to open a Portal to another world had been foiled when Hal and Simon took down Hargash Barsaka. But the Portals had been opened. Simon still had the strange otherworldly weapon Glendowyn had brought through one, locked in a strongbox in a secure Stonebender Hall storage room.

Joby's plan was to open a Portal big enough to take his 'Select' through to a world where Orcs ruled without Elves, Dwarves or Men. Mad but understandable. What was in it for Flandyrs? Destabilizing the Commonwealth? There was no chance that any conflict with the Azeri's could do lasting harm to the country. We'd assumed he was simply motivated by the money he could make on war profiteering. Fair enough. But why involve Aspenwald and Alorton and Kershaw?

He spent an hour reading through the final reports on Hightower, but nothing resonated with the feeling of unease that had haunted him since the previous night. It was clear that Glendowyn had made the Fire grenades for Barsaka, but only as a way to get money and victims for her Portals. She had no interest in Blackpool's escape or Barsaka's revolution. So how had Flandyrs connected the two of them in the first place? *I'm missing something important here.*

He picked up his mirror and summoned Hal. "Yes, lad?" answered the old Dwarf.

"Hal, I'm going over the Hightower case from last year. Snick was the source who told you about the farmhouse, right?"

"He did, but it was actually his cousin who made the delivery of the aquamarine."

"What was his name?" Simon asked.

"The cousin? I don't recall," said Hal. "Why?"

"Because something's not right here." Simon sighed. "How does a High Elf end up making Fire grenades for an Azeri revolutionary? How did Flandyrs connect them?"

"Flandyrs was a Ranger," said Hal. "Likely he had informants in the Orc community, maybe in the Brigades. He could have reached out to Barsaka through them."

"What about Glendowyn Hightower?"

Hal laughed. "He already had the Steward's ear. How else would he contact her."

"But the family disowned her when she left the Havens to do her research in the Commonwealth," said Simon. "I doubt she'd spoken to her brother in years."

"He'd still be able to find her, offer her the farmhouse for her work and a supply of expendable Orcs to open her Portals."

"Maybe, probably," said Simon. "I still feel like I'm missing something."

Hal shrugged and reached to close the connection, stopped and looked thoughtful. "Bogwood," said Hal. "Glesel Bogwood was Snick's cousin."

"Bogwood? That tickles a branch." Simon shuffled through the reports in front of him. "Glesel Bogwood was the Orc in the suicide vest that I took down in front of King Olaf Hall. He's Snake Clan. Hargash Barsaka was trying to assassinate the Crown Prince, probably on information leaked by Alorton to Flandyrs."

And if the Crown Prince had died, it would have left Princess Rebeka as the heir. With her abdication, the assassination of the King could have ended the Fangbern Dynasty. Under the Accords, the Justice Ministry would have control of the succession, giving Alorton control of the country. That was Flandyrs's end game. It resonated with his hunch. It felt right, but he had no real evidence. Something was still missing.

"Gotta go, Hal. Thanks for the name," said Simon.

He put away the records and sat at his desk going over what he knew and thought he might know. He moved on to the attacks on the King and Queen and the explosion at the Justice Ministry. The weapons had come from the Havens, that much was clear from the official investigation conducted by Bendict Hammersmith. He'd traced the neutral iron from the

Free States, through the Havens to an Orc owned shipping company out of West Faring. The actual assembly had been done in a cobbler shop south of Knacker run by a Snake Clan subchief.

But how did they know how to make the weapons? Hells, I couldn't reconstruct the weapon I have, and I'd never seen the ones they made until Sylvie brought one to the Hall. So how did they make them? And what's in that explosive black powder? Where did these things come from? There was only one explanation. Someone was opening other Portals.

He looked at his timepiece. It was now just before 15th. Still time to call Hammersmith. He summoned the advocate's mirror.

"Simon," said Hammersmith. "How's your head today?"

"Just fine, Bendict, how are you?"

"A little under the rocks, truth be told. Not used to drinking that much. What can I do for you?"

"I'm interested in the explosion at Justice," said Simon. "Are you all good to talk about it?"

"All good. What do you want to know?"

"Did your people analyze that black powder that caused the explosion? Or did they turn it over to our forensics Mages?"

"We turned it over to the Peacekeeper CSA Mages," answered Hammersmith. "But we got a report. It's a combination of materials that are pretty much inert individually. About three quarters of it is a potassium salt containing nitrogen, the rest is a ten to fifteen mix of ordinary sulfur and charcoal."

"Thanks, Bendict," said Simon.

"Wait, why do you want to know?" asked Hammersmith.

"Just nailing down a few loose boards, that's all. Good parting."

"Good parting, Simon," said Hammersmith, still

sounding doubtful.

Simon closed the connection and stood, pocketing his mirror. He passed through the outer office as he donned his uniform jacket. "I'll be leaving for the day, Lessa. Have a good evening."

"Good evening, LT," said Lessa, hardly looking up from her work.

Simon descended the main stairs to the lowest level and made his way to the morgue. As he'd expected, Evarts was at his desk. Simon knocked on the doorframe before entering the office.

"Simon, to what do I owe the pleasure?" Evarts set down his stylus and leaned back in his chair.

"Nothing sinister, Kyle. Just a routine inquiry," said Simon with a wink. "Remember the explosion at Justice a couple of months ago?"

"Of course," said Evarts. "They asked my team to do the forensics. Not that we learned much."

"How so?" Simon asked.

"There wasn't enough left of the Orcs who set off the explosion to analyze, none of the damage had any sort of magic aura, and the powder that seemed to be the explosive agent was like nothing anyone has ever seen before."

"So Bendict Hammersmith tells me," said Simon. "No magic at all?"

"None. Totally inert materials. Until they're combined that is." Evarts shook his head. "The different substances weren't simply mixed randomly, either. This was a very specific mixture that was molded into cakes and then ground to make it granular rather than a simple powder."

"You can tell that just by looking at it?"

"Give us some credit, Simon," laughed Evarts. "The process isn't mysterious, just the ingredients."

"But how would someone learn how to make this stuff,"

"That's what you and your people are supposed to find out." Evarts cocked his head. "Any ideas?"

"Not a one," said Simon. *Could someone learn this by looking through a Portal? I need to talk to Gran Swampwater.* "Thanks, Kyle. We still need to get together for that dinner."

"Anytime."

Simon made his way through the booking level and the locker rooms to the stables where he found his Oxley. He settled behind the yolk and took out his mirror again. He found Yondell Greenmire's locus in the record scroll and summoned it.

The Southern Reservation Marshall answered and peered at Simon. "Buckley, is that you? Long time. What can I do for you?"

"Good meeting, Marshall Greenmire," said Simon. "How are things on your beat?"

"All quiet, Sergeant," said the Marshall. "No wait, I hear it's Lieutenant now. Congratulations." His voice took on a slight edge. "Now what do you want? Big city Keepers don't call the likes of me unless they need a favor."

"I do need a favor," Simon admitted. "I'd like to have a conversation with Gran Swampwater."

"And you want me to arrange it." Greenmire sighed. "I'll ask. No guarantees. But she seems to like you for some reason. Maybe she'll say yes. Wait for my summons." He broke the connection.

Simon had almost reached the stables at Stonebender Hall when his mirror chimed. He swiped it on and said," Marshall Greenmire. That was fast."

"Gran Swampwater will see you tomorrow at 11th. Don't be late." He shook his head. "She said to tell you Happy Pairing. Are you getting married?"

"Yes, I am, but how did Gran Swampwater know?"

"I don't ask," said Greenmire. "Just be here by ten till so I can check you in."

"Will do," said Simon. "Thank you, Marshall."

CHAPTER TWENTY-ONE

Simon rose before dawn and got on the road to the Southern Reservation. He wanted to be South of Bowater before the Ring Road and the S393 jammed up with commuter traffic. He'd be early for his appointment but didn't care if he had to wait. He reached the town of Fernhill on the outskirts of the reservation by half past 9th. He found a small café that advertised Azeri coffee and Dundarian sausage and stopped. Both proved excellent, the sweet thick coffee perfectly complementing the spice of the sausages.

He arrived at the Reservation gate exactly ten minutes before the hour, wide awake and well fed. Greenmire waited in the parking area in front of the government administration building. Simon removed his badge, sidearm and mirror and locked them in the compartment between the seats of the sled.

"Good meeting, Buckley," said Greenmire, after Simon climbed out of his sled. "Nice slide. Tornado?"

"Yes," said Simon. "Last year's model. A bit showy,

I suppose, but I like it."

"I'm more at home in a utility sledge, or a patrol car, myself." He pointed up a well-tended gravel walkway. "You know the way to the Spirit House. Gran Swampwater and the crones are expecting you."

Simon made his way along the path, through a screen of birch trees and up a small hill. The living walls and gate of the Spirit House came into view. The House lay within a low wall of mud and willow. Living dogwood trees formed the corners, and branches of dogwood and willow arched over the cold iron gate at the entrance. He approached the intertwined iron fronds that formed the gate with his hands held down and out from his sides, palms facing outward, Orc body signals for peaceful intent. Gran Swampwater herself waited for him just inside.

"Welcome to the House of the Earth Spirits, Simon Buckley." Olega Swampwater smiled pleasantly. "Will you join me for tea?"

"Thank you for seeing me, Gran Swampwater," said Simon. "Tea would be welcome."

He followed her through the center courtyard to the small comfortable room where he had met her the first time he'd visited. A plain pottery teapot and small cups waited for them. He sat across from Gran and she poured for them both. He took a sip as she did the same.

"How is Lady Graystorm?" Gran said without preamble. "I understand you are to be married soon. Her *strahk* is of Fire and will augment your own. Your children will make a mark on this world."

Simon shifted in his chair. "We hope the union will be blessed with children."

Gran smiled knowingly but said nothing. They finished the tea in comfortable silence. After a slight pause, Gran said, "You have questions."

"I do. About the Portals," said Simon.

The old Orc shaman folded her hands on the table in silence.

"If someone were to open a Portal, what could they learn of art or artifice from the other side?" Simon asked. "Could they obtain detailed knowledge simply by observing?

"Yes, if one observed carefully," Gran answered slowly. "There is no way one could know in advance what would be learned in such a way, but it could be so."

Simon thought about that. "What if you could watch for a long time, or could watch the same thing over and over again?"

"Doubtful." Gran shook her head. "These other worlds as you choose to call them don't lie side by side like pages in a book. Think more of a ball of twine where they overlap and repeat. Even we, who do this magic all the time, can't control what we see."

"Would you and the others here know if someone else opened a Portal using a sentient being, like Glendowyn Hightower did? A Portal that could pass an object?" *Or gods forbid, a person.*

Gran hesitated only a fraction of a second. "If the spell were close enough or powerful enough, yes. But you can feel the twist and spin of magic as it is cast as well as we. What have you felt?"

Simon's mouth went dry, and he looked down at the tabletop. It was one thing to have a vague feeling that he kept to himself. It was another to admit it to an Adept as powerful as Olega Swampwater. "Something is not right, Gran Swampwater," he said softly, his voice a hoarse whisper. "I've been looking for days but can't find anything definite. It's just a feeling in my gut that something is wrong."

She closed her eyes and muttered a few words in a language Simon didn't recognize. She lifted a hand and held it toward him, just above the tabletop.

"Your *strahk* is in turmoil," she said, opening her eyes. "You look too hard for facts and evidence. What you feel is a lack of balance."

"Balance?"

"All Magic derives from the Earth," said Gran. "You humans insist that your classes and probabilities and mathematical formulas are separated from this basic truth. Using Magic draws from the strength of our Mother Earth, and that strength is restored to the Mother from your own essence, what we call *ghiras*. All remains in balance. Even the violence of a Portal opening is balanced by the life force of the sacrifice."

Simon recognized the root of his unease in her words. "But something is not in balance, is it?"

"That is what my sisters and I fear. There is something here in our Mother that does not belong."

Simon sat back in his chair. "Something or someone, Gran Swampwater? We know Glendowyn brought objects through the Portals. That didn't seem to cause much imbalance."

"Glendowyn Hightower gave much of her own life force to maintain that balance," Gran pointed out. "She was already dying on the night you encountered her."

"Could someone else open a Portal large enough to pass a person? Joby Blackpool was confident he could do it."

"That would require the Blood sacrifice of several living people," said Gran, her voice stern. "That is an abomination we will not contemplate. I leave such things to the likes of Men or Elves."

"We likewise consider such things abomination," said Simon, defensively. "But there are Men and Elves who would not be stopped by that."

They sat silently for several minutes. Gran refilled their tea, and they sipped it. Finally, Simon drained his cup and set it upside down on the table. He rose and bowed.

"Thank you for the tea, Gran Swampwater," he said. "And for the information. I will take my leave now. I have leads to pursue."

"Take care, Simon Buckley," she said. "The thing you pursue may be something you don't wish to find."

Simon sighed. He made his way slowly out of the Spirit House and down the hill to his sled. Greenmire waited there, looking grim. "Did you learn anything useful?"

"Maybe," said Simon. "Disturbing, but maybe useful." He noticed Greenmire's expression. "What's troubling you?"

"You need to understand my position here, Buckley," said the Marshall. "I'm supposed to be the law, but everyone knows Gran really runs things. It's hard enough to keep a lid on the drinking and the family feuds, the poverty and hopelessness. When you show up and I defer to you and let you meet with the Spirit Crones alone, it makes me look weak, or at least irrelevant."

"I'm sorry, Yondell," said Simon. "I don't mean to make your life more difficult."

"I know that. Doesn't change anything." He turned and began walking toward Simon's sled. "Gran likes you, seems to think you're important somehow. And she's the power here."

They reached the sled and Simon climbed behind the yoke. Simon extended his hand and after a second, Greenmire took it. "Oh, hells," he said. "Who am I to question Olega Swampwater? As long as she keeps the lid on around here, it's a fairly peaceful job. Take care of yourself, Buckley."

The trip back to Glenharrow seemed to take longer than the trip down. *How could Flandyrs have known how to build the weapons, to make the black powder? A book? That would do it. But it seemed unlikely based* on what Gran said that they could open just the right Portal to find such a thing. *How likely was it that a person could survive passage through even a very large Portal and have the right knowledge to build those weapons?* His head spun with the questions. He needed to try to find where the Portals were being opened. If in the Commonwealth, he might be able to find a pattern. If they were in the Havens, could he use the Cabal to contact Barca?

He pulled into the stable at Stonebender Hall a few minutes before 18th hour to find Sylvie standing in the postern door, waiting for him. He climbed out and walked toward her, palms out. "Am I in trouble?" he asked.

She laughed. "Not with me, but Molly's got a burr under her corset about finalizing some wedding plans." She kissed his cheek. "What did you learn from Gran Swampwater?"

"That she's very scary," he said. "She knows we're getting married. She say's our children will make a mark on the world."

"How..."

"Interesting?" offered Simon.

They held hands and entered the kitchen together. "There you are," said Molly, standing with her hands on her hips. "Both of you sit down. We have things to decide. There's less than two weeks to go, and we still don't have the guest list finished, I don't know who will be standing with you, and we need someone to be the Stranger."

"Calm down, love," said Hal, coming in from the outer hall. "We have room for everyone who wants to come, invited or not. The food is ordered, enough to feed the entire Force, and Simon has already made it clear that Brackenville is to be his Second." He grinned and drew himself up. "And he's asked me to be Guardsman."

Sylvie reached out and took Molly's hand. "I was hoping you'd be willing to stand with me as Matron, Molly. It would make me very happy."

"Oh, my dear." Molly's eyes filled with tears. "It would be my honor."

"Do you think it would be all good if I asked Wills and Mery if Jasmine could stand with us as the Virgin?"

Molly laughed. "That would be perfect. We'll ask them this Weeksend."

Simon caught Hal's eye, and they moved to the other end of the table as Sylvie and Molly talked about wardrobes and place settings and whether the weather could be counted on to allow an outdoor wedding.

Hal poured ale for them both. "I hear you went to see the Swampwater witch today. What was that all about?"

"She's not a witch, Hal, she's a respected shaman," said Simon. "I needed some information about Portal magic."

"Portal magic? Why?" asked Hal. "The Hightower case is closed. Portal magic died with Joby Blackpool."

"I'm not so sure, Hal." Simon sipped his ale. "Someone else has opened a Portal just like Glendowyn Hightower. It's the only way Flandyrs's people could have learned how to make those strange weapons and the black powder that makes them work."

Hal thought about that. "How do you figure?"

"Look at the weapon that Sylvie brought. Its purpose is obvious, but the mechanics aren't like anything used in the Commonwealth. The design, the parts, all may be handmade, but there has to be a master template. Where did that come from?"

"Does it matter?" asked Hal. "Flandyrs is dead, Sylvie is safe, the plot against the king and queen was stopped, and now that we know what to look for, we can prevent them from trying again." He grasped

Simon's shoulder and held his eye. "Let it go, Simon. At least for now. You're getting married in ten days. Worry about that, not some vague notion about other worldly Portals."

CHAPTER TWENTY-TWO

Over the next several days, Simon spent his afternoons pouring over reports of missing persons, especially Orcs, looking for some sort of pattern. First, he looked for clusters, people who went missing at the same time, either from different places or from particular locations. He set aside files of pairs or threes reported missing on the same date, or similar numbers reported from the same locations over a short time. Several times, he thought he detected a pattern, but when he looked at the reports, they proved to be ordinary. Husbands leaving wives, young people leaving home, itinerant workers moving on. Even those that appeared to be truly missing had no links to other cases.

He finally admitted defeat and began to look for another way to track missing Orcs. *I need inside help. Maybe Lily can point me in the right direction.* He checked his timepiece. It was after 16th hour. He debated a trip into the Hollows to Lily's Tavern but decided against it. There would be time later. Sylvie was expecting him to help with a final guest list and Stenson Harold planned to come by to discuss security for the Crown Prince's visit.

Harold's green and gold official sled awaited Simon in front of the Hall. Simon parked in the stables and entered through the postern door. Harold sat comfortably at the kitchen table with a plate of flatbread and cheese in front of him. Molly and Sylvie sat close by.

Harold looked up as Simon walked in. "Ah, Buckley, good meeting. I was just going over the security plan with Mistress Stonebender. Perhaps, you can explain some of the realities of Royal protocol and security."

"Dreck and tailings," said Molly. "Stonebender Hall is as secure as the Palace. I won't have our guests subjected to security scans or have armed guards on the dais."

"I see," said Simon. "Stenson, I think you and I should work this out, try to balance what is ideal with what's practical."

They adjourned to the library and talked for nearly two hours. In the end, Simon agreed to a security screen at the entrance to the Hall, snipers stationed on top of the Hall and in a large oak behind the dais where the prince would stand, and armed security patrols around the perimeter of the property. Many of the guests would be active Peacekeepers, which made it easier to convince Harold to back off of his original plans.

"Liam and Becky will be here for the wedding," said Simon as he escorted Harold to the front door. "I hope you'll be able to spend some time with them."

"I will. What about you, Simon? Will you take some time with your bride and put off whatever quest you're currently on?"

Simon smiled at him. "How do you know?"

"You have an air about you when you're on the hunt," said Harold. "Does this have anything to do with the Royal Family? Anything that I need to know?"

"Not immediately," said Simon. "It's about the weapons the Azeri's used to try to kill the King and Queen a couple of months ago. I'm trying to find out where they came from and how anyone knew how to build them."

"It doesn't matter, does it?" Harold asked. "Any ongoing conspiracy against their Majesties surely died with Flandyrs. And now that we know what to look for, they won't get by us again."

"Maybe not, but the knowledge is out there and unless we know how Flandyrs came by it, there may be other surprises waiting for us."

Harold considered that for a few seconds. "In that case, good hunting Simon." He extended his hand and Simon shook it. "I'll see you in a few days."

Simon returned to the kitchen where Sylvie and Molly were deep in conversation, something about the proper flowers and greenery for the canopy. Hal had retired to the library. Simon thought about joining him but decided to shower and change out of his uniform first.

He was just drying off when the summoning tone on his mirror chimed. He swiped the screen and Lily Ponsaka gazed out at him.

"Mistress Ponsaka." Simon angled the mirror to focus mainly on his face as he wrapped the towel around his shoulders. "This is unexpected. What can I do for you?"

"If this is a bad time, it can wait until tomorrow," said Lily looking away from the mirror.

"Not at all," said Simon. "In fact, I was intending to pay you a visit tomorrow. I was hoping you could help me with an inquiry."

"Of course you were," she said with a roll of her

eyes. "But I need your help first, unless investigating crimes against Orcs is beneath you now that you're a Lieutenant."

Simon frowned. "You should know better than that by now, Lily. What sort of crime?"

"Kidnap, maybe murder," said Lily.

"Maybe murder? Is someone dead or not?"

"They're missing, and the Orc who got kidnapped is certain they were killed," Lily finally met his eye. "It's best you come down here and see for yourself."

"When?" asked Simon.

"Tomorrow, 8th hour. Come to the back door."

Simon agreed and closed the connection. *Could this be related to the Portals?* He shook his head. More likely it was just Orc on Orc crime, the kind of thing most Keepers dismissed with little real investigation.

The next morning, he approached the back door to Lily's Tavern only a few minutes after 8th hour, having rescheduled his team briefings for the afternoon and letting Hal know where he'd be. Lily opened the door before he could knock.

"Come in before someone gets the wrong idea," Lily said, checking both ways as she closed the door.

"And a good meeting to you, Mistress Ponsaka." Simon didn't try to keep the sarcasm out of his voice. "You called me, remember?"

"Don't mean I want the whole neighborhood to know I'm talking to a Bluebelly." She pointed to a table in the far corner of the kitchen. "Jontry is over there. I'll bring some coffee."

Simon approached the table. An Orc sat with his back against the wall, slightly hunched over the table. He furtively regarded Simon, dark eyes watching him from beneath a prominent brow above a sharply hooked nose. Simon pegged him as being from the Southern reservation, lately come to the capital looking for work only to wash up in Lily's place like so many other castoffs and refugees.

Simon stopped a few feet from the table and stood with his hand at his sides, palms out. "Jontry is it? I'm Simon Buckley. Lily says you're the victim of a crime. Would you please tell me about that?"

Lily bustled up and set three mugs of coffee on the table. "Sit down, Simon," she commanded. "This is Jontry Hillcrest. Jontry, you need to tell Simon about what happened to you."

"You never said he was a Bluebelly." Jontry's voice was sullen, the accent pure Southern Rez.

"Well, who the hells else can help? Your *kharo* told you to come to me. This is what I've got for you." Lily spoke as if addressing a recalcitrant child. Simon stifled his grin.

"Why don't you start at the beginning, Jontry?" said Simon. "You came up from the Southern reservation, I'm guessing somewhere near Fernhill? Looking for work here in Cymbeline."

"You know Fernhill?" Jontry asked.

"Pretty well. I've had coffee and Dundarian links at the Rose Café, just past the A393 turnoff."

That seemed to resonate with the Orc because he gave a short nod and began speaking. "I had work lined up through an overseer when I left Fernhill. Working in a rope factory down near Eastmark on the riverfront. Found a room close enough by I could walk to the job. Started getting paid and could send some money home to my Ma. I weren't looking for trouble. I ain't nobody special, not even down on the Rez."

Simon nodded but didn't speak, sensing Jontry would tell the story in his own time.

"Things go on like that for two, maybe three months. I keep myself to myself. I just want to make some money to send home. Once in a while, I go down to a place where they serve drinks and food. Sort of a treat to myself." He paused to sip coffee. "Anyway, one night this cobber comes over and sits down next to me, starts chatting like he knows me. I try to ignore him, but he knows my name, knows where I'm from. I tell him to bugger off; I don't want what he's selling.

'But what if I could show you how to make twenty Crowns for a single night's work?' says he.

'Not interested,' says I. Anything pays that much ain't legal.

'Suit yourself,' says he. 'I'll give your regards to your Mam, next I see her.'

Well, that stops me. He knows how to get to my Ma. 'What do you want from me,' says I.

'Just a little bit of lifting and toting,' says he. 'Some cargo coming in by boat from the East. Cargo that nobody needs to know about.'

'Twenty Crowns? One night? You ain't gonna keep coming at me after this one time?'

'Hand to Durlash, one night,' says he.

So, he gives me this address, an old boathouse down by the Cut. Says be there by 1st hour the next day. He gives me two Crowns, the rest when the job is done. I ain't stupid. I know this ain't legal, and I know once I do this, they'll be back like they own me. But I figure with twenty Crowns I can take my Ma and get away, start over somewhere, maybe northwest, where the Clans ain't that strong."

Simon interrupted. "Clans? How did you know he was with the Clans?"

"Had the tattoos, din't he. Snakes all up and down his arms." Jontry drank more coffee. "So, I go to the boathouse, and at first there ain't nobody there. I try the door, but it's locked. Then this big black sled pulls up and the cobber with the tattoo climbs out and waves me over. Points to a dock alongside and says to wait there. So, I do. Two more cobbers walk over, Orcs like me, street trash. I watch the sled and two Men in black coats get out and unlock the door and go into the boathouse.

"A few minutes later we hear a boat coming close. One of the cobbers with me must know boats because he catches a line and ties it off. Nobody gets off and we get waved on. At the back of the boat there's two long boxes, about as long as you are tall and half an arm wide. We pick them up, two to a box and start off the boat. I'm on one end and Tattoos is on the other and just as I get my foot on the dock, the load shifts, like something inside rolled around. I slam my end against part of the dock, and I hear something inside cry out. There's somebody in the box. I get my end up again and we carry it into the boathouse. The other two cobbers are already there. Tattoo counts out money for them, then he waves them away.

"Now it's just me and Tattoo. He looks me in the eye, and he knows. 'What are you going to do there Jontry?' asks he.

"'Get paid and leave town,' says I. 'You'll never hear from me again.'

"The next thing I know I've been wacked on the head and trussed up like a Year's End pig. I'm on the floor with two other cobbers, tied just like me. I try to talk but they've stuffed a gag in my mouth. I'm groggy, but I know this ain't ending good for me.

"The other two are just lying there. They're awake, but they've given up. I start moving and can tell the ropes are too tight for me to wiggle out. But the way I'm tied, I can just reach my boot. I've got a knife there and Tattoo didn't take it. I push a bit and get it out just as Tattoo and a man walk in. The man's in a mask, can't see his face, but he looks strange, like his arms and legs don't match. He says to Tattoo, 'Bring the Earthborn first.'

"Tattoo bends down and picks up the Orc next to me, tosses him on his shoulder like he don't weigh nothing. He follows the Man into another room. I manage to get my ropes off and go to the other cobber in the room, make to cut him loose but he shakes his head and rolls away, moves his head to tell me to run. I move to cut him loose again but hear the door rattle. I scarper out of there. I thought Tattoo would be right on my tail, but nobody follows."

"When was this" asked Simon.

"Five days ago," said Jontry. "First, I hid out in the East End. Couldn't go to work, couldn't go back to my room."

"Why didn't you come to the local Keeper station?" Simon asked.

Lily and Jontry scoffed in unison. "I don't have no time for Keepers. Like as not they lock me up."

"You need to understand your place here, Buckley," said Lily. "You and I have history. You have street credit down here. Orcs like Jontry, fresh off the Rez, got no reason to trust the Keepers."

"I get that Lily, but he's here now." Simon held out a hand. "What should I do about that?"

"He's here because he got smart and approached a *kharo* down on South Canal. Asked where an Orc in trouble could hide out and maybe get help." There was a note of pride in Lily's voice. "Everyone knows this is neutral ground."

Simon faced Jontry. "What you saw may be very important to a case we're working. Can you tell me exactly where this boathouse is?"

"I'll tell you an address, but I ain't going back there." He recited the address of the boathouse and Simon wrote it down.

"That's fair," said Simon. "In return I can call some people, get you and your mother safe and protected."

"I don't want to be tagged as no weasel," said Jontry. "You put me in Keeper protection, and nobody will ever believe I ain't working for you."

"No Keepers. The people I have in mind are all

Orcs. They'll see right by you." Simon rose from the table. "Stay here at Lily's until she vouches for the Orcs who'll come for you."

Lily followed him to the door. "What's this about, Simon? You believe that tale he spun?"

"I do Lily, and he's in great danger. I need to reach Kermal Brackenville. I may have to involve the Cabal in this. But if someone is using Earthborn Orcs for Blood Magic, there's only one thing they can be doing."

Lilly took a half step back. "Blood magic? Like those poor children from a few months ago?"

"Different spells, and far more dangerous." Simon looked back at Jontry, small and miserable at the dark table. "Watch over him, Lily. Kermal should be in contact before the day is out."

He left quickly, driving up Canal toward Tanner. He entered the last mirror locus he had for Kermal, hoping it was still valid. Kermal answered on the first tone.

"Hello, Simon," he said cheerfully. "What's happening?"

"I need a favor, Kermal, a rather big one, and it's time sensitive," said Simon.

Kermal's face grew serious. "Name it, Brother."

"I have a witness, an Orc, who has information about illegal Portal magic and the Blood sacrifice of at least two Orcs. Some very powerful people, possibly with the Serpent Clan, and at least two highly placed Human agents are looking for him. I need him protected, taken out of the capital, and his mother from down Fernhill way picked up as well." Simon paused. "I know I already have a debt owed to Chief Forsaka. Tell him to put this on my account."

Kermal was silent for long enough that Simon feared he'd say no. "The first part isn't hard. I assume he's in a safe place right now?"

"Lily's Place. She's the one who called me about

this."

"All good. I can get him out of Cymbeline on my own hook." Kermal shook his head. "But hiding him and his mother long term, I'll need to run that by the Chief. You're sure about the Portal magic?"

"My man says the people he's running from specifically mentioned Earthborn Orcs. I believe him. His story is too detailed, checks too many boxes to be anything else."

"All good," said Kermal. "I'll go to Lily's myself. We'll get him out."

"Thanks, Kermal." Simon closed the connection and increased his speed toward Wycliffe House.

He arrived just after 11th hour and made his way to the office. Lessa met him as usual with dispatches and a mug of coffee. He thanked her and sat at his desk, reading the dispatches. Midday came and went, along with reports from Gervis Birchfield and Jason Hanks. At a little after 13th, Hal came in and pulled up a chair.

"We're close to closing three of our current cases. Three more are going to trial in the next ten days, and we'll be ready for them all. So, what more can I tell you?" Hal sat back with his hands folded over his belt.

"How's the team doing, Hal? Is Jack solid?" Simon asked.

"He's solid. Sonia keeps him grounded and Handel is a crack investigator." Hal cocked his head. "We've been over this. Why are you asking?"

"I need a team right now for a priority case," said Simon. "Are you up for it?"

"Oh, hells, yes," said Hal. "What have you got?"

"A location where someone may have performed a Blood sacrifice to open a Portal, just like Hightower did," said Simon.

Hal gave a low whistle. "I thought that died with Joby Blackpool. Someone else is involved in this madness?"

"So, it would seem," said Simon. He quickly filled Hal in on Jontry's story.

"I'll mount out the team. Full kit?" said Hal.

"No, just basic badges and sidearms. I don't expect armed resistance. They think they're safe." Simon checked his timepiece. "Meet me in the stables in thirty minutes. And put Kyle Evarts on alert. We may need a CSA team."

They slid out of the stables below Wycliffe House in an unmarked Faleron. Simon drove with Hal next to him. Sonia Milhaven, Jack Ironhand, and Handel Brookstone sat in the rear seat, slightly cramped, but all together.

Simon had a good idea where the boathouse was but wasn't sure of the best route. He crossed the Cut on the Handleford Bridge and turned south along the frontage road that ran parallel to the Cut. The Cut ran straight, but the road wove in and out between quays and warehouses. Simon watched the street numbers and turned left at a nondescript corner. After half a block, he swung right and found they were headed straight to the River Finnegan. The street ended at a tumble-down boathouse built partially out over the water with a pier extending out into deep water next to it.

The team climbed out and spread out in an arc, covering the door. Simon stepped forward to the door. He tried the handle, but found it locked.

"We treat this as a crime scene," said Simon. "As soon as we clear the building, we secure the scene and call in the CSA teams. If what my source tells me is true, at least two Orcs were killed here within the past week."

Simon pulled back and readied a kick to force the door, but Jack held up a hand.

"Let me try, LT." he said. He pulled a set of lockpicks

from his back pocket and went to work on the door. Less than a minute later, he had it open and it swung inward.

Simon raised his needler and sighted along the barrel. "King's Agents!" he shouted as he rushed the door. Hal and Jack followed close behind, clearing the space to his left and right. Directly across the room was another closed door. Simon paused and surveyed the room around them. Empty and devoid of furniture, it was pretty much as Jontry had described. Scratches on the rough wooden floor showed where the three Orcs had lain. A long drag mark led from one deep scratch to the second door.

Simon reached out and checked the handle. Not locked. He pushed the door inward and rushed into the room. "King's Agent." He called out, but there was no one in the room to hear him.

Hal stepped in behind him. The team spread out and checked the rest of the room. "Gods above and below, Simon. It's like that farmhouse."

Glyphs and symbols were etched into the floor, outlined by the silvery residue of platinum. Instead of a stone slab, a metal table occupied the center of the room, blood-stained gutters around three sides emptying into a funnel. The floor under the table extended out over the river, the hole under the funnel emptying directly into the water.

"Alright people, this is a crime scene. You know what to do." Simon walked around the table, taking in the restraints, the blood stains. He looked around at the walls, noted the scorch marks. Multiple sets, some close to the table, but others at the limits of the room. Simon remembered the marks in Hightower's lab where he'd confronted Joby Blackpool. These were even wider.

He took out his mirror and summoned Kyle Evarts. "Hey, Kyle," he said when the mage answered. "I've got a crime scene for you, illegal Portal magic with a Blood sacrifice. Interested?"

"Like the Hightower case? Hells, yes."

Simon sent him the address. "Roll a full team," said Simon. "Unfortunately, there's no body, just trace."

"You'd be surprised what my guys can do with trace," said Evarts. "Thirty minutes."

CHAPTER TWENTY-THREE

Simon left Hal and the team to secure the building and walked down the small quay to the dock. The boathouse projected over the water and had two boat bays under the main deck that were suitable for maintenance or boat storage but not ideal for loading and unloading. The adjacent dock would serve for that purpose. Jontry had said the boat approached from downstream, moving slowly and quietly. The Finnegan estuary was broad, deep, and slow moving here. One could row against the gentle current, so any powered boat could easily travel upstream from points East all the way from the sea at Kingsport. Along the course of the river were dozens of small cities and towns, any one of which could be where the boat originated.

Hal approached from the side of the boathouse. "I thought we'd finished with this deviltry. How did you know, lad?"

"The black powder, Hal," said Simon. "There was nothing in the farmhouse or in Hightower's lab that even hinted at such a thing. So where did it come from? There had to be some other Mage doing Portal magic and bringing this stuff through."

"Portal to where?" asked Hal.

"Hells if I know," said Simon. "Gran Swampwater says we create new worlds with every spell cast, every major decision we make. She says they twist and tangle around one another like a ball of twine. She doubts anyone can reliably access the same place twice." *But Joby Blackpool could do it! He'd seen the world he planned to enter. Maybe these people, whoever they are, have figured that out as well.*

Simon heard the sound of an approaching sledge and turned as the CSA team slid up. He headed over and met Kyle Evarts at the door to the boathouse.

"Thanks, Kyle," said Simon. "The first room is pretty bare. My witness tells me he and two other Orcs were held there, tied up and gagged. The inner room looks a lot like the farmhouse where Hightower did her casting. Glyphs etched on the floor and a sacrificial table in the center of the room. Lots of dried blood but no corpses. They took those with them or dumped them in the river."

"Did you call a water search team?" asked Evarts.

"No, should have thought of it though. I'll get Hal on it right away." Simon led the way into the first room and Evarts detailed two of his team to start sweeping for loose material and taking scrapings from all surfaces. They opened the door to the second room and Evarts stopped and surveyed the floor. "Kia," he said to the technician behind him. "Get images of this before we go in." He crouched and looked over the floor from several heights and angles, then stood and backed out, pulling Simon with him. "I'll need aural exemplars from anyone on the team who was in that room. On the surface, it looks the same as the farmhouse, but I think some of the glyphs are drawn differently, and a few are clearly different."

"Meaning what?" asked Simon.

"Hells if I know," said Evarts. "I don't understand this Magic and don't know if it's just a difference between Mages, or fundamentally a different spell."

"Any chance you can find trace on the Orcs who were held in this room." Simon gestured to the floor. "Enough to get some idea where they came from?"

"Won't know until we process it. Want me to copy you with the reports?"

"Hal has point on this, he'll let me know if you find anything." Simon looked around but couldn't see anything he could do to help. "I'm heading back to Wycliffe House. Let Hal know, will you?" Evarts nodded, already absorbed in his task.

He reached the stables at Wycliffe just before 17th. He climbed the stairs two at a time and made his way to Axhart's office. Elvira Cairns was just packing her carpet bag when he opened the outer door, breathing hard.

"Is he still in, Mistress Cairns?"

"He is," she said. "And what would you be wanting with him?"

Simon slowed his breathing and drew himself upright. "We have a serious new case in Eastport that the captain needs to know about."

She regarded him skeptically for a moment, then waved him toward the office door. He crossed and entered.

Captain Axhart looked up from the papers in front of him. "I'm assuming you said something to Mistress Cairns that convinced her to let you in here." He pointed to one of the chairs in front of the desk. "Sit. Tell me."

Simon settled himself into the chair. "Hal and his team are at a crime scene in Eastport. Two Orcs were murdered there in a Blood magic ritual to open a

Portal. It isn't the first time that site has been used. There are marks on the walls of at least three other Portal spells."

Axhart exhaled and pushed the paperwork aside. "Are you certain? I thought the knowledge of that particular spell died with Blackpool."

"With respect, sir, it couldn't have," said Simon. "The black powder that was used to bomb the Justice Ministry came from somewhere. It's a combination of magically inert materials that becomes something deadly when they're mixed. No one from this world would have the knowledge to make it."

"What do we know?" asked Axhart.

"Not very much, so far," Simon answered. "We have a witness who saw the two victims and confirms that one was what the Orcs call an Earthborn. That's apparently important to opening the initial Portal. Our witness also saw two Humans who seemed to be the Mages casting the spells. Beyond that, we haven't much. Kyle Evarts is processing the scene now. He may be able to tell us more."

"Do you need more people?"

Simon shook his head. "Not as yet. Hal and his team can handle it. If we learn more about the victims, we may need more picks and shovels but for now we're good."

"Keep me informed," said Axhart.

"Aye, sir." Simon rose and took his leave.

He returned to his office, Lessa had already gone home, so he checked his messages. There was no news from Hal or Evarts. He decided the best he could do was to go home. Until the forensics came in or the water recovery team turned up a body, there would be little go on.

He slid into the stable at Stonebender Hall at a few minutes past 19th hour. He noticed Wilston and Mery's big Faleron sled in the center spot next to an

Oxley Sprinter. He smiled. Katya was here. She must have driven all the way from Bolton in the Northwest Territories. Ilsa was supposed to arrive from the East in a couple of days. Liam and Becky were expected at any time as well. Simon settled his Tornado next to Katya's more modest Sprinter and canceled the Air spell. He had just climbed out when the postern door opened, and Katya herself stepped into view.

"I thought I heard an intruder out here," she said.

"Katya!" Simon opened his arms to embrace her. Two years older than Simon and the youngest of his foster siblings, she held a special place in Simon's heart.

She returned his embrace. "Congratulations, little brother. Your lady is something special. I'm happy for the both of you."

"Thank you, Katya," said Simon. He draped a hand on her shoulder as they started for the postern door. "What about you? Anyone special in your life? What about that defense advocate you brought by at Years End?"

She waved a hand. "That was never serious. I'm all good. I'm happy the way I am."

They entered the kitchen to a muted cheer from the table where some sort of game between Jasmine and Mery was going on. Jasmine danced a small jig and pointed at her mother who hung her head in mock dismay. Wills and Molly laughed. Sylvie grinned and patted Jasmine on the back.

"Look what I caught sneaking around the stables," said Katya.

"Uncle Simon!" shouted Jasmine, running toward him. "I beat Momma at Three Fingers! You should see my dress! It's so pretty. I can't wait for the wedding."

"Jasmine," said Mery. "Let your Uncle Simon breath. I'm sure he's tired from work. He'll see your dress soon enough." She gave him a hug. "Hello,

Simon."

"Hello, Mery. Hey, Wills," said Simon. He cocked his head at Molly. "Hal not home yet?"

"No, he called about a half hour ago," said Molly. "Said he'd be home before 22nd. What have you got him working on?"

"Portal magic. Best I not say more right now." Simon found a chair and sat next to Sylvie. He leaned over and kissed her, causing Jasmine to giggle. "We'll talk later."

"Not just the two of us," said Sylvie. "Liam and Becky are here. I left them getting settled in their room. They came a bit earlier than we expected, and you'll never guess who's with them."

As if on cue, Liam and Becky entered from the front hall. Simon watched them, still surprised at how they had changed since leaving the Commonwealth. Rebeka Aster, formerly Crown Princess Rebeka Fangbern, looked relaxed and happy on the arm of her husband. Her head was high, and she exuded a quiet confidence. Liam matched her air of calm confidence, a far cry from the uncertain new Fire Mage he'd been a year ago. Simon rose and shook Liam's hand and accepted a kiss on the cheek from Becky.

"You two are looking well," said Simon. "I'm so glad you're here."

"We're glad to be here," said Becky. "Father issued a writ of special immunity, so you needn't worry about security breaking up the wedding to arrest me. I'm still a criminal, after all." Only a couple of months earlier Rebeka had revealed to the public that she was a Fire Mage and had confessed to arson in a series of fires down in the Hollows.

"I hope you don't mind," said Liam over Becky's shoulder. "But we brought a couple of extra guests."

"Don't look at me. That sort of thing needs to be cleared with Sylvie and Molly." Simon grinned at his fiancé. "Who did you drag along?"

Sylvie punched his arm lightly. "It's Hamil Fairborn and *Syr* Tandril Misthaven, Simon. They came down with Becky and Liam but likely will stay here in the Commonwealth. Molly and Hal have extended them sanctuary."

"Of course, they're welcome," said Simon. "We'd never have gotten home without them."

"Enough talk," said Molly, setting a plate of flatbread and *kalam,* shredded spiced pork, in front of Simon. "Eat something. Sylvie, pour Simon some cider."

"Jasmine," said Mery. "Tell your Uncle Simon good night. It's time to get ready for bed."

"But, Momma," the girl protested. "I wanna hear about Uncle Simon's new case."

"Sorry, Jasmine," said Simon. "It's classified. Keepers only."

She leaned in and said, "I'll be a Keeper when I grow up."

"I'm sure you will." Simon gave her a squeeze. "Good night, Jasmine."

She followed Mery out of the kitchen, calling over her shoulder, "Good night, Aunt Sylvie. Good night, Papa."

Katya stood and embraced Molly. "I'm going to go to bed, too, Momma. It was a long drive and I'm done in. Good night, all."

Everyone wished Katya good night. Wills excused himself to join Mery and the children. Simon mopped up the last of the pork with a square of flatbread and washed it down with some cider.

"Talk, Simon," said Sylvie. "What's this about a Portal Magic case?"

"I talked to a witness early today who barely escaped a boathouse in Eastport where he was held with two other Orcs. We found solid evidence of Blood sacrifice and Portal magic. At least three Portal spells were cast in the same place. This didn't die with Glendowyn Hightower and Joby Blackpool."

"Do you have any idea who's casting these spells?" asked Sylvie.

"Not a clue," said Simon. "But they've been in contact with Flandyrs and his people in the Havens. It's the only explanation for the special weapons Flandyrs built and the black powder. We found nothing about either in Hightower's or Blackpool's notes."

"You think someone found the instructions for making these things through the Portals?" asked Sylvie.

"They must have; how else did they get them? How many of those special weapons did Flandyrs have?"

"Several dozen at least," said Sylvie. "He bragged about how he was going to have a whole army equipped with them. But producing them was taking longer than he liked. He convinced the Steward that they were going to make the Havens invincible."

Simon shook his head. "That doesn't make a lot of sense, Sylvie. Think about it. As scary as those weapons and the black powder seem, when you get right down to it, they're not more effective than conventional weapons. Less so, actually. They're single shot, and don't seem easy to reload. They're weapons of assassination, not weapons of war."

"They were good enough to almost kill the King and Queen," Sylvie pointed out. "And you at the Justice Ministry."

"My point exactly," said Simon. "What would happen if Flandyrs and a dozen men brought weapons like this into a High Council meeting? What if they killed the Steward and his supporters?"

Sylvie paled. "The government would be crippled. The Havens doesn't have an established rule of succession, not like the Commonwealth. Any major House with enough influence could take the Scepter."

"I think I need to talk to Tandril Misthaven," said Simon. "He knows more about the politics of the High Council."

"Tandril and Hamil should be down in a short while," said Becky. "Tandril wanted to speak to Hal in person before accepting his offer of sanctuary."

"Tandril is Progressive, but certain things are important to him and need to be done with respect for tradition," said Sylvie. She looked up as Hal came in from the postern door.

Molly went to him. "You look tired, love. Sit and have some pork *kalam* and cider.

Simon moved over and Hal sat next to him. "Any news from Eastport?"

Hal gulped cider and smiled up at Molly as she set a plate in front of him. "The water recovery team dragged up a dead Orc if that's what you're asking. Throat cut, likely one of the poor sods killed for that cursed spell. Evarts is having the corpse sent back to Wycliffe."

"Sorry to drop this on you, Hal," Simon said with a sigh. "But I need your experience."

"I know, lad. I wouldn't want to put this on any other team. We caught the Hightower case; we need to finish this business ourselves." Hal scooped a huge portion of the spiced pork onto a chunk of flatbread and ate it, chasing it with cider.

"Did they have the same setup as the farmhouse?" asked Liam. "Room with glyphs etched on the floor, table in the middle?"

"Aye," said Hal. "Is that important?"

"Maybe." Liam scratched his head. "Hightower's lab had the same setup as the farmhouse. I think the spell needs to be anchored somehow in order to work. Unless these Mages have another site, you may have shut them down at least for a while by finding this boathouse."

"Well, here's hoping that Evarts can find something that gives us a lead on these snakes," said Hal, raising his mug of cider. "He wants Simon to stop by after watch change tomorrow."

"Will do." Simon looked up as Hamil Fairborn and Tandril Misthaven approached.

Sylvie jumped up and rushed to embrace them both, and Simon stood and extended his hand. "Well met, Hamil, and welcome, *Syr* Misthaven. I'm surprised but gratified to see you as well."

Hamil returned Sylvie's embrace then took Simon's hand. "Glad to be here, Simon. I trust my information proved useful."

"Essential," said Simon. "We'd never have gotten close to Sylvie without it."

Hal rose and faced Misthaven. "*Syr* Tandril Misthaven, House Stonebender welcomes you and offers you the sanctuary of the Hall. Meat and mead, fire and fellowship be yours."

Misthaven bowed deeply. "I accept your sanctuary, Haldron Stonebender. I will place myself and the resources of House Misthaven, such as they are, at your disposal."

"Ha! Enough ceremony," said Hal. "Sit. Have some cider."

Misthaven sat next to Sylvie and accepted a mug of cider, clearly a bit nonplussed by Dwarfish hospitality.

Sylvie grasped his arm. "I'm glad you decided to leave the Havens, Tandril. I know what it must have cost you."

"The mist started to clear when they detained Ciara Leafgreen and confiscated her estates," said Misthaven.

"Ciara Leafgreen? On what grounds?" Sylvie shook her head. "She was always openly Progressive but never a threat."

"After Flandyrs was taken, the Steward began to

see enemies in every shadow." Misthaven sipped cider carefully, then smiled and sipped more. "Anyone who didn't support him became suspect. Those of us who could, fled to our estates or left the country."

"So, who is left of the High Council?" asked Simon.

"No more than a half dozen of the Steward's closest followers," said Misthaven. "It's just enough for a quorum. The Steward can rule without opposition."

Was that Flandyrs's plan from the beginning? Isolate the Steward so he could influence the government? But he couldn't ensure he'd be the only one with the Steward's ear.

"Sylvie," said Simon. "Where did Flandyrs keep his cache of special weapons?"

"I heard they were stored in the armory of the High Tower itself." She thought for a second. "I think some may have been kept at the Graystorm armory as well. I wasn't allowed into that area but overheard a couple of guards speculating about a restricted room."

"*Syr* Misthaven." Simon used the honorific to indicate a formal question. "What would happen if the Steward were to die in office?"

"The High Council would meet and select a successor. The Steward's designated choice would be given preference, but the choice isn't guaranteed." Misthaven paused. "The process is supposed to be collaborative, but currently, I don't know who the Council would choose."

"What if a team of Flandyrs's henchmen, or partners, brought these special weapons into the High Tower and managed to kill the Steward and the remaining Council members?" asked Simon.

Misthaven paled and Sylvie gasped. "That's what Flandyrs planned all along. It would be chaos. Anyone could claim the Scepter."

"Who would have the power to do that and enforce it?" Simon reached out and took Sylvie's hand as he asked the question.

"*Syr* Berland Graystorm," said Misthaven grimly. "I'm sorry, Sylvie, but you know it's true."

Sylvie nodded. "Of course it is. It's why my father took Flandyrs in to begin with. He's always coveted the Scepter but could never gather the political support to take it."

"I fear all the Steward has done by purging any opposition is to isolate himself and make himself more vulnerable to such an attack," said Simon. "The question is, should we try to warn him? I'm not a friend of the current Steward, but the potential chaos of a coup may be worse than the beast we know."

"I will try." Misthaven spoke softly. "I have always been truthful with him. If I write him under the seal of House Misthaven, he may pay attention."

"Thank you, Tandril," said Simon. "I fear this is bigger than just the Havens. We narrowly escaped three assassinations here in the Commonwealth."

"Three?" asked Hal.

"Aye. First was the attempt to firebomb King Olaf Hall during an Azeri trade fair. The Crown Prince had scheduled a surprise visit, and the Brigades were tipped off. An Orc with a Firebomb vest came close to detonating it near the Royal Coach. Second was the attempt on the king in Parliament, and the third was the queen the same day. If they'd succeeded, the succession would have been thrown into turmoil, and under the Accords, the Justice Ministry would choose a new King. Except the Justice Ministry was almost destroyed by a black powder explosion the same day."

"Listen to yourself, Simon," said Becky. "You make this sound like a conspiracy to wipe out my family and the Steward at the same time. It's too fantastic."

"It happened, Becky. The threat was real and it's only good fortune that it didn't succeed."

"Good fortune and good Keeper work," said Sylvie.

"You've made a good case, lad," said Hal. "Now what do we do about it?"

"We work the case we've got," said Simon. "We reach out to the Steward through Tandril, and we warn the Crown Prince that this didn't end with Flandyrs's death."

Molly stood and cleared away Hal's empty plate. "All good. But you're getting married in three days. You have tomorrow to work your case. After that you will be here helping your bride prepare for the ritual and vows."

"Yes, Molly," said Simon.

CHAPTER TWENTY-FOUR

Simon flipped through the morning messages as he sipped coffee. About halfway through, he found what he'd hoped he would. The short note from Kermal confirmed that Jontry Hillcrest and his mother were safely on their way to Canfield, a small city in the Northwest.

We also have a possible name for the overseer who approached Jontry. The description fits a former kharo from Eastport named Damier Bogrunner, second cousin to your old friend Dirking Bogrunner. Last known to follow. Kermal

The last time Simon had seen Dirking Bogrunner, he'd abandoned him to the mercy of the crones in the Spirit House. Bogrunner had been responsible for the death of Gran Swampwater's grandson, so Simon didn't imagine that he had fared very well. Dirking hadn't been directly involved with Glendowyn Hightower, but he'd been an overseer and had lured a number of Orcs away from the Reservation with promises of work. It looked like Damier was in the same line of work.

Simon checked in with Jason Hanks and Gervis Birchfield but neither had much progress to report on their active cases. He briefed them on the new Portal magic case and reassured them that Hal would give them details later.

Hal strode into the office a few minutes past 10th looking tired. He dropped into one of the chairs in front of Simon's desk.

"What's the latest, Hal?" Simon asked.

"Forensics are still pending, but we did confirm that the dead Orcs likely came from one of the towns along the Finnigan, East of the Cut. Something about the composition of the mud on the floor of the room. The dead Orc the water recovery team dragged out of the river had no detectable aura, which Evarts says is strange. Likewise, the blood on the table. Something about that Portal spell destroys aural trace." Hal paused and consulted his notes. "Nothing firm on the glyphs on the floor, but there was some trace fabric embedded in the wood next to the table. Evarts is running that through a registry of known materials. As to the boathouse, we tried to trace ownership, but the last known owner died intestate three years ago. Legally, the place belongs to the city of Eastport. Practically, it's abandoned property. Another dead end." Hal closed the notebook and looked up. "What have you got, lad?"

"Jontry and his mother are safe and headed to the Northwest," said Simon. "And Kermal has a possible name for the overseer who recruited him for the job at the boathouse. He's an Orc named Damier Bogrunner. Kermal's working on getting us a last known address."

"I'll have Sonia start asking around the neighborhoods," said Hal. "Bogrunner? Any relationship to old Dirking Bogrunner?"

"Second cousin." Simon thought for a minute. "The

family likely comes from down south. Not Azeri by birth but apparently recruited by Snake Clan sometime in the past. Might be worth an inquiry with Handel Greenmire, the Marshal down on the Southern Rez."

Hal nodded and made a note. "An outsider recruited by the Snakes isn't common. Usually reserved for Mages or assassins. Should give us a lead. Anything else?"

Simon leaned back with a sigh. "Nothing I can put my finger on, Hal. But that boathouse makes me uneasy. I've felt for a while that something just wasn't right. The signs in that boathouse mean something important, but I can't figure out what. Gran Swampwater says the whole world is out of balance somehow and that's what I'm sensing."

"Don't put any stock in the rantings of an Orc witch," scoffed Hal. "Still, I trust your sense of stone. If you think something's off-kilter in the shoring, run it down. Better a blind tunnel than a cave in."

They agreed to check in with Evarts later in the day. Hal took his leave, and Simon reluctantly sorted through some of the administrative paperwork that seemed to make up more and more of his job as a Lieutenant.

He worked through midday until he was interrupted just after 14th hour by the summoning tone of his personal mirror. He swiped the screen on and was surprised to see Kermal's face.

"Good meeting, Kermal. What's happening?"

"I have a location for Damier Bogrunner, Simon. You're going to want to send a team and forensics."

"Where, and why the forensics?"

"Bogrunner's dead," said Kermal. "Your team will find him in a vacant house three blocks south of Wheelwright in Eastport." He gave a street number. "He's hanging upside down from the ceiling in the kitchen. His throat's been cut, and his eyes gouged out. One of Forsaka's people found him. I'd put it about that I wanted to have a word with him."

"Traitors death?" Simon tried to wipe the image of Sanjik Clearwater hanging upside down, mutilated in the same way, from his mind. "Did Serpent Clan claim responsibility?"

"No," said Kermal. "And the Cabal would know if it was done under Clan sanction. It could be *kanly*, a personal feud, but that generally doesn't warrant the traitor's death. A knife between the shoulder blades is usually enough."

"Could someone be trying to make it look like a Clan execution by staging it that way?" speculated Simon. "Maybe as a warning to others to keep quiet?"

"That would shut down any idle curiosity," said Kermal. "But it would have to be someone with knowledge of Clan ritual to stage it properly."

"Whatever," said Simon. "It leaves us without a light in a very confusing tunnel."

"Sorry to spoil your afternoon," said Kermal. "And if you could keep me and the Cabal out of this, I'd appreciate it."

"Will do, Brother. This was an anonymous tip." Simon broke the connection. He summoned Hal's mirror and relayed the street address and the fact that their best lead was dead. They agreed to meet in the morgue to talk to Evarts at 16th hour.

Simon made his way down to the lower levels a little early. He checked Everts's office, but the forensics Mage wasn't there. Simon found him in the morgue sewing the chest incision closed on the corpse of an Orc laid out on the steel exam table.

"Is that the Orc the water recovery team fished out of the river?" he asked, causing Evarts to turn and fumble a stitch.

"Gods above and below, Simon," said Evarts. "A little warning next time. And yes, it is."

"What can you tell me about him?"

Evarts tied the last stitch. "He was about twenty-five years old, healthy, ate Azeri blood sausage for his last meal. He died from a deep slash wound across the neck that severed both carotid arteries. The wound was a single smooth stroke, no hesitation, delivered from left to right. Almost all his blood was drained, and I can find no detectable life aura. Any identification will have to be by facial recognition or dental analysis." Evarts paused and pointed to the Orc's wrists. "He was bound with his hands behind his back using common hemp rope. The same bindings were used on his ankles. Any other useful trace was washed away in the river."

Simon looked closely at the Orc's pale face. His cheekbones were high and his eyes large and round. His nose was sharp but not large, and his thin lips were pulled back over even flat teeth. "He was from the Eastern provinces. You can see it in the shape of his eyes and his long face." Simon lifted the Orc's right hand, noting the ligature marks. "He's well-muscled and his hands have thick callouses. He was a laborer or farmer."

Evarts grinned. "You'd make a good forensics tech. I agree. More likely a farmer; there was both dirt and animal manure under his fingernails."

"He was the Earthborn they sacrificed to activate the Portal spell," said Simon. "That's why there's no life aura. All his *ghiras* went into the Portal."

"If you say so." Evarts stripped off the gloves he wore and turned to a nearby sink where he began washing his hands. "You seem to know a bit about this Portal magic."

"Only what I've picked up talking to Gran Swampwater and her sisters at the Spirit House." Simon shivered as if cold. "Enough to be afraid."

"Afraid?" Evarts picked up a ragged towel and dried

his hands. "Afraid of what?"

"It sounds crazy, but I think someone, or something, came through one of these Portals from somewhere else into our world," said Simon.

"I was always taught that passage through a Portal was fatal," said Evarts.

"Ordinarily, it is," replied Simon. "But it's the light the Portal emits from its boundary that's deadly. Make the opening big enough and there's a clear zone in the center; that's how Joby Blackpool planned to escape to his Orc paradise. Something has come into our world that doesn't belong here."

"Now you do sound a bit fanciful," said Evarts. "But not entirely crazy. There was a scrap of fabric recovered from a sharp edge on the table. It's very weird, like nothing I've ever seen. It's soft and smooth textured, like silk, but the individual fibers in it are perfectly round and uniform in diameter."

"How is that weird?" asked Simon.

"No spinning technique that I know of can make thread that is perfectly round and uniform. There's always variation in the diameter of individual threads." Hal stepped into the morgue and nodded to Evarts to continue. "I can't figure out what the threads themselves are made from. It certainly isn't cotton or flax or any known plant we have catalogued. It isn't silk, or gut or hide either. My reveal spells keep indicating glass, which makes no sense."

"It's not of our world," said Simon. "Like that weapon and ammunition and the strange mirror device we found in Hightower's office. I don't know if it came from the same place, but it came through a Portal from somewhere outside."

"Like I said, fanciful but not entirely crazy."

"Did you find anything that could lead to an identity for this poor sod?" asked Hal.

"No," answered Evarts. "If you get a name, we can

try to verify with dental records, but there was no life aura and none of the Civil registries have an image that matches his face, at least not on preliminary facial recognition spells. That's not very reliable, though. Random searches without a name have almost thirty percent false negative rates."

"Then I'd best get the team out East beating the bushes," grunted Hal. "Thanks, Kyle. See you at home, Simon."

Simon took his leave as well and made his way back to the Command floor. He stopped by his own office and sent Lessa home, telling her he wouldn't be in the next day. He walked down the hall to Axhart's office and briefed the captain on the discovery of Bogrunner's name and the fact that it was a dead end since the Orc was already dead.

"Seems someone is covering their trail," said Axhart. "I take it Evarts hasn't found anything in forensics to point us down a new tunnel."

"No, sir," said Simon. "I have some outside sources looking into Bogrunner's activities but no new light."

"Just make sure anything Brackenville or the Cabal uncover can be verified," warned Axhart. "Otherwise, the KP's office will throw it out as hearsay."

"Aye, sir." Simon took Axhart's nod for a dismissal and turned to leave.

"Simon," said Axhart. "You're getting married in two days. I expect you to concentrate on that and not on this case. Understood?"

"Aye, sir." Simon grinned. "You sound like Molly Stonebender, sir."

"Who do you think ordered me to say that to you? Now go, and we'll next see you at the wedding."

Simon arrived home at half past 17th hour to find the Hall in a kind of organized chaos. Sylvie, Mery and Katya bustled about storing food in cupboards, chillers, and pantries under Molly's sharp eye. Simon was dispatched to find Willston and help with the setting up of the outdoor dais and canopy where the ritual and vows would be conducted. Meanwhile, Hervik had arrived and oversaw setting up seating for the hundred or so expected guests. Tradesmen and workers drifted in and out, all carefully vetted and watched by a contingent of Palace Security guardsmen posted at the entrance to the Hall.

The open meadow behind the Hall, freshly mowed with a graveled walkway laid down the center, served as the venue for the ritual and vows. At the end of the gravel, Willston directed a couple of carpenters constructing the raised dais and canopy where Simon, Sylvie, their attendant avatars, and the Crown Prince would stand. Simon paused and looked around. *This really is going to happen.* He felt a small thrill of anticipation.

"Hey, Wills," he said. "Molly sent me to help. What can I do?"

"Simon, good to see you finally. The canopy will need to be dressed once Clarence there gets it tied down. Do you know where Ma and Sylvie stored the garland?"

"Aye, it's in the long shed behind the stables. I'll fetch it." Simon set off, happy to have a task.

The evening passed quickly after that. After the light faded and the outdoor work stopped, they came indoors. Most of the tradesmen had finished and the family gathered around the long kitchen table. Ilsa and her husband, Gerold, had arrived that afternoon from the Eastern Borderlands. Molly was disappointed that they'd left their children with Gerold's mother, but Ilsa shrugged it off.

"I couldn't face that long trip with a pair of restless two-year-old girls," Ilsa confided to Simon. "I love my children, but this will be more enjoyable without them. Besides, their grandmama deserves a chance to spoil them."

Molly beamed as the family sat down to dinner. Hervik stayed and promised that his family would come to the prewedding feast the next day. Wren and Thorston were also expected. *This is Molly's dream come true,* thought Simon as he accepted the good wishes and gentle jibes of his siblings. *All the family gathered at her table. It doesn't happen often enough.*

Sylvie held his hand under the table and beamed almost as brightly as Molly. "Gods, this feels good," she whispered to him. "I've never had a real feeling of family. Thank you, Simon."

They spent the rest of the evening laying out the ritual costumes for the wedding. Simon reverently opened the large chest in which they were stored. Kermal, as Second, would wear the leather apron and tool belt of the Smith. Hal tried on the ancient Stonebender chainmail and greaves he'd wear as the Warrior. He opened a polished oak box and drew out the sword his forefathers had used to fight Orcs when both races had contended for supremacy in the deep places of the world. As Guardsman, he'd protect the wedding couple from the Stranger who lurked in the darkness to bring death to everyone eventually.

Molly drew out the distaff and kettle she'd carry as Matron. Jasmine could hardly contain her excitement as she stood on a stool in the sky blue and argent dress she'd wear as the Virgin. She swished her willow wand around until Mery chided her to hold still so she could sew the final pleat into the skirt.

Hervik made a show of jumping out from behind Hal, wearing the black cloak and death's head mask of the Stranger. Jasmine shrieked in mock fear and waved her wand more vigorously to drive him off. Mery laughed and just managed to snip the last thread she was using before Jasmine began to chase her Uncle Hervik around the kitchen.

Molly finally restored order. Hervik shed his costume and folded it carefully into the chest. Mery packed Jasmine off to bed and Hal wrapped the armor in its oiled cloth. Simon and Sylvie said their good nights and climbed the stairs to their room.

"Tell me again about the ritual, love," said Sylvie as they settled into bed.

"But you know it already," protested Simon.

"But I want to hear it from you. Elves follow the Silver Lady, if they worship at all. I love the Dwarf ways. Tell me." She held his hands and gazed into his eyes.

"All right." Simon sighed and began. "When the world was made, the Father and the Mother of All knew Dwarves would need guidance to make their way. Men as well, but they came about later. So, the Gods created avatars of themselves to embody the virtues the Dwarves would need. The Smith, to build and create, to teach the crafts and the virtue of work. The Warrior, to defend hearth and home, to teach courage and honor and duty. And the Father, to hold them all together, to teach and raise the children. The Mother of All created from her own breast the Mother, to have children and be a partner and helpmate to the Father. From her grew the Matron, to make the hearth and home a place of welcome and safety. But the Mother had a dream of innocence and wildness, and as she slept, the Virgin appeared, to remind all that youth and innocence were virtues as well and hold the power to drive off despair. And so were created the Six: Father, Smith, and Warrior; Mother, Matron, and Virgin."

"And we celebrate these in the wedding," said Sylvie. "I think it's a wonderful ritual."

"Don't forget the Stranger," said Simon.

"Why do you call death the Stranger?" asked Sylvie.

"The legend is that, in the beginning, there was

no death. Dwarves were as constant as the hills and mountains where they made their homes," said Simon. "But Darkness existed, hiding in the deep. The Dwarves, in their drive to tame the world, disturbed its peace, so it created its own avatar to show the world that nothing can be forever safe or permanent. And so, the Stranger stalks us all and will eventually take us into the darkness. But the innocence and joy of the Virgin and the courage and honor of the Warrior can hold the Stranger at bay, at least for a while."

"Jasmine takes her role in the ritual so seriously," said Sylvie with a smile. She snuggled into his shoulder. "I love all of it. It's a celebration of life and love and family. Elf weddings are legal affairs, contracts with expiration dates and obligations spelled out in great detail. About as joyful as a business meeting."

Simon held her close. "You don't mind the open-ended promises?"

"No, love. We'll share *ghiras* for as long as we can and take joy in it." She kissed him gently. "Now sleep. We have a lifetime ahead of us."

CHAPTER TWENTY-FIVE

The next day started early and became a whirl of activity as final preparations were made. Tables were set up in the vast audience chamber at the center of the Hall. Outside, chairs and awnings sprouted like toadstools in the space where the ritual would take place. Simon was pulled this way and that as the security team and Molly battled over access to the Hall. In the end, Molly had her way, but Simon had to personally guarantee that he and a Peacekeeper squad would sweep the venue for any threats before Harold and his force arrived.

By 14th hour, all was in place and the caterers and tradesmen were gone. Kermal arrived a short time later. He strode down the gravel path with barely a limp, although he still used a walking stick. Simon greeted him with an embrace.

"Thank you for being here, Brother," he said.

"Try to keep me away," said Kermal "But we need to talk. It'll keep, at least for a while."

The wedding party gathered under the canopy to rehearse the ritual for the next day. Kermal took his place next to Simon as his Second, and Hal stepped up beside Kermal. Sylvie took Simon's hand facing him and Molly and Jasmine stood at her side. Thorston stood in for the Crown Prince, reading the words of the ritual. Hervik played his part, moaning and roaring as the Stranger until Hal and Jasmine drove him off. Molly pronounced herself satisfied and ordered them all to get cleaned up for dinner.

Kermal pulled Simon aside and he waved for Hal and Sylvie to join them. "We may have a lead on a name," he said. "The boathouse was owned by a man named Kendal Degarlis until he died about three years ago."

"We know that," said Hal. "Degarlis died without an heir. The boathouse reverted to the city of Eastport under a tax lien."

"Degarlis may not have had an heir, but he did have a business partner," said Kermal. "He wasn't listed on the boathouse deed, but they co-owned a cargo barge."

"So, who is this unnamed partner?" asked Simon.

"Fenrik Avila," said Kermal. "Just after Degarlis died, Avila and the barge dropped out of sight."

"Do we have a line on Avila?" asked Simon.

"Nothing solid. Street talk is that Avila went into the smuggling business and has been moving both goods and people between Kingsport and the Cut with the boathouse as one of his transfer sites. The Cabal has put it about that they have some business for Avila. If he makes contact, I'll let you know."

"All good, Kermal," said Simon. "Let's put it aside for tonight. Molly wants us at the table."

They joined the rest of the family around the extended table. Everyone was there: Hervik, his wife, Gayla, and their grown sons; Thorston and Helga;

Wren and her husband, Tomsa: Katya; Ilsa and Gerold; Willston and Mery sat next to Molly with Jasmine and Glory on her other side. Hal occupied his place at the head with Simon, Sylvie, and Kermal to his right.

Food was passed and eaten with joyful conversations as family news was exchanged. Simon had eyes only for Sylvie. Kermal had an animated conversation with her about the plight of Orcs in the Havens. Jasmine and Glory chattered and laughed with Molly, enjoying the privilege of being at the adult table. Finally, Hal stood and pounded on the table for attention.

He raised his tankard. "Charge your glasses," he said in a deep voice. When everyone had raised their glasses or mugs, he said, "I give you Simon and Sylvie, may the Gods bless them and their union." There were shouts of approval as people drank. Hal remained standing and waited until there was a moment of quiet. "To the Six Gods, King Thorston, and House Stonebender," he said solemnly. Everyone echoed his toast and drained their glasses.

The food was cleared away, but the family lingered about the table talking, drinking, and enjoying the company. It was near 23rd hour before Simon and Sylvie were able to say good night.

They were awakened the next morning by an urgent knock on their door. "Simon, Sylvie," said Kermal from the other side of the door. "Come downstairs quickly, things are happening in the Havens."

They dressed and joined Kermal, Hal, Hamil Fairborn, and Tandril Misthaven in the library. The large mirror over the mantle showed a news reporter in front of the West Faring border crossing.

"Details are sparse," the reporter said. "But it appears that last evening, during a special meeting of the High Council, a group of assassins entered the Council chamber and killed the Steward and ten Councilors. *Syr* Berland Graystorm, who had the good fortune to be absent from the chamber has assumed the Scepter until the High Council can be reconstituted."

"It seems your concerns were well founded, Lieutenant Buckley," said Misthaven. "And my warning was too late."

The image cut to a street scene in Portalis. Orcs stood lined up against the fence separating the Orcish district from the rest of the city. Elves in tactical gear and holding D'Stang heavy bolt throwers herded them into transports. The reporter's voice continued, "These images were released by the official Haven Information Service. According to Genna Silverthorn, newly appointed Chief Ranger, an Orcish Liberation Front headed by Kaldan Barca is responsible for the attack on the Council. Barca is wanted for interrogation and known associates are being detained by Gray Rangers from the Security Services."

"That snake," muttered Sylvie. "She'll say anything to get ahead. The Orcs had nothing to do with this."

"You know this Chief Ranger Silverthorn?" asked Misthaven.

"We were stationed together at the Borderlands," said Sylvie. "She weaseled on Hamil and me when we planned our escape. She delivered Rulanis Summerfield to the Traditionalists on charges of assisting me. She obviously got her reward."

The reporter reappeared. "His Majesty's Foreign Minister has yet to respond to our request for a reaction, but the Armed Forces and Security Services are reportedly on high alert. Yesina Welborn, the Palace Information Secretary, has promised an official statement from His Majesty this afternoon. We will provide further details as they become available."

Simon's mirror chimed and he swiped the screen. Stenson Harold's face appeared. "Hello, Simon. You've heard about the coup in the Havens?"

"Aye, we're watching the news services now."

"His Highness is ignoring my recommendations and is determined to be at Stonebender Hall this afternoon for your wedding," said Harold. "Just letting you know. And tell your foster mother that we will have additional security on hand whether she approves or not."

"I'll handle Molly, Stenson," said Simon. "I need to speak with his Highness regardless, so it's just as well he'll be here."

Harold frowned. "Anything I need to know?"

"No immediate threat. I'll brief you along with the prince." Simon broke the connection.

Molly had prepared a large family breakfast, and they all sat around the kitchen table to eat, although the mood was subdued. As the morning passed without further information out of the Havens, attention shifted to preparing for the wedding.

Harold and his security team arrived at 13th hour and set up their patrol and overwatch locations. Harold and a pair of technicians swept the seating area and the dais as well as the banquet hall. Molly huffed at the sweep through her kitchen, but Simon calmed her down.

Guests began arriving at 16th and were efficiently cleared by the team at the front of the Hall. Many were Peacekeepers from Simon's teams or friends of Hal's, and they accepted the screening with good grace. Their curiosity was satisfied at half past the hour when the Royal limousine and two chase sleds slid into the driveway in front of the Hall. Harold and two armed and armored security guards met the sleds and opened the door of the limo. Crown Prince Henrik climbed out and greeted Harold. He wore the black and gold robe of a Chief Magistrate with a red sash draped around his neck. He turned and waved to several of the guests as they waited for the security team to pass them in.

Simon stepped out of the Hall and approached the Crown Prince. He wore his dress uniform with the Legion medal around his neck. Henrik reached out and shook his hand.

"Welcome to Stonebender Hall, your Highness," said Simon. "If you'll come with me, I'll introduce you to Haldron and Molly Stonebender, Master and Mistress of the Hall."

As they walked side by side, Simon lowered his voice. "With your permission, your Highness, I'd like a word in private with you and Stenson Harold. It concerns events in the Havens and their possible impact here."

The prince touched Simon's arm. "We'll make time after the ritual. You need to put everything else aside." He reached into the breast pocket of his robe and pulled out an envelope. He handed it to Simon. "Speaking of which, a mutual acquaintance asked me to give you this."

Simon broke the seal and looked at the contents. It contained a bank draft for fifty thousand Crowns and a short note.

Loot, this is your share of the bounty on Flandyrs. You earned it. If that makes you uncomfortable, just think of this as a wedding gift from the team. Congratulations to you and your Noble Lady. Josen Taylor

Simon nodded to Prince Henrik and tucked the note and the draft into his pocket.

The security team passed them through, and they found Hal and Molly waiting in the entrance hall. Hal wore the legacy armor of the Guardsman and Molly the long skirt and apron of the Matron. They both took a knee as the Crown Prince approached.

"Your Highness," said Simon. "Allow me to present Haldron Stonebender, Master of Stonebender Hall and Patriarch of House Stonebender. At his side, please meet Mistress Mariadoch Stonebender, Mistress of this House and Matriarch of House Stonebender."

"Rise Haldron and Mariadoch," said Henrick. He lowered his voice to a familiar tone as he reached out to shake each of their hands. "If I may, Hal and Molly. Your foster son is a tribute to your family. He's one of the finest men in our service and a credit to the Peacekeepers."

Hal inclined his head. "Thank you, your Highness. His foster mother and I are rather fond of him."

The prince laughed. "Come, friends. I believe we have a wedding to attend."

They passed through the center of the Hall and out to the meadow. The wedding party assembled in a closed tent behind the seating area. Simon presented Willston, Mery and Jasmine to the prince who greeted them with the familiarity of a close friend. Jasmine, completely smitten, asked the prince if she could sit next to him at the wedding banquet. Henrick graciously thanked her for the honor but said he was unable to remain after the ritual due to affairs of State. He turned and shook hands with Kermal, greeting him with a familiarity that surprised Simon. The two had obviously met before.

Sylvie entered the tent and bowed to Henrik. She smiled. "You honor us, your Highness," she said as he took her hand.

"The honor is mine, Lady Graystorm. You and Lieutenant Buckley have performed invaluable service to the Crown, and I only wish to acknowledge that." He laughed. "Besides, I promised Top I'd make sure Simon actually went through with this."

Simon for his part was speechless. This was the first time he'd seen Sylvie in her wedding dress, and she took his breath away. The dress, all smooth sky-blue satin and white lace, fit her perfectly, complementing her slim figure and her light coloring. Simon took her hand and tucked it under his arm. The rest of the wedding party formed two lines behind them. Kermal gripped Simon's shoulder in support as he took his place.

"Ready?" asked the prince. When everyone nodded, he took his place in front of Simon and Sylvie and opened the front of the tent. Soft lute music began to play as he led the group down the gravel path to the dais.

They walked sedately to the dais and stopped. Prince Henrik slowly mounted the platform and took his place behind a plain wooden lectern facing the assembly. He beckoned the rest of the wedding party forward and they climbed the short stairs. Simon and Sylvie stood in front of the prince, facing each other, hands clasped. The others spread out to stand at their shoulders. Prince Henrik raised his arms, and the music stopped.

"Mother and Father of All," he said in a loud, formal tone. "Bless this couple and this gathered congregation as they celebrate their union." He lowered his arms and gripped the sides of the lectern. "Welcome all," he said. "We gather as family and friends to celebrate and bear witness as Simon Buckley and Sylvie Graystorm speak their vows of fealty to one another.

"Since the beginning of all things, the gods recognized that this union of two people, founded in love, gave strength when it was needed, comfort when times became hard and joy when good times were at hand. To help them in this life, they created the Six. The Father to provide guidance and strength, the Mother to nurture and love unconditionally, the Smith to build and craft the essentials of life, the Matron to keep the hearth and teach the crafts of the home, the Warrior to safeguard all, and the Virgin to remind the rest that innocence and joy are the antidote to despair."

He paused and touched first Simon and then Sylvie on the forehead. "Simon Buckley, will you have this woman as your partner in all things, as your helpmate in life, honoring her, lending her your strength when she needs strength, your love when she needs love and your wisdom when she needs guidance?"

"I will," Simon said with a nod.

"Sylvie Graystorm, will you have this man as your partner in all things, as your helpmate in life, honoring him, lending him your strength when he needs strength, your love when he needs love and your wisdom when he needs guidance?"

"I will." Sylvie's answer was clear and firm.

"Extend your hands," said the prince. They did so and he took the red stole from around his neck and wound it around their clasped hands three times before knotting it. "By this knot are you joined as one until death shall cut this cord and separate your mortal bodies."

On cue, there came a rattling and moaning from the back of the assembly. Hervik, costumed as the Stranger in black with a death's-head mask and festooned with bones and thorny stakes, advanced down the path toward the dais. Jasmine waved her willow wand and rushed toward him followed closely by Hal, armor gleaming and sword drawn. As they approached, the Stranger recoiled. Before Simon's eyes, he seemed to grow in stature and take on a distorted shape with short bandy legs, shoulders that stuck out at an odd angle and arms that stretched impossibly long. Simon gasped and blinked his eyes, and the form became his foster brother once more. He slowly withdrew, pursued by Jasmine's wand, until he disappeared into the tent at the rear. Jasmine and Hal linked arms and returned to the dais.

"Having freely exchanged vows and being joined by the knot of life, you are now husband and wife."

Henrik raised his arms again and the entire assembly stood. "The gods bless this union, keep them safe from all evil, and bring joy and honor to their family."

Simon and Sylvie exchanged a kiss and turned to face their friends and family, raising their linked hands above their heads. A cheer answered from the crowd. Hal and Jasmine, arms linked, led the way as they stepped down from the dais and walked up the gravel path to enter the tent. Simon and Sylvie turned and once again waved their linked hands to their guests.

Kermal reached out and embraced them. "All the best to the both of you," he said. "I can only stay for the banquet and the toasts. Chief Forsaka wants me up in the Borderlands as soon as possible."

"You're not going into the Havens, are you?" asked Sylvie.

"Not as yet. Forsaka wants me in West Faring to handle any refugees, especially any of Barca's people." Kermal shrugged. "I hope he makes it over the border. His capture would set the Cabal's efforts back years."

Prince Henrik approached them. "Forgive me for overhearing, Mr. Brackenville. Am I to take it that the Cabal is actively working against the Steward's government?"

"I must decline to confirm or deny that, Your Highness," said Kermal with a deep bow.

Henrik smiled. "Of course. Do be careful in your travels."

Kermal bowed again and moved away to where Hal and Molly were replacing their costumes in the family trunk. Sylvie gave Simon a nod and joined him.

"I fear I must take my leave soon," said the Crown Prince. "Events are moving quickly, and we must be ready with a response." He lowered his voice. "You wanted to speak with me and Captain Harold?"

"Yes, your Highness." Simon waved to Harold who had entered the tent and stood guard near the entrance.

Harold inclined his head respectfully to the prince, then shook Simon's hand. "Congratulations, Simon."

"Thank you, Stenson. Your Highness, I assume you were briefed on the Hightower case a year ago?" The prince nodded and Simon continued. "We all assumed that the ability to cast Portal spells that would pass solid objects died with Hightower and Joby Blackpool. It did not. As recently as a few days ago, someone has been casting those spells here in the Commonwealth. They used them to transport either an object such as a book or paper, or, as I believe, a person into our world. This resulted in the transfer of knowledge about the explosive black powder and the special non-magical weapons it powers from that place to here."

"You're certain of this?" asked Henrik.

"Of the transfer of knowledge, yes," said Simon. "As to how, I am not sure but strongly suspect that a living person survived passage through a Portal and is now here, in our world."

"I thought passage through a Portal was fatal," said Harold. "Something about disrupted probability streams."

"Actually," said Simon. "It's the light emitted by the Portal that kills. It takes the Blood sacrifice of an Earthborn Orc to open the portal, but the sacrifice of any sentient after that will enlarge it. Make it big enough, and there is a safe zone in the center where a person might survive a passage. Joby Blackpool planned to use that to escape this world. The same could have brought an outsider into it."

"This is disturbing news," said Henrik. "But how does it concern us?"

"Because there may be other knowledge that we can't predict, but that could be used against the Royal family. They've already overthrown the Steward." Simon held the prince's eye. "You are vulnerable, your

Highness. Not just to physical attack, but to political attack as well."

"How so?" Henrick asked.

"You are your father's only heir and yet you personally control the Ghost Teams, which operate outside the law. What would happen if your role in ordering extrajudicial executions became public knowledge? Your father would be forced to disavow you. You'd have to abdicate, leaving the Crown isolated and at the mercy of the Anti-Monarchist party."

"That's why you were sworn to secrecy, Lieutenant," the prince said sharply.

"And I would never reveal that secret," said Simon. "But I was able to uncover much of the story of the Ghost Teams by ordinary investigative methods. If I can do it, others may as well. You need to insulate yourself against that, your Highness. With respect, you can't afford to be Colonel Fangbern anymore."

"First Sergeant Taylor and I have said as much before this, your Highness," Harold said quietly. "Simon is right."

"But how can I ask anyone to assume the responsibility of ordering another person's death?" There was real anguish in Henriks quiet question.

"There are those of us who would volunteer for that duty if only you would ask it," said Harold. "Men of integrity who would take the responsibility as seriously as you yourself. And take the sole blame if discovered. You need but ask."

Henrik looked at the ground for a long moment, then raised his eyes to Harold. "I will consider it. Thank you, Stenson, and you as well, Simon. Your courage and honesty are appreciated, but I must think about this."

Simon bowed. "That is all I ask, your Highness."

Henrik grasped Simon's shoulder. "Go, enjoy your guests and your Lady. Come, Stenson, we must be on our way." And with that he strode from the tent, waving to the crowd as he made his way to the waiting Royal sleds.

Sylvie came over to his side and took his arm. "Did he listen?"

"He listened," said Simon. "But he didn't say he'd step away from the Teams—only that he'd give it serious thought."

"You did what you could, love." She squeezed his arm. "Come, we must lead the procession into the banquet, or no one can eat. Our guests are getting restless."

CHAPTER TWENTY-SIX

Simon whistled as he climbed the staircase to the Command level at Wycliffe House. He and Sylvie had just returned from three days at a country inn midway between Cymbeline and the Borderlands. It was a place they knew well, and the innkeeper had reserved their favorite suite for them when he learned of their wedding. Sylvie was making the rounds of the administrative checks she needed to formally become a King's Peacekeeper.

Lessa greeted him as he entered the outer office. "Welcome back, LT." She handed him a mug of coffee. "Dispatches and messages are on your desk."

"Thank you, Lessa," he said as he entered the inner office. He slid behind his desk with a sigh and sipped his coffee. He flipped through the messages and reports, skimming rather than reading them in detail. A report from Eastport of a possible sighting of Avila's cargo barge moving downriver toward Kingsport caught his eye. Attempts to verify the sighting at points downriver failed to turn up anything. He made a note to get Hal's team on it when he took reports later in the morning.

He finished his coffee as Lessa leaned into the room, a worried look on her face. "LT, Captain Axhart wants to see you in his office right away."

Simon sighed. "On my way. Let the sergeants know I'll be late."

He made his way down the corridor to Axhart's office and opened the door. Sylvie sat in one of the chairs in the anteroom. Simon shot her an inquiring look, but she just shrugged.

"Sit," said Elvira Cairns pointing to the chair next to Sylvie. "He'll see you in a few minutes."

Simon sat. "Have you any idea what this is about?" he whispered.

"Not a clue," said Sylvie.

They both looked up as Hal stepped in. He frowned and turned to Elvira. "What's going on here Elvira? Why are we here?"

"He doesn't tell me everything." She crossed the room and opened the door to the inner office. "They're all here."

"Send them in," said Axhart from the depths of the inner office.

The three of them filed in and stood in front of Axhart's desk, not quite at attention. Axhart looked up and laughed. "You should see yourselves. Feeling guilty about something?" he waved at the chairs and sofa that flanked the green carpet in front of the desk. "Sit, all of you. I have news." They settled into the chairs, and Axhart came around the desk to join them.

"What's this all about, Gelbard?" asked Hal.

"A new assignment," said Axhart. "The Crown Prince and the Justice Ministry have proposed a new Peacekeeper team composed of experienced investigators to focus on illegal Portal magic. You three were selected specifically by His Highness, subject to my approval and your willingness to volunteer. Bendict Hammersmith from Justice will be the fourth member of the team and will be the liaison with the Ministry."

"What about our current duties?" asked Simon.

"Those will be turned over to the Keepers replacing you," said Axhart. "Hal, you are now a lieutenant. Sonia Milhaven will be promoted to Sergeant and will assume leadership of your team. A new armorer will move up to the team to replace her. Simon, you and I will need to discuss a current sergeant to promote to lieutenant in your stead. I will assume temporary command of the teams until then."

"When will this team stand up?" asked Hal.

"That's the shale in the dig," said Axhart. "The Crown wants you operational immediately. The logistics are still in play, but there is space assigned to the team in the Justice Ministry. Clerical and equipment support is still in process but should be in place within 48 hours. You'll all retain your rank and pay through the regular Peacekeeper force structure. Sylvie, you'll be brought in at the rank of lieutenant with today as your date of rank. All I need from the three of you is your agreement to serve on this team."

"I'm in," said Hal. "Milhaven will make a fine sergeant and is already a better team leader than I am."

"I agree as well," said Simon. "With one request."

"What's that?" Axhart asked skeptically.

"I'd like Lessa Greenwater to be assigned as administrative lead for the office staff. She's more than qualified and has earned the promotion."

Axhart smiled. "I think that can be arranged."

"Of course, I agree," said Sylvie. "When do we start?"

"Immediately," said Axhart. "Get yourselves organized, decide who will take the lead. See Elvira when we finish here. She has dispatches from Eastport about the Portal mages Simon and Hal uncovered." He stood. "You are dismissed. Simon, if you could remain for a few minutes."

Hal and Sylvie rose and filed out. Simon remained seated. Axhart sat across from him. "The Crown has made a special request, actually the Crown Prince himself. He wants you to establish a link with the Cabal through your relationship with Kermal Brackenville."

"What sort of link?" asked Simon. He was already uncomfortably indebted to Forsaka and the Cabal.

"The prince sees the Cabal as a possible partner in an effort to develop intelligence sources inside the Havens. The Crown can't officially approach the Cabal. Hells, the Peacekeeper Force has officially designated the Old Men as a criminal organization. We can't officially have any dealings with them."

"The enemy of my enemy is my friend," said Simon. "Captain, my relationship with Kermal Brackenville is personal and already complicated for both of us. We share information when it doesn't compromise our positions. There are certain things we simply can't talk about."

"The prince and I won't ask you to compromise your friend."

"You won't ask it, no," said Simon. "But you can't control every situation. Kermal and I will work together when it's mutually beneficial, and I'll keep the team informed when I can."

"That's really all the Crown asks," said Axhart. "Just let the Cabal know the Crown is open to cooperation in the Havens."

Simon nodded but said nothing more. Axhart stood and nodded his dismissal.

He joined Sylvie and Hal in the outer office. "Anything in those messages?"

Hal nodded. "You know about Avila. His barge has been sighted near Kingsport. No confirmation that he's aboard, but it's the right barge."

"So do we head for Kingsport?" asked Sylvie.

Simon shook his head. "Too far for too little information. The Avila connection feels right but is tenuous. And nothing connects him to this mysterious stranger that Jontry saw at the boathouse."

"What's our plan here, lad?" asked Hal.

"Keep Sonia and the team working Eastport. See if they can find out more about Avila," said Simon. "Meanwhile, we need to get our base of operations squared away." He checked his timepiece. "It's just past 10th. Let's head over to Justice and speak to Bendict Hammersmith. Even though we'll be a Peacekeeper unit, we'll be based on his turf. We'll need to figure out how to fit in."

Over the next several days, Simon and the team settled into their space in the Justice Ministry. They had a large suite of three individual offices around a central reception area. True, it was in the basement of the East building, right under Bendict Hammersmith's office, but it was right next to the archives and had its own exit to the side street behind the building.

Lessa Greenwater proved to be an excellent administrative lead, organizing the office and clerical staff into an efficient team. She still favored Simon with early morning coffee and managed to route messages and reports to each of them flawlessly.

Slowly, they built a profile on Fenrik Avila. Sylvie worked with Sonia Milhaven and her team and uncovered sources in Eastport and downriver with surprising speed. It appeared that Avila managed to avoid official notice but had alienated many of the low-level smugglers and drug dealers along the river, especially among the Orcs. He undercut most of the rivermen, offering transport at prices no one else could match. Rumors of outside money allowing him to operate at a loss were rampant, but there were no solid leads.

More intriguing to Simon were whispers of a black hooded partner, who was rarely seen and who never spoke, but to whom Avila deferred and even seemed to fear. Avila was no Mage, so this hooded stranger must be the one casting the Portal spells. There were only sparse reports of his appearance, but all seemed to suggest that he had some sort of deformity of his legs. Lately, Avila had taken to wearing a hooded cloak as well, concealing his face and body behind a thick swath of material.

Ten days later, Simon felt like the team had its feet on the ground. By unspoken understanding, he found himself as team leader. They were all of equal rank, but Hal had no interest in leadership and Sylvie was the newest on the force. Hammersmith still had his regular duties.

He had just settled into his new office with the first mug of coffee of the day when the summoning tone on his handheld mirror chimed. He swiped the screen. "Kermal," he said. "Good to see you, Brother. What's happening?"

"I have a lead on Avila," said Kermal. "You interested?"

"Most definitely."

Kermal checked something off to his right, then looked back at Simon. "I don't have much time, so listen. The Cabal, through Wind clan, put the word out that we wanted to move some people down river and out of the country through Kingsport, no questions, no official notice. Avila got in touch, and we negotiated a price for his barge. He's meeting our people tonight and moving them downriver. You and the team can hit him in Kingsport and arrest him on a smuggling charge." Kermal looked off to his right again and made a small wave of his hand.

"Thanks, Kermal." Simon frowned as his friend

shook his head at someone out of view. "Where are you? Is everything all good?"

"Can't talk right now, Simon. All good. I'll get in touch soon. The barge is picking up our people at the boathouse at 23rd hour." He broke the connection.

Simon sat back in his chair. *What's going on with Kermal? He said at the wedding that Forsaka might need him up in West Faring. I hope to the gods that he's not going into the Havens.* He shook his head. He needed to get the team mobilized.

***

"Hal, this is Sylvie. In position." Simon heard her voice, soft and clear, over the FS net. It was twenty minutes before 23rd hour, and the team had set up around the boathouse. Sylvie sat in a nondescript Faleron two-seater at the head of the street leading to the quay. Hal was stationed behind a cluster of trees twenty yards downstream from the southeast corner of the dock with a clear view of the river.

"Aye, I'm set in the trees. Let me know when Kermal's people arrive." Hal's answer was louder in Simon's ear.

"Hal, Sylvie," he answered over the net. "I'm approaching the Cut. I'll be in position in two minutes." He concentrated on piloting the small skiff down the Cut and out into the current of the Finnigan. While Hal and Sylvie watched from shore, Simon would maneuver to a position just upstream from the boathouse and observe from the West side of the Cut with a long-distance imager to record the boarding of Kermal's "escapees" and the exchange of money for their passage down river. The team would then track the barge to the harbor at Kingsport and take them as they unloaded their "cargo" and charge them with trafficking in people. Simon hoped to use the trafficking charge to pressure Avila to talk and reveal the identity of the Mage casting the Portal spells.

"Sled coming your way, Hal." Sylvie's voice was a soft whisper over the FarSpeaker receiver clipped to his ear. "I recognize the driver. He's Snake Clan, used to work with Bogrunner." Hal tapped his FS stone twice to indicate he'd received the message.

"Sled has parked," said Hal, a few minutes later. "Four Orcs getting out. Heading for the dock."

"I've got them," said Simon. He watched as the four dark figures crouched at the end of the dock, waiting.

Time seemed to drag, but Simon knew only five minutes had passed. Then Hal said, "Boat coming upstream."

Simon raised the imager and activated the magnifier. He could see the barge approaching, a dark robed figure at the helm. He shifted to the dock and watched the four Orcs come to their feet. The barge approached, slowed, and edged up to the dock. A rope was thrown and one of the Orcs caught it and secured it to a bollard.

The figure in the dark robe shut down the barge's water impeller and climbed out onto the dock. He spoke to the Orcs and pointed to the stern of the craft. Three of the Orcs climbed aboard and sat down on the rear deck near the stern. The dark man and the remaining Orc conferred for a minute. Simon began recording images of the exchange. The Orc held out a thick packet which the man accepted. He turned to reboard the barge, and his hood fell back. Simon got a good image of Fenrik Avila's face, clearly identifiable, before he jumped down to the helm. *Shouldn't have much trouble ID'ing him. Not with those scars.* The left side of Avila's face was a rope of scar, as if he'd been badly burned at some time in the past. The Orc on shore untied the rope and tossed it aboard.

Avila powered up the water impellers and allowed

the current to turn the craft's bow away from the dock and downstream. He advanced the throttle, and the barge gathered way as it headed away from shore into the middle of the river.

"Hal, this is Simon. I got good images of the exchange and a clear view of Avila's face. We're done here. I'm heading into the Cut and will catch up with you and Sylvie at the rally point."

"Copy," said Hal. "The last Orc is back in his sled. He should pass Sylvie momentarily."

"I have him," said Sylvie. "He's heading for the main road."

"Take him," said Simon. "Hal, back her up. Meet me at the rally point."

Their rally point was a small pier on the West side of the Cut. Simon arrived twenty minutes after Hal and Sylvie, who stood leaning against the Faleron. An Orc sat at their feet, hands flexcuffed behind him. As Simon got closer, he saw that the Orc was leaning his head forward as blood flowed freely from his broken nose. He looked up at Simon through his right eye, the left being swollen shut, and spat blood on the ground at his feet.

Sylvie cuffed him in the left ear. "None of that," she said. "That's my husband you're spitting at."

"Thanks for waiting," said Simon. "Who is this charming gentleman?"

"Chanze Gronska," said Sylvie. "Snake Clan and a business partner of Damier Bogrunner."

"I weren't never," said Gronska. "Bogrunner was a traitor what got his due."

"And yet you and he recruited Orcs from all over the East End for Fenrik Avila. And some of those poor sods were never heard from again." Sylvie cuffed him again. "Did you kill them? Or was that Bogrunner's thing?"

"Them as disappeared weren't down to me or

Bogrunner," grumbled the Orc.

"Who then?" asked Simon.

Gronska looked up at him again. "Not worth my life to say, Bluebelly. I want me an Advocate. I ain't saying nothing more."

"Have it your way," said Simon. "But I doubt Avila and the Stranger in black will bail you out."

The Orc's eyes widened with fear briefly before hardening and looking away.

"Where to," asked Hal looking down at Gronska.

"Maybe the River?" suggested Sylvie. She brushed her hair back behind her ear and for the first time Simon saw the livid bruise on her cheek.

He leaned toward her. "Are you all good?" he asked with concern.

She nodded. "Can't believe this son of a gnome got the drop on me, but I'm all good."

"It'll take Avila twelve hours to navigate downriver to Kingsport," said Simon. "We can do it in eight on the E46. We have a little time to safeguard the images and gear up. Back to Wycliffe House with this one. We'll start for Kingsport in two hours."

"Best alert the Chief at Kingsport station that we're coming and get her people involved in watching the river," said Hal. "We don't know where Avila will tie up, even if we know what ship he's supposed to meet."

They abandoned the Faleron and climbed into the Peacekeeper patrol sled they'd prepositioned at the rally point. Hal drove with Sylvie next to him. Simon sat in the rear with Gronska. The Orc was cuffed hands and feet and leaned against the door, pulling as far from Sylvie as possible.

Simon leaned forward and spoke softly to Sylvie. "Are you sure you're good? Just the bruise, nothing else?"

She shook her head. "Nothing hurt but my pride." She turned to look at him. "Really Simon. I'm fine. But if we're going to make this work, you can't hover and fret when I'm on the job. It isn't safe for either of us."

Simon blinked, a little stung by her tone. *But she's right. I can't always protect her. Maybe this working on the same team isn't such a good idea.* He kept that thought to himself and they rode the rest of the way to Wycliffe House in silence.

Even though they'd established themselves at Justice, vehicles, tactical gear and weapons were still maintained at Wycliffe House. They turned Gronska over to the booking sergeant for holding, at least until they got enough evidence to formally charge him with trafficking.

Simon found Sylvie in the locker room, examining her bruised cheek in a mirror. To his eye, it had already started to fade. She frowned at the look on his face.

"I said I was fine, Simon. It takes more than a street rat like Gronska to hurt me. I was stupid and let him get close before I tried to restrain him."

"Look, I'm sorry if my concern comes across as hovering or overly protective," said Simon. "I know more than anyone that you're capable in a fight. It's just that after almost losing you once, I can't bear to think of it happening again."

"Do you think it was easy for me? Locked up, knowing you'd move heaven and all the hells to come get me and afraid all the while you'd get yourself killed in the process?" She sighed and closed her locker. "We work at a dangerous job, Simon. If we're going to be partners in this, we have to trust one another to be able to look out for ourselves. We have each other's back, yes, but just like on the teams, you have to let me do my job and I have to let you do yours."

He nodded and she reached out to embrace him. "Come on, let's find Hal and get on the road."

They signed out the sled for a trip to Kingsport, drew tactical vests and D'Stangs as well as their personal needlers. Simon slid his Gallinberg Reaper saber into the rear storage of the sled and noted that Sylvie's Whirlwind rapier was already there.

They slid out at ten past 2nd hour. Avila had a three-hour head start, but the Finnigan didn't run straight between the Cut and Kingsport. The E46 highway did. They were confident they'd beat the barge to the seaport with time to spare.

CHAPTER TWENTY-SEVEN

They reached the outskirts of Kingsport just before 10th hour. Simon was behind the yoke, having relieved Hal about halfway through the trip. A call to Bendict Hammersmith just after 7th had updated him on their progress and ensured that he'd call the Justice liaison in Kingsport. The Peacekeeper contingent and the Customs Service had been alerted. Both shores of the Finnigan, as well as the harbor, were watched.

"Let's check in at Kingsport Central first, lad," said Hal. "Haley Reinbern is an old friend, but she won't take kindly to us showing up in her garden unannounced."

Station Chief Reinbern greeted Hal like an old friend, but was less than enthusiastic about a special operations team on her turf. "We'll help out, of course," she said. "But you could have handled this with a mirror summons. We're capable of picking up a fugitive on our own, Hal."

"I know that, Haley. But this one's a bit special. High brass jingle, if you get my drift."

Simon gave Hal a sharp look but let the jibe slide.

"Have you got a picture of this person?" she asked.

"Coming your way," said Simon. He forwarded the image from the dock.

"Ugly mug; clear enough for an identification, but not exactly booking cell quality," said Reinbern. "I'll get it out to my people."

They exited the highway at Commercial Street, which took them through the center of the city to the Harbor. Traffic was heavy, and the short trip to the Customs Building harborside took over thirty minutes. They showed their badges at the entrance desk and were directed upstairs to the Harbormaster.

They entered a cluttered office with a wide window looking out over the docks and quays of Kingsport harbor. The Harbormaster was a sturdy Dwarf with long mustaches and side-whiskers. The nameplate on his desk read, "Hiram Stonechild." He rose as Simon and company entered.

"How can I be of service to the King's Peacekeepers today?" His voice was pleasant, but held a touch of sarcasm.

Simon smiled and extended his hand. "I'm Lieutenant Simon Buckley, Special Detail out of the Justice Ministry. These are my partners, Lieutenants Graystorm and Stonebender. We're pursuing a trafficker named Fenrik Avila. He should be arriving soon from upriver on a commercial barge. He's wanted for questioning in a double murder, but he's also smuggling three Orc fugitives on his barge, which is the cause for detention on our warrant."

"Aye," said Stonechild. "And can I see that warrant?"

Hal pulled the warrant form from the pouch of his tactical vest and handed it across the desk. Stonechild glanced at it and handed it back. "Looks in order. Most River traffic docks a ways upstream at the fishing dock. River barges aren't allowed down here on the ocean quays. You'll have to check up there. It's only about a quarter mile up Harbor Street."

"Thanks," said Simon. "The fugitives Avila's carrying are supposed to meet the RMS *Speedwell* bound for Zahkaria in the Azeri Empire. Can you point her out?"

Stonechild looked perplexed. "You're out of luck there, Lieutenant. *Speedwell* sailed with the tide last night around midnight. She'll be well out to sea by now."

"That's ill news," said Hal. "Was that a scheduled sailing?"

"No, but she was fully loaded, and all scheduled passengers and crew were aboard. Her captain took advantage of the flood tide to get out of port and avoid the heavier daytime traffic."

"I need to let Kermal know about this," said Simon quietly to Hal and Sylvie. "And see if he has a way to contact the Orcs on the barge." He looked across the desk at Stonechild. "Are there any other scheduled sailings for Zahkaria or points Southeast."

Stonechild consulted a large chart on the desktop. "Not Southeast. A lot of coastal traffic, mostly small craft and short run freighters. RMS *Albatross* is due to sail for the Spice Islands, but that's all the way across the Eastern Sea. The only other departure scheduled is the *Silverseed,* but she's an Elf ship out of Talien. I doubt your Orcs would be welcome aboard her."

"*Silverseed* is likely part of the Trelawney Conglomerate," commented Sylvie. "All their ships are named for seeds. And the Trelawney's are staunch Traditionalists. Unless they're adding slaving to their business model, no Orc would be allowed to book passage with them."

"Thank you, Harbormaster," said Simon with a short bow. "We'll check out the fishing docks. Also, is there somewhere we can get passenger manifests for ships sailing today?"

"Customs can help you with that," said Stonechild. "But only foreign nationals are required to register with them. Commonwealth citizens are free to leave as they please."

Simon thanked him again and they returned to the Customs desk on the ground floor. Their badges got them the manifests but, as expected, neither Avila nor a trio of Orcs was listed.

Simon pulled out his Mirror and summoned Kermal. When he finally answered, he looked tired and harried. "Simon, what's wrong?"

"Do you have a way to reach the Orcs you planted with Avila? The *Speedwell* sailed early, and we haven't heard from them."

"They were due to check in an hour ago," said Kermal. "I wasn't too concerned, since they need to maintain their story as fugitives. Have you sighted Avila's barge, yet? Maybe they're just slower than we expected."

"We've got the local Keepers as well as Customs watching the waterfront," said Simon. "We're going ourselves to the docks where barges usually put in. I'll be in touch if we sight them." Kermal nodded and broke the connection. Simon again wondered if his friend was all good.

They took the sled up Harbor Street rather than walk, just in case they needed to go farther upstream or cross to the other shore. The fishing docks were so named because much of the commercial fishing fleet unloaded their catch there, but the complex also had quays and docks that extended for almost a mile along the shore of the Finnigan. River traffic bound for the city offloaded here, as did export items that were transshipped by smaller harbor boats or sledge to the bigger ocean-going freighters at the Harbor docks. The buzz of activity defied the team's efforts to pick out any individual barge.

Simon sighed in frustration. Behind him, he heard the summoning tone of Hal's mirror. He couldn't hear the conversation but clearly heard Hal's curse. "Thanks Haley," Hal said as he came to Simon's side.

"Trouble?"

"Aye, lad," said Hal. "Reinbern's people found a barge half submerged about a mile upstream from here. There's three dead Orc's in her stern cabin."

"Where is this place?" asked Simon.

"Spot called Granbier Creek. Reinbern said to stay on Harbor, it'll take us right to it."

The cluster of Peacekeeper sleds and the orange crime scene ropes left no doubt that they'd reached the right location ten minutes later. They climbed out of their sled and immediately a sergeant approached them.

"You the team from Justice?" he asked.

"Aye," said Hal. "What've you got?"

"They're towing the barge ashore right now. Don't know if it's the one you're looking for, but my Boat Team found it adrift, water up to the gunnels. They took it in tow and checked aboard. Found three dead Orcs in the stern cuddy cabin, all with their hands tied and their throats cut." He shot the team a hard look. "Just what sort of trouble did you bring to my River?"

"More than you want to take on, Sergeant," said Simon. "Any sign of the owner of the barge? A man named Avila." He took out his mirror and showed the man an image of Avila.

The Sergeant pursed his lips. "I think you need to talk to one of my lads," he said. "Handel! Where's that fisherman you talked to?"

A young Keeper near the winch that was pulling the barge ashore looked up and called back, "Up by the sleds, Sarge. I told him to stick around in case we had more questions for him. Name's Riverstone. He's an Orc; lives just across the creek from here."

They found Riverstone sitting on a large rock near the cluster of Patrol sleds, smoking a battered pipe. He looked them over as they approached, stood, and knocked out his pipe on the rock.

"Mr. Riverstone?" said Simon. "I'm Lieutenant Simon Buckley and these are my partners Lieutenants Stonebender and Graystorm. We understand you may know something about the barge over there?"

"That I do," said the Orc. "Called the Bluebellies myself, din't I."

"What can you tell me about it?"

"Well sir," Riverstone said. "I was fishing the mouth of the Creek, like I always do of a morning, when I seen that barge drifting downstream. She was down by the head and turning sideways-like in the current."

"Did you see anyone aboard?" asked Simon.

"Nope, but I seen two men pulling away from her in a small rowboat like they didn't care that she was going down."

"Where did the rowboat go?" asked Sylvie.

The Orc pointed downstream. "Just a ways downstream. Put ashore just across from where Pirie Street joins Harbor, near the bend in the River. They walked off like they was in a hurry."

"I'll go," said Sylvie, heading to check out the rowboat.

Simon gave her a nod and returned to Riverstone. "Can you describe these men?"

"Not so's you'd know them." The old Orc shook his head. "They was bundled in dark clothes with hoods on their heads. One was tall and lean. The other was short and wide and looked kinda funny. Bandy legs that was too short for the rest of him. He didn't have no trouble keeping up with the taller fella though."

Simon cursed under his breath. He checked his timepiece. It was just noon. The high tide would be

257

turning any minute.

"Sylvie!" he shouted. "We need to go, right now." He shook Riverstone's hand. "Thank you, Mr. Riverstone. You've been a big help. Come on, Hal" He started to jog toward their sled.

Hal ran to keep up. "What's going on, lad? Why the rush?"

"Avila and the Stranger with him are cutting their losses. They plan to sail on the *Silverseed* with the noon tide and get away to the Havens," said Simon between breaths.

They reached the sled just after Sylvie. Simon told her what he'd told Hal, and they climbed in. Simon turned the sled around and activated the lights and siren as he accelerated down Harbor Street, back toward the Customs House.

Traffic delayed them despite the lights and siren, and it took almost twenty minutes to reach the control gate leading to the quays. Simon showed his badge to the guard, then drummed his fingers impatiently on the steering yoke as the man walked back to the controls and opened the gate. They heard a klaxon sounding at the far end of the quay as the gate finally opened enough to let the sled pass.

Simon sped down the quay, dodging stevedores and cargo loaders, and drawing shaken fists and curses. He pulled up at the end of the quay and jumped out of the sled without canceling the air spell.

A large cargo ship slid slowly away from them, the gap between the hull and the quay already a hundred feet and increasing. Simon looked up at the ship's rail and saw two figures watching them. One threw back his hood and waved. It was Avila. His dark-hooded companion stood for a moment as if recording Simon's face, then turned and walked away.

Simon looked around frantically, saw an officer in a Customs Service uniform and ran over to him. "We have to stop that ship," he said to the man. "There are two dangerous criminals aboard."

"Sorry, mate," the man said. "She's already been cleared by the port authority and sounded her klaxon. Can't board or stop her without a direct order from the Harbormaster."

Simon watched as the *Silverseed* lowered her huge impellers into the murky water. She'd be underway on her own power in a moment. There wouldn't be time to reach Stonechild and get the order before the ship cleared the outer range buoys.

Sylvie and Hal came up. "Can we stop the ship?" Sylvie asked.

Simon shook his head. "We're too late. By the time we can get an order to stop, she'll be at sea. Stopping a foreign flagged ship would require the Coast Guard or the Navy, and we don't have enough evidence on Avila to justify that kind of action."

He sighed as he watched the ship move smoothly through the water. "Maybe Kermal can get word to Barca. Avila and his friend will be in Talien in a few days, and maybe Barca's people can track them from there."

Sylvie shook her head. "Talien's a strongly Traditional district. My cousin Nura lives there, but she's firmly in my father's circle. I doubt she'd even talk to me, much less help. Avila will be in Tintagel before the month is out."

Black storm clouds loured on the distant horizon. Simon shivered as a feeling of dread washed over him.

He took Sylvie's hand. "Let's go home.

...

ACKNOWLEDGMENTS:

This is the fourth book in a series of connected stand-alone novels. It also completes a story arc involving Simon and Sylvie. The entire series was actually planned that way: as a series of cases, each involving the school of magic specific to the metal in the title. I have spent the last couple of years deeply involved in building this world, and I hope that dedication to detail comes through.

I've had help from a number of people, many of whom I have acknowledged in past novels. As always, my heartfelt thanks to Sharon Skinner for her editorial expertise and often pointed recommendations. Thanks also to Bob Nelson of Brick Cave Media for his continued support and belief in my work. I must also acknowledge Brad Faliks, my dedicated and perceptive beta reader. His cogent suggestions and observations have made all the difference in several of these novels.

Finally, to my wife Michele, thank you for your love, your tolerance and your support.

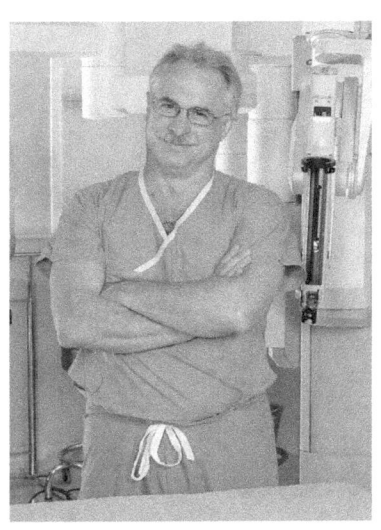

ABOUT THE AUTHOR:

Bruce Davis is a writer of Science Fiction and Fantasy. His current books, published by Brick Cave Media, include the Magic Law series of which Silver Magic is the third installment. It, along with Platinum Magic and Gold Magic are a mash-up of High Fantasy and Police Procedural set in a modern world. Also published by Brick Cave are his Profit Logbook series of SF novels about Zach Mbele, former Martian special forces commando and captain of the fast freighter, the Profit.

In his day job, he is a Trauma and Critical Care surgeon at a Phoenix area Level 1 Trauma Center. His independently published non-fiction memoir Dancing in the Operating Room is a glimpse into the life and training of a Trauma Surgeon.

He lives in Mesa, AZ with his wife who tolerates his passions for writing, science fiction conventions, kayaking, and collecting functional swords and custom knives.

www.ingramcontent.com/pod-product-compliance
Lightning Source LLC
Chambersburg PA
CBHW060625260626
47161CB00008B/2807